# Brotherly Love

SCEPTRE

*Also by Elizabeth Pewsey*

Children of Chance
Divine Comedy
Unholy Harmonies
Volcanic Airs
Unaccustomed Spirits

# Brotherly Love

## ELIZABETH PEWSEY

SCEPTRE

First published in 1998 by Hodder and Stoughton
A division of Hodder Headline PLC
A Sceptre Book

A CIP catalogue record for this book is available
from the British Library.

ISBN 0 340 68566 2

Typeset by Palimpsest Book Production Limited,
Polmont, Stirlingshire
Printed and bound in Great Britain by
Clays Ltd, St Ives plc

Hodder and Stoughton
A division of Hodder Headline PLC
338 Euston Road
London NW1 3BH

For Mavis, the ghost

ı ∫

'Your mother's done a flit.'

'Flit?'

Edmund passed the phone to Mimi, who took it, looking puzzled. 'Hello?' she said. 'Oh, it's you, Vincent.' She began to untwirl the cord as she listened to the voice at the other end.

Edmund settled himself at the kitchen table, seemingly to lose himself in the excitement of the local paper, but in reality to listen to at least one end of the conversation going on between his wife and her elder brother.

'Mimi?' Vincent's cool voice showed no concern. 'Ma's gone.'

'Gone where?'

'Don't ask me. She seems to have done a bunk. All her papers and books have gone, and most of her possessions. I thought she might have ventured north to stay with you.'

'No, I haven't seen her. I spoke to her last week, she didn't say anything then about going away. How mysterious. Don't Ferdie and Benedict have any ideas?'

Vincent was scornful; he had a low opinion of his and Mimi's younger brothers. 'Them! Ferdie's gone off with some of his revolting friends, and I believe, but can't say for sure, that Benedict's on retreat with those ghastly monks of his. In Scotland,' he added with distaste.

'Hasn't she left a note, some kind of message?'

'It depends what you mean by a message. There's a strange scrawl on the noticeboard in the kitchen. Written in giant letters, announcing that one Mr Mapleton will be here tomorrow at ten, and we must attend upon him.'

1 •

Mimi rubbed at a piece of candlewax which had stuck to the oilcloth on the kitchen table. 'Who is Mr Mapleton?'

'Haven't a clue,' said Vincent.

Mimi raked her memory. No, the name Mapleton rang no bells. Could it be the tax man, one of Her Majesty's Grabbers as her mother always called them?

Vincent thought not; there was no way Ma would let a tax man over the threshold of her flat. 'No, she's up to something,' he said. 'She finished her book and simply had a brainstorm, that's what I think.'

'She had definitely finished the book?'

'She took a fat parcel to the post office two days ago. I assumed she was sending the book off to her agent as usual.'

'I expect she's gone on holiday. I could ring Junius Paxley later, he may know where she is.'

Junius was their mother's literary agent. Vincent pooh-poohed Mimi's suggestion. 'You know what a clam the man is, he won't tell you his own name if he doesn't have to. He may know where she's gone, but if he does, he won't tell you. Or me.'

'Will you be there for this Mapleton?'

'Sorry, no,' said Vincent in his disobliging way. 'I'm going to an auction down in Sussex, off at the crack, can't help. You'll have to come up to town if you think it's important.'

Mimi banged the phone down. 'That's so typical of Vincent, how can he think I'd go all the way to London at such short notice? I've got work to do.'

Edmund had made himself some toast, and he was now spreading it thickly with jam, taking care it went right to the edge of the crust. 'Your brothers aren't interested in what you've got to do. Your brothers are only interested in themselves and what affects them directly.'

'Mapleton may affect them, for all we know. But how are we to find out, if there's no one there when he comes?'

'He'll call again if it's important.' He finished his piece of toast and rose from the table, licking some stray jam off his fingers.

'Do take your plate to the sink,' said Mimi automatically. 'Are you working at home today?'

Edmund put his plate into the dishwasher with a defiant clatter. 'Possibly.'

'I'll bring you some coffee later on.'

He bent to kiss the back of her neck, and left just as a wiry young man came through the door. 'Good morning, Gerry,' said Edmund, tucking the newspaper under his arm.

'The literary genius off to his study to read the paper?' asked Gerry as Edmund shut his study door across the hall with a loud bang.

'That isn't kind. He has to get into the right mood to work.'

Gerry was an old friend of Mimi's, going back to their student days, but he knew better than to criticize Edmund. So he forbore to mention that it was taking him a very long time to get into the right mood. Eighteen months, to be precise.

Now in his late twenties, Gerry was a designer and artist. He had a compact and competent look about him, with nothing of the dreamer or romantic in his appearance. At the school where he worked two days a week, visitors usually took him for a teacher on the science side, with perhaps responsibility for hockey coaching in the afternoons. They were surprised to find that he belonged to the more laid-back and scruffier world of the art department. He worked for Mimi for the remaining three days of the week, doing her designs and lending a hand with the paperwork when it threatened to spill out of the in-tray.

'What's up?' he asked. 'You look troubled.'

Mimi had unrolled some drawings on the worktop under the window, pinning the corners down with pebbles from a jar on the window sill. She was studying them with an intent expression on her face. Gerry went over to her.

'Problems with the council fountain?'

'No, it's nothing to do with the fountain. Vincent rang, and he says that my mother's gone off somewhere, without leaving a forwarding address.'

'Gone on holiday most likely, keen to get away from Vincent and those other brothers of yours,' said Gerry caustically. 'No idea where she's gone?'

Mimi shook her head.

'I wouldn't worry about her. Finella's well able to take care of herself, and I don't suppose there's anything you can do about it until she chooses to get in touch.' He carried the remaining bits and pieces from the kitchen table to the sink and then wiped the oilcloth with a sponge. He had brought a portfolio with him, which was propped up against the door. Now he took it to the table and drew out some sketches and diagrams which he laid flat on the table. 'You go through these, then give me a shout. I'll be in the office.'

'Yes,' said Mimi, her thoughts and attention elsewhere.

She gazed blankly at the sheets of diagrams and figures, hearing her mother's scathing tones ringing in her head. Her mother had been furious when she'd begun to work with fountains; she could not have disapproved more. Mimi, she said, was an artist. A musician. A pianist. It was folly to give that up simply because she'd got a friend's fountain working, through sheer luck, and liked to spend time among the pipes and taps and up to her elbows in water.

You couldn't explain anything to Finella Ostiman. Driven by her own daemons, she never stopped to pay attention to anyone else's. Mimi had tried.

'I like fountains. They fascinate me. Lots of people want fountains, it could be a good business.'

'Business!'

Nothing would persuade her that Mimi didn't want to be a pianist. That there was no place for her in a ruthless and competitive world where only the greatest talent and nerve made any impression.

'You can train as an accompanist.'

'You have to do what other people want all the time if you're an accompanist. I like to be in charge.'

This was the moment when her mother moved into tragic mode. 'I have sacrificed my art to provide for you children. I once dreamed of literature, but circumstances forced me to turn my pen to a lowlier form, to oblige my agent and my publisher, to consider money before expressing my soul.'

What nonsense it was. Her mother had a genius for writing horrific crime stories, and no one who watched her at work could doubt that she loved every gory minute of it.

'If it's so terrible to provide what other people want and not write what you want, then why expect me to follow in your footsteps?'

'We who serve art must be content to linger in the foothills if that is where our humble talent and circumstances lead us.'

The difference was that her mother's foothills were made of gold. Mimi knew that the life of a good but not outstanding pianist was not likely to be rewarding financially.

Her mother came back to the horrid matter of business. 'I brought you all up to cultivate the higher side of life. Art, culture, the things of the spirit. Business is so materialistic.'

'Business is fun.'

Then had come the predictions of the awful people she would mingle with; no chance, among such a money-grabbing crowd, of finding a soul-mate.

Mimi thought of her mother's booky parties where all the writers ever talked about was money, but held her tongue.

And her mother couldn't have been more wrong. She had met Edmund while fixing her friend Sylvester's fountain. Covered in cobwebs and stone dust, she had wandered into the kitchen at Midwinter Hall with a lead pipe in her hand and found this most interesting-looking man pacing up and down and holding forth at length about private life in mediaeval France to Sylvester, Sylvester's housekeeper Lily and a large black cat.

The dark and interesting man had found her just as interesting, and having wrung her address out of Sylvester, had arrived on her doorstep in London one Sunday afternoon.

'Fluke,' her mother had said. 'Besides, he's a northerner, I told you what would happen if you moved up to those parts.'

Her mother had a very out-of-date and unreasonable view of the north of England. Edmund said it might have been a valid viewpoint in the eleventh century after William the Bastard had laid waste the northern half of his kingdom. 'But possibly a little far-fetched today. There's not that much difference between north and south, now admit it.'

'The north is greatly overrated,' said Finella in dramatic tones.

Mimi told her mother not to exaggerate and hastily took Edmund out of the house and into a nearby pub, where he could recover from the shock of meeting Finella.

# 2 ∫

There were sounds of arrival in the hall and Mimi came out of the kitchen to see who it was. A large figure stood there, sliding a cello case off his shoulder and taking off his voluminous mac. It was Sylvester.

'You're looking very serious,' he said. 'Gerry let me in, he told me you'd heard some disconcerting news about your mother, and you were worrying about her. I wouldn't worry about Finella if I were you, I never knew a woman more able to look after herself.'

'Not worrying, exactly. More mystified. She's gone off without saying a word to anyone.'

'So Gerry told me.' He looked attentively at Mimi. 'There's something different about you. Have you changed the colour of your hair? A new shade of red? It seems more vibrant than usual.'

'I went to a new hairdresser,' said Mimi. 'He specializes in colouring and tinting. Do you approve?' She spun round.

'Exactly the same colour as your shirt, very smart. Mind you, it's a good thing you gave up the idea of a career on the concert platform. That hair wouldn't go with Beethoven, you know how stuffy classical music audiences are and how staid we musicians have to be. Now, I'll have some coffee, I can smell it, so delicious, and you can tell me if there's anything I can do for you in London.'

'London? Are you going to London?' Mimi followed in Sylvester's wake as he headed purposefully for the coffee jug.

'Yes, I am, for a concert.'

Her old friend Sylvester Tate was a distinguished cellist who chose to escape from the pressures of the international concert world by living in the remote village of Midwinter. He loved the fells and the space of the countryside, and adored the goings-on, gossip and intrigue of the nearby city of Eyot. 'Very convenient for roads and trains, excellent place to live,' he would say. 'And a good long way from my agent.'

'When is the concert?'

'Tonight. I'm catching the midday train. I'll be coming back tomorrow, but I don't mind what train I catch.'

'Where are you staying in London?'

'Off Marylebone Lane.'

Of course it was a family matter, but Mimi sometimes suspected that Sylvester knew more about her family than she did. And he had offered. 'Listen, that's not far from Mother's flat. Could you be there at ten tomorrow morning?'

'Why?'

'Apparently there's a Mr Mapleton coming at ten, and there'll be no one there.'

'Who is Mr Mapleton?' Sylvester took the cup of coffee which Mimi had poured out for him and gave it a brisk stir.

'Nobody knows. At least, my mother must have known, because she left a message to say he'd be there at ten, but she didn't say who he was, or why he was coming.'

'What about your brothers?'

What about them, indeed. Never there when they were wanted, always happy to leave anything inconvenient to others. 'Away. At least, two of them are, and Vincent's got to go off early. So he says.'

'You've got a key, presumably?'

When Edmund had acquired his redbrick, neo-gothic Victorian house near the river in Eyot, it had been in a dreadful state. So he had done it up entirely to his own taste, with many happy finds from a friend who dealt in architectural salvage, especially from churches. Edmund felt that ecclesiastical details went with the house and they had the advantage of not costing a lot. As well as unexpected arches and pillars and strange grilles over radiators, Edmund had bought all kinds of bits and pieces from St This and St That, as and when modernizing vicars arrived and threw out all the old pews and stuffy fittings so as to be able to praise the Lord in a functional, modern, hygienic way. The line of hooks which ran all along the hall wall had come from the robing room of a Victorian church, and little silk and velvet bags hung from them, full of household flotsam and jetsam.

Mimi pulled open a black and gold brocade pouch and rummaged among a selection of keys. 'Here you are. This does the main lock, and then it's this one above it.'

'And no idea at all as to the nature of Mapleton's business?'

She shook her head.

'Let us trust that it's drains, and that he isn't the mad axeman of Wigmore Street.'

'Sylvester, you don't really think . . .'

He leant down from his considerable height and gave her a hug. 'Don't fuss, he won't be. Now, I shall gather up my cello from your hall and be on my way. Give my regards to Edmund.'

There was no need; Edmund appeared in the hall as Sylvester was leaving.

'Sylvester's just off to London,' said Mimi, hoping that Sylvester would keep his mouth shut about his intended visit to the flat. Edmund would not have approved. He felt that Mimi's family took up far too much of everyone's time and energy.

'I'm going to the university now,' Edmund said.

'Ah.'

'Work to do,' he added.

'Will you be back for lunch?'

'No, no, don't expect me. I'll have a sandwich there.'

With Inez, no doubt, thought Mimi resentfully, as she closed the door on both men. She resolutely put her worries about her mother and about Edmund and Inez out of her mind, and turned her attention to her work. She must concentrate; there were costings and all kinds of details to be worked out for a new civic fountain, commissioned by the city council for the forecourt of their new offices.

'Nothing too fancy, mind,' Councillor Henthorpe had warned her. 'None of your naked doxies writhing about in the foam. There's enough of that sort of thing going on in the city without drawing attention to it outside the council offices.'

Gerry had been very amused when she'd passed the message

on, and promptly sketched a riot of plump ladies disporting themselves with lascivious delight in the company of well-endowed tritons and a staggering Neptune.

'I'm not sure I could find a customer for that,' Mimi had said, pocketing it. 'Meanwhile, something staid, reflecting the civic pride of our ancient city.'

'A grasping hand?'

'I think they'll go for something symbolic, something exemplifying the historic past of the city.'

'Oh, bugger,' Gerry said without rancour. 'It's that bloody boar again.'

'They do like the boar. It doesn't have to be realistic, though; Councillor Henthorpe prides himself on being modern.'

Councillor H would like what Gerry had done, she thought, as she looked again at his drawings. She tucked them back in the portfolio, and settled down to cope with the technical specifications of a new pump.

# 3

'You'll have trouble with that boar,' said Edmund that evening when he caught sight of Gerry's design for the council fountain.

'Trouble? Casting him? I don't think so.'

'I don't know about the technical side, I'm sure Gerry knows what he's doing. No, it's the boar himself. He's far too rampant.'

'In the heraldic sense?'

'No. He breathes male hormones. He is a masculine, bristling, phallic kind of boar.'

'He's called Klaus.'

'What?'

'Gerry drew him from a boar called Klaus. He lives at Upperby End, he's the Hazletons' prize boar.'

'Well, Klaus is clearly a fine fellow, and doubtless well up to his work at Upperby. But he won't do for the council.' Edmund put the bottle of wine he was holding down on the table and went to the cupboard in search of glasses.

'Councillor Henthorpe likes him.'

'Councillor Henthorpe is but one among many. Wait until the full council claps eyes on Klaus here. The chamber will be in uproar.'

'Oh, nonsense,' said Mimi. She hoped Edmund was wrong. This was an excellent commission, both in terms of fee and publicity. She looked down at Gerry's vibrant boar. 'Councillor Henthorpe was worried about naked ladies. He didn't want naked ladies.'

Edmund was hunting in the drawer for a corkscrew, but

he looked up at that, much amused. 'No, he's got something far wilder. Tell you what, there's something about that boar's expression that reminds me of Valdemar.'

'Val does not look like a boar.' Mimi had her own opinion of Edmund's cousin Valdemar, but no one could say that he was boar-like; he was very good-looking, quite apart from being disturbingly attractive.

'No, but there's something about him which is similar. Probably the look of lustful intent.' He was wrestling with a rebellious cork now, which came out with a sudden rush, causing the corkscrew to inflict a deep scratch on his hand. 'Ouch,' he said, sucking it. 'Do you think you can get tetanus from a corkscrew?'

She ignored the dripping wound. 'Gerry's boar is hardly full of lustful intent. He is symbolic of historic and civic pride.'

The civic pride came from the boar being the chief emblem on the arms of the city of Eyot, which dated back to the days of Richard III, known locally as Good King Richard.

Edmund's cynicism was not reassuring. 'Ha, just you wait.'

# 4 ♪

Mimi awoke the next morning to a feeling of uncertainty and oppression. She told Edmund so, and he looked at her in an endearingly sleepy way before he sloped off to his shower, humming tunes from Gilbert and Sullivan as he went.

She bunched the covers back over her shoulders, reluctant to get up and face the day.

Bother her mother. Bother her for vanishing like this. Bother her brothers for being so generally unhelpful.

'Working at home today?' she asked Edmund at breakfast.

'No, another day at the university for me.'

'You always say the university here is hopeless for Templars.'

'It is, it is, but there's plenty on the rest of the period. Inez has dug up some fascinating family papers for me.'

'Grrr,' she said as the door shut behind him.

'Fretting about Inez?' enquired Gerry, sliding into a pew and reaching for the coffee pot.

She wasn't exactly fretting. Why should she? She didn't have any doubts about Edmund's affection for her, what nonsense that would be. Though one had to remember that she'd only been married to him for three years. He and Inez had been together for at least five years, she knew. Perhaps even longer; it wasn't something they ever discussed. And Edmund and Inez had spent quite a lot of time over those years in bed together. Not to mention holidays abroad, dining out, theatres, trips abroad . . .

'And, of course, picnics.'

Gerry looked at her in surprise. 'What is there about a picnic to rouse your ire?'

'Inez makes wonderful food for picnics.'

In her mind's eye, she could see them. *Déjeuner sur l'herbe,* naked figures sporting on the bank as a dappled river flowed serenely by. Caviar and champagne in a Fortnum's hamper on the rug, a scene of archaic, pastoral depravity. Dark Edmund gazing adoringly at Inez's pink and white body; all right, so Inez was a brunette, but she could still be pink and white. People with bosoms like that would surely be pale-fleshed, with the languorous look of the boudoir.

She knew quite well that Inez rose early to jog, wearing a firm sports bra, played tennis, ditto, had muscular brown limbs and would consider frolicking by the river a waste of time.

Even so, the images had power to alarm and disturb.

'Inez knows how to please men,' said Gerry.

'Too true, and I wish she didn't want to please my husband.'

'Must have been a shock for her when you two whizzed off to the Registrar and got hitched.'

'I did have hopes of that new economist, just her type I thought. But it didn't last, so I suspect it's back to Edmund.'

'Trust him,' said Gerry. 'He's in love with you, why should he succumb to the delights of Inez?'

'Habit. And possibly greed.'

'Buy a new cookbook.'

It was all very well for Gerry to be so flippant. He didn't understand the perils of being so much in love with your rather older husband, and wondering always what he'd been up to in those thirty-plus years before he knew you. Especially when he was a Mountjoy; the Mountjoy men were famous for their wild amours and numerous infidelities.

'They can't all be like that,' said Gerry. 'I remember hearing that the last Lord Mountjoy, Magdalena's previous husband before she married Valdemar, was a devoted husband. Every time.'

'It's in their blood.'

'You're quite lively yourself; I think Edmund should be the one to worry. Anyhow, he hasn't got time for anything on the side right now, isn't he under tremendous pressure to get this book of his finished?'

'Oh, that's no problem. I know he doesn't seem to be getting on with it, but he is. He says it was just the same with the last two, and they got written all right. He's the procrastinating sort of writer.'

Gerry was too wise to suggest he knew more about a husband than his wife did, so he kept his doubts to himself. He was an artist, which Mimi wasn't, and he knew only too well about the dark and sterile days which could descend without warning, and go on for lengthy periods of time. Years, in some cases.

'I wouldn't worry about him straying, though. He's got too much on his mind, take it from me.'

There was nothing like an old friend for giving you cold-water advice.

She and Gerry had met on a typing course which took place in a strange little room in a decrepit building off Oxford Street.

'A peck, N peck, T peck,' Mimi said, pulling off her earphones at the end of a session. 'No way for human beings to spend their time. Have you noticed the strange way the voice talks when it dictates names? Falling minor thirds, and then a major third to finish off.'

'You must be a musician.'

'Sort of.' She held out a hand. 'Mimi Ostiman.'

'Gerry Wilkins. Mimi? Is that your real name?'

'Nickname,' she said, digging into her large red leather shoulder bag and pulling out a Mars Bar. She broke it in two and gave half to him. 'For Miranda. My mother's keen on Shakespeare.'

'Ah.' Gerry took a big mouthful of Mars Bar and licked a trail of toffee from his top lip. 'Why are you learning typing?'

She took another bite of Mars Bar. 'To fill in time. And it means you can always get temp work.'

'I'm doing it for a bet,' he said. 'My elder brother said I could never learn to do anything practical. I said I could, he said prove it, so here I am. My parents are paying for the course, and if I finish it, my brother's giving me fifty quid. He's in the city, big earner. You don't just want to temp, do you? What about the music?'

'I go to the London College of Music in October.'

'I'm starting at art school. What do you play?'
'Piano.'

She and Gerry had kept up the friendship when they started at their separate colleges that autumn. They used to meet for cheap student lunches and went to the cinema together, sharing tales of woe about studies and lovers.

They had been so full of hope and plans for the future, thought Mimi, gazing into the dregs of her coffee. It had only taken her a term, though, to realize that she wasn't going to make it to the big time as a pianist. She knew it, her teachers knew it, all her fellow students knew it. And it was the same for most of them.

'What are you going to do if not the piano?' She had left her seedy, cold digs and taken up the offer of a room in the house which Gerry rented with other student friends. It had a huge basement kitchen where they all congregated and discussed life, sex and their futures.

'I'll stick it out there and get my piece of paper. You never know when a qualification will come in handy. Then, well, I don't know.'

'I'll consult the cards,' said Molly, a serious student of Theology at London University. 'See what comes up.'

'Cards?'

'More efficient than tea leaves.'

Mimi had thought Molly was joking, but she wasn't. Molly had read the cards for her, persuaded her to stay with her music for the time being, enjoy it as much as she could, insisted that something would happen while she was at the college which would change the pattern of her life.

She had been sceptical. 'If something's going to happen, it'll happen wherever I am.'

'Not so.'

Molly had been right. The mother of a fellow student, a tuba player, ran a shop, and Mimi, short of money, had gone to work there on Saturday mornings. A warren-like emporium of ceramics and glass, the shop had numerous fountains trickling in odd corners and in the central courtyard. The fountains were always going wrong, and she found she had a knack for getting them working again. She grew bolder, reading up on pumps as well as unblocking the loo and mending the taps in the tiny kitchen.

She installed a new, improved fountain at the entrance. The grateful proprietor smelt a business opportunity, and ordered a variety of fountains from Spain and Portugal and Italy.

'I'll sell them, and you can install them,' she told Mimi. 'I'll give you commission on each sale, and you charge whatever you like for getting the thing up and working.'

The books of studies and Beethoven sonatas lay unopened on the piano as she flew from lion heads to dolphins to nymphs bearing dribbling shells.

Her mother was furious. 'Darling, what a waste with such a talent as yours.'

'Not much of a talent,' said Mimi firmly. 'A good ear, excellent teachers – thank you for that, Mum – and hours and hours of practice. It isn't enough, you see. No stardust on me, and that's what you need.'

'I'll sell the piano,' her mother had threatened.

'Why not? I'm going to be tremendously successful, and I shall buy one of my own.'

Her mother had kept the piano then, but she had no room for it, nor for most of her other furniture when she decided she had to move from her large and comfortable Kensington house to a very small flat.

Mimi had been aghast at the dramatic clear-out. 'Mum, sell all your lovely things? But why? You're making a fortune with your crime horrors.'

'It isn't money, darling, it's the boys.'

'Are they costing you a lot?'

'Only my sanity.'

Mimi hadn't fully appreciated the strain on her mother of having three fully grown sons on the premises. Their father had left years before, soon after Benedict was born, finding four children more than he could take. He lived in Mexico with a circus artiste, took no interest in his offspring, and sent

Finella occasional sums of money. It was his departure that had led Finella to take up writing to supplement her irregular income.

She had sent the boys away to boarding school and then they had moved on to their respective universities and colleges. Naturally, they had their rooms at her big house in Kensington, where they spent their holidays and vacations. When they graduated or qualified, they would, their mother assumed, do as young men did, and move out. They would find a flat with friends, share a house, move in with a girlfriend. Finella was all for a spot of living in sin.

Not so.

They tried moving away from time to time, but always came back.

'So much more civilized here,' said languid Vincent, who had drifted into the world of antiques. 'I do need to be surrounded by beautiful things.'

'Solly refused to do any more of my washing,' said Ferdie the sculptor. 'I've dumped it by the machine for whiz Marje to do, is she coming in today?'

Benedict insisted in his gentle, obstinate way that the light in the attic room which he had made into his studio was not to be found anywhere else in London. He was a painter, with quite a lot of illustration work coming in from publishing houses. 'And if I'm working upstairs, it's much easier to live here as well, you do see that.'

Still not reconciled to Mimi's being in business rather than the arts, Finella had nonetheless generously bestowed the Steinway on her as a wedding present. She sent almost everything else to Sotheby's and found herself a flat off Marylebone High Street.

'Perfect,' she said. 'A bedroom and a little study for me, a tiny dining-room, a sitting-room and a spare bedroom for a friend. Marje can come and give the flat a good clean once a week, what a relief.'

In no time at all, Vincent had installed himself in the spare bedroom. 'Just for a week or two, Ma, until I find the right place.' Benedict came back from a retreat suffering from severe spiritual panic and took up residence on a pile of cushions under the table in the dining-room. Then Ferdie arrived back from France in the dead of night, with nowhere to go.

'There's a little hotel just round the corner,' his mother said. 'I'll pay, and then tomorrow you can find somewhere more permanent.'

'It's all right,' said Ferdie. 'I've got a sleeping bag.'

# 5

They were gathered in the big sitting-room in Edmund and Mimi's house.

Several years before, Edmund had come across yards and yards of deep red and gold heavy velvet curtains which were being tossed out from a theatre. This, with glowing Persian rugs on the floor, a Knole sofa upholstered in a rich brocade and several deep armchairs, gave the room an opulent, oriental feel.

Mimi loved the sitting-room, and although Edmund had offered to redecorate it when they married, she had wanted it all left just as it was. The only change she made was to install her piano, and the gleaming blackness of it suited the room. She was sitting on a favourite floor cushion, covered in Indian fabric with black and red elephants stamping round the border, looking very exotic herself in a brief red skirt and embroidered waistcoat.

Her mother had criticized her short skirts earlier that year. 'You're twenty-seven, too old to show your knees.' Very old-fashioned, not to say unkind. Edmund had expressed no such concern when she asked his opinion; he liked to see her comely legs.

'Why your brothers want to live like that beats me,' said Sylvester, who had been playing a Bach fugue on the piano. He came over to the table and helped himself to another ginger biscuit, dunking it in his tea.

'Laziness,' said Gerry.

'It's cheap,' said Edmund.

'They like being at home,' said Mimi, and got three disbelieving looks.

Edmund lifted the lid of the pot to see if there was any tea left. 'Don't be sentimental.'

'Come on, Sylvester,' said Mimi. 'You arrived gasping for tea, we've made it and you've drunk two cups. Now stop munching ginger biscuits and tell all. Did Mapleton show?'

'He did.' Sylvester dug into his inner pocket and flourished a card. 'John Mapleton, of Gastwick and Mapleton. Estate Agents to the Gentry.'

'Sylvester, it doesn't say that.'

'No, not gentry, you're right. But Mr Mapleton is an estate agent.'

'So Mum's planning to sell the flat. Where's she moving to? And where is she now?'

'A bed-sit, eight-by-eight and no facilities might get rid of those three,' said Gerry. 'Might, mind you. They'd probably find bunk beds and move them in.'

'Not *going* to sell.' Sylvester was enjoying himself. 'Has sold. Completion next Wednesday, and did I know what arrangements Mrs Ostiman is making for the furniture if she is away at present.'

'Sold the flat?' She couldn't believe her ears. '*Sold* it? Without saying a word to us?'

'Smart work,' said Edmund. 'Take everyone by surprise, a fait accompli, and do a scarper so that she isn't there to catch any flak.'

'I asked Mr Mapleton what was happening to the proceeds of the sale. Oh, I said I was Finella's brother, by the way, Mimi. I knew you wouldn't mind, and I wouldn't have got anything out of him otherwise. He was a willowy man in a navy overcoat, who oozed discretion.'

'I'd like you for an uncle,' said Mimi. 'I never had any, and you'd count as several.'

'I shall ignore that remark. Anyway, I made the guy some coffee, and he unbuttoned a bit. Money and all correspondence to Junius Paxley. Those were his instructions.'

'He's sending the money to my mother's agent?' She was disappointed to hear that, because she knew he would button his mouth and refuse to tell her anything about what her mother was up to.

'And there was a letter for you on the doormat,' said Sylvester. 'Which appears to be from Finella.'

'Hand it over.'

'Perhaps I'd better read it first,' said Edmund. 'In case it contains shocking news.'

Mimi took the letter from Sylvester, flicking Edmund's cheek with the envelope before opening it. The three men sat and looked at her, for all the world like a row of expectant birds, she thought as she drew out a single sheet of paper.

'Well?' said Gerry, after some moments' silence while they watched Mimi read the letter.

'Well, nothing, really.' What had got into her mother, to do such a daft thing? 'She's gone off on a banana boat.'

'Where to?'

'She doesn't say.'

'May I?' said Sylvester, consumed with curiosity. He plucked the sheet out of Mimi's hand and perched a pair of tortoiseshell specs on his nose. 'She could have typewritten it, what terrible handwriting. Now. "By the time you read this, I shall be far away . . ."'

Edmund said one had to admire her organization. 'She's thought it all through. And I'm glad she said you could have the winged chair, Mimi. I've always found it very comfortable. I shall put it in my study here.'

Mimi's mind was on other things. 'Nothing for the boys, they won't be happy.'

Sylvester could see problems ahead. 'Who's going to see to all this? If Ferdie and Benedict are away, who's going to move their stuff out? And be there when the packers come to take your mother's things into storage? And someone will have to arrange for the rest to go to the saleroom. Moving everything out of even a small flat is no joke.'

'Vincent's at home,' said Mimi.

'Vincent!' said Sylvester and Edmund together.

'He won't help,' said Gerry.

'He'll be livid,' said Edmund, not sounding very sorry for him. He found Vincent very hard to take.

'Nasty one, that,' said Sylvester with a hoot of laughter. 'Your ma saying she's had an inventory done. No use Vincent thinking he can get his hands on anything.'

'Vincent wouldn't,' said Mimi, summoning up a vestige of sibling loyalty.

'Oh, yes he would,' said Edmund. 'Leave it to me. I need to spend some time in the British Museum, I can see to the flat while I'm in London. Then you can get on with your boar, Mimi.'

'Boar?' said Sylvester interested. 'Something new?'

'I'll show you,' said Gerry, getting up. He was back almost immediately, with the drawing in his hand.

'Ha,' said Sylvester. He tapped the boar's head. 'He's a good specimen of bristly boarness. One of your best, Gerry, no doubt about it. Who's he for?'

'New city council offices.'

Sylvester looked startled. 'Council? Is this quite their style? Rather virile, isn't he?'

'That's just what Edmund thinks, but Councillor Henthorpe likes it,' said Mimi looking up from a second reading of her mother's letter. 'He's in charge of the commission for a fountain.'

'Old Henthorpe would like it. He's got some go-ahead ideas, has Henthorpe. But the rest of them . . . Well, you know what they're like.'

'What's wrong with it?' asked Mimi, joining the large cellist and Gerry as they stood at the heavy refectory table under the window, the design spread out before them. Bother them; first Edmund and now Sylvester sounding so doubtful about the boar.

'Nothing wrong with it. I like it. I'd have him at Midwinter Hall if I could afford another fountain. A fine boar, as I said. And these shrubs are good, with the little hillock. Where does the water go?'

'It comes out here,' she said, pointing to a rocky outcrop. 'Then it splashes down on the boar's back. And some will come out of his mouth, round his tusks.'

'Unruly kids will put foam in the water, to make him froth at the mouth,' Edmund predicted.

'I like the idea of that,' said Mimi.

'The council won't.'

'You're all being very negative,' said Gerry. 'I reckon they'll like the boar, they'll think he's heraldic and noble.'

'Possibly,' said Sylvester.

'Philistines, that's what you and Edmund are.'

'My advice is, if you want your money, stick to one of those depressing martyrs from the seventeenth century. One of those flattened Catholics. You can't go wrong with a squashed young woman.'

Mimi was speechless.

'Funny you should say that,' said Gerry. 'It's what the Mayor suggested.'

'I shall put it away,' said Mimi. 'It's better not to mix work with pleasure, I don't want you getting het up about the boar.'

'If pleasure means you getting in a state about your ma, then I'm off,' said Sylvester. 'Oh, she didn't say what's happening to the loot from selling her furniture.'

'You didn't read the PS,' said Mimi. 'It's to go to charity.'

'Doesn't sound like your mother,' said Edmund. 'Which one?'

'Help the Homeless.'

# 6 ♪

Edmund had told Mimi he would go straight to the British Museum from King's Cross station, put in a few hours work, and then go round to Finella's flat.

He did no such thing. Outside the station, he sniffed the familiar traffic-laden air, picked up his bag and made for the taxi queue. He waited impatiently behind an argumentative Arab family, three Danish girls with huge rucksacks and two sweet-looking old ladies, who fought to the bitter finish for the taxi that drew up beside them.

The smaller and more elderly of them won and drove triumphantly off, leering vindictively through the window at her vanquished opponent. Two more taxis drew up in quick succession. The Danish girls hung back, not wanting to take on the old lady, but she was in, quick as a flash, and the Danes only just made it into their taxi before the Arabs snatched it.

Edmund didn't have to fight anyone for his taxi. Tall, dark and purposeful-looking, he wasn't the sort taxi-snatchers would mess with.

'Wimpole Street,' he said, sitting back and stretching out his legs.

Desmond Fuseli never changed, thought Edmund, as the little man bounced up from his substantial leather chair and greeted him with cries of delight.

'Family all well?' he enquired, placing a pristine pad of paper in front of him on the desk. 'I saw Val the other night, at the opera. With Magdalena. He said they were going to spend a week or so in the north. At the castle, between lets.'

'Ah,' said Edmund. 'I'll go over to Mountjoy in that case.'

He and his cousin Valdemar got on well enough, but made no particular effort to see each other. They drifted in and out of each other's lives as the Mountjoys all did, although Edmund always had the feeling that Val, a great gossip, knew exactly what everyone was up to.

'And Justinia was there. With that peculiar woman she studies with, what's her name, Yseult something. Justy was in very good looks, I thought. That Gervase fellow was there with her, too; I suppose she'll marry him in the end. Although after Digby, perhaps . . .'

As Dr Fuseli enquired about other members of Edmund's family, he mused on Mountjoy marriages, past and present; he knew a great deal about them all. The recent and dramatic break-up of lively, musical Justinia and oppressive Digby, a Philistine to his toe-nails, had come as no surprise, no surprise at all.

The niceties over, he fixed a sharp professional eye on Edmund. 'Looking tired,' he said. 'Not sleeping? Troubles in the sexual area? You have a young wife; that can be a problem when you get to your age.'

Edmund was furious. 'No such thing. Not at all.'

'Good, good,' said Dr Fuseli. 'So what can I do for you?'

'It is sleep, in a way,' said Edmund, not quite sure how to come out with it. It seemed strange at two in the morning in distant Eyotshire. Here on a bright summer's day in central London, it was preposterous.

'Trouble getting to sleep? Or waking up in the early hours? Driven by a need to urinate?'

The fellow seemed to be fixated on that part of his anatomy. Edmund glared at him. 'It's the other end,' he said shortly. 'Inside my head.'

'Headaches? Ringing noises in the ears?' Fuseli leaned forward with enthusiasm. 'Eye strain?'

'No, no, nothing like that.'

'Do tell me about it,' urged the doctor. 'I'm sure I can help.'

Edmund was beginning to feel that he certainly couldn't, that it had been a major error of judgement to come here and consult this little doctor who had treated all the Mountjoys for all their sundry ailments over the years. He would take a bet that he'd never been consulted about this one before.

'All right,' he said, after a long pause. 'It's a presence.'

That did startle the good doctor. 'Presence?' he repeated.

Edmund shifted in his chair. Fuseli had luxurious black leather to sit on; his patients had to perch on a tightly upholstered wooden chair. 'Presence. I wake up, or don't even get to sleep, and I think; no, I *know* that there's someone in the house. Moving about.'

'Burglars?'

'Burglars? Burglars! Night after night, and I'd just feel they were there? Hardly.'

'No, no, you misunderstand me,' said Dr Fuseli gently. 'Is it fear of burglars? Do you imagine there is an intruder, come to steal or commit mayhem? It isn't such an uncommon fear, especially these days. Although I would have thought that in Eyot . . .'

'It's nothing to do with burglars. I'm not in the least frightened of burglars. If we had one, I'd deal with him. Besides, I lock up every night, why should we have burglars? And what burglar would pad about in my study, opening drawers, taking books off the shelf, switching on my tape recorder?'

'Dear me,' said Fuseli, beginning to sound alarmed. He wrote busily on the pad in front of him, the heavy gold nib of his black fountain pen making expensive squeaking sounds as it travelled across the sheet. 'Every night?'

'Most nights,' said Edmund, shifting in his chair, relieved to have got it out, relieved to have told someone, relieved that Desmond Fuseli hadn't immediately pressed a buzzer to summon help and call for the plain van and men in white coats.

'Very fanciful,' said Dr Fuseli, tut-tutting. 'Mentally ill people are not treated like that these days, and besides, I do not for a moment believe that you are mentally ill.'

'Thank you,' said Edmund, meaning it.

'First, I shall give you a thorough physical examination.'

'No, you won't,' said Edmund, who hated, as he put it, being flapped at and manhandled by the medical profession. Or by anyone else, except a woman. A picture of his wife in déshabillé rose unsummoned to his mind, followed less forgivably by the sensation of Inez's memorable breasts. He adjusted himself in his chair, trying to pull himself together and focus on the matter in hand.

Dr Fuseli was regarding him with quizzical eyebrows and a knowing smile on his moist little red mouth. Edmund had the uncomfortable feeling that he knew just what images had flitted through his patient's mind.

'No?' the doctor said.

'No. There's nothing wrong with me physically. Except that I could do with a bit more sleep, as I said.'

'You wake, then, hearing a noise?'

Edmund paused before answering. 'I hear nothing. I tell you, it's a presence. A knowing that someone is there. That there's, well, a personality loose in the house.'

'A personality? That's very interesting.' More brisk hieroglyphs joined the others on the paper. 'However, you hear and see nothing? No shadowy shapes, no footsteps?'

'No.'

'Do you smell anything?'

'Smell?' Edmund stared at the doctor. Was the man joking?

'There is no smell? It's a serious question. You must answer my questions if you want me to help you.'

'No smell.'

'So no physical manifestations at all.'

'No.'

'You mentioned drawers being opened, things disturbed in your office.'

'Yes.'

The doctor was clearly waiting for more details. He sat with his head slightly on one side, all attention, his pen poised above the paper. 'Go on.'

'It was as though someone was looking for something.'

'Very, very interesting.' Dr Fuseli's eyebrows were nearly at the top of his head.

'Annoying.'

Dr Fuseli sat forward, his elbows on the desk, his fingertips pressed together. Edmund, so much the taller, stared at the top of the doctor's balding head.

'This physical disturbance has only happened in your study?'

'Yes.'

'Have you tried being in your study at this time of night? Rather than retiring.'

'Yes.'

'And?'

'And, I fell asleep. To wake up feeling, as usual, that there was someone there, in the room with me.'

'But there wasn't?'

'No. The light was on, the room empty. And I had locked the door, the windows were shut and locked. In case of burglars,' he added snappishly.

'And the room was undisturbed?'

'No. My papers had all been disarranged, several books had been taken from the shelves, and the drawers were all open. As usual.'

'Nothing missing?'

'No.'

'You raised the alarm?'

'I did not.' Edmund found that an appalling thought. Mimi rushing in, insisting on calling the police. Tranquillizers being offered, the Neighbourhood Watch all in a jitter; fuss, fuss.

'What did you do?'

'Poured myself a whisky and went to bed.'

'Ah.' Fuseli swung himself round, and looked out of the window behind him, tapping on the window sill with his firm, stubby fingers while he pondered. He swung back, and looked at Edmund, almost sternly. 'The books which are pulled out. Are they a random collection?'

'Now you come to mention it, no. They're all on the same subject.'

'What is that?'

'The period I'm working on at present; I'm doing another book, you know. Twelfth, thirteenth century. Financing of the crusades, economic patterns; it was a bad time in Europe.'

'I believe so,' said Dr Fuseli, dismissing the famines, plague and wars of that turbulent time with a nod of his head. 'Well, now, Edmund. Illusions in the brain, hallucinations, hypnogogic images in a tired mind, sleepwalking, all these could be investigated.'

Edmund made a grunt of protest. Fuseli raised a hand.

'Could be, I said. Could be. It is not, at the moment, what I would recommend.'

'Good.' For one awful moment Edmund had thought Fuseli had been going to refer him to a psychiatrist. He told him so, adding that he wouldn't go near any of them. 'I was at Oxford with Herringbone.'

Fuseli's face brightened. 'Herringbone,' he said admiringly. 'Outstanding in his field. Top of the trees, none better.'

'Mad as a hatter.'

This was not a subject for jest as far as Fuseli was concerned. He looked severely at Edmund. 'Were I to feel that these areas warranted attention, I would send you rather to a psychologist. Possibly advise a course of psychoanalysis.'

'Like hell you would.'

'However, I have a strong suspicion that this would be barking up the wrong tree.'

'Good.'

'What you need is a different kind of specialist. Someone who is knowledgeable about the paranormal.'

'What?' Edmund couldn't believe his ears.

'Quite outside my own area of expertise, but I know that there are some very reputable people who could help you.'

'What on earth are you talking about?'

'To be brief, Edmund, I think that what we are dealing with here is a poltergeist.'

# 7 ∫

After his session with Dr Fuseli, Edmund walked to Finella's flat in Marylebone High Street. He was in a thoroughly bad mood, and not prepared to put up with any nonsense from Mimi's bloody brothers.

Vincent had been loud in his protests over the phone to Mimi, and unaware that Edmund was not approaching this matter in a spirit of tolerance, he was just as argumentative now.

'We're sitting tenants. Ma has no right to do this to us.'

'Sitting nothing,' said Edmund brutally. 'Where's your agreement, rent book, lease and whathaveyou?'

'It's a family matter,' said Ferdie resentfully.

'Which is why it's staying in the family, and you lot aren't going to kick up a fuss about it. I'm not having Mimi upset. Now, the van from the auctioneers will be here first thing in the morning. Are the pieces of furniture ready to go?'

Vincent shrugged. 'Not my problem.'

'They're all empty,' said Benedict with his charming smile. 'Ma must have cleared out her things before she left, and I've seen to the rest of it.'

Vincent cast a cold eye on his younger brother. 'Benedict is unbearably smug,' he observed. 'That's because he's fixed himself up in a cosy hole with a strange young man from Poland.'

'Adam is not strange,' said Benedict, without resentment. 'A fellow artist,' he explained to Edmund. 'He says I can use his studio while he's away for a week or so. It will give me time to find somewhere more permanent. Although it is very difficult in London, on what I can afford. And it's a bad time,

I have sixteen illustrations to finish by next month. For the Fogarty Press.'

Ferdie shrugged. 'I can hardly sleep at the old warehouse where I do my work. I shall be in a cardboard box on the street, I dare say.'

Edmund was unsympathetic. 'I doubt if it will come to that. How about you, Vincent?'

'I have friends,' said Vincent.

'Older women,' said Ferdie confidentially. 'They'll look after him, in return for a bit of action between the sheets.'

'Don't be coarse,' said Vincent. 'At least my tastes are normal. At least I don't go round London lusting after ugly men.'

Benedict broke into what was developing into a promising, and, Edmund felt, familiar quarrel. 'Furniture tomorrow, then what?'

'Mimi's arranged for a firm of cleaners to give the place a going-over.'

'Mimi would. Why doesn't she come and greet the new owners, scrape the ground in front of them?' said Vincent bitterly.

'Oh, shut up,' said Edmund, bored with their hostility. 'So I take it you'll move your things out tomorrow?'

Their assent was muted and unenthusiastic, but they knew when they were beaten.

It was a good thing he'd come to London and not Mimi; they'd have had her feeling sorry for them in no time. She seemed to find it impossible to see her brothers as they really were, and would have been incapable of the necessary ruthlessness.

God, what a trio they were. How had Finella put up with them for all that time? No wonder she had hared off into the deep blue yonder, he thought, as he walked briskly in the direction of the estate agent's office to leave the keys.

Edmund was staying with his cousin Virginia Luthier and her husband Ralph, and he was glad to sink into the subdued luxury of their flat and be greeted with civilized offers of refreshment and an intelligent interest in his doings.

Ralph laughed when Edmund told him about his encounter with Mimi's brothers. 'I've run across Vincent once or twice,' he said. 'Never met the other two. Hard on Mimi, Finella taking off like that, but I can't blame her. Remarkable woman, Finella,' he added.

Virginia was an old friend of Finella's. 'She put up with those boys for far too long,' she remarked, crossing her elegant legs and looking, Edmund thought, quite terrifying.

'I remember how pleased she was when she sold the house and felt she was going to be on her own. That didn't last long. Those boys would still be with her if she moved into a cupboard.'

'Maternal affection, very laudable,' said Ralph. An attentive host, he topped up Edmund's whisky and passed him a garlic titbit.

'Maternal nothing,' said Virginia sharply. 'Sheer selfishness and laziness. I can't think what's going to become of them.'

'They'll have to find their own places now,' said Ralph. 'I expect they'll get married.'

'Vincent might, if he can find someone classy and rich enough who's willing to take him on. I suppose Benedict might at a pinch, although it can go either way with him. Ferdie, of course not, but there's no reason he can't move in with one of his muscular boyfriends. Of course, they're all quite hideous; it might be a shock to the system waking up beside one of them morning after morning.' Virginia rose and beckoned to the others. 'Let's eat.'

# 8 ∫

Far away in Eyot, Mimi was missing Edmund.

She liked her own company, but nonetheless felt lonely in the house by herself. She settled down in her office and forced herself to work, getting a formidable amount done. Then, pleased with herself, she pushed the papers aside, yawned, got up and stretched wildly.

She listened to the sounds from outside. Birds trilled as they hopped around in the courtyard. She heard doves calling in the trees of the garden over the garage wall, and a large and attractive bee buzzed past the open window.

Summer; it felt as though summer was coming at last.

She considered what to do next as she finished up the glass of orange juice on her desk. She needed a break from work. She would go out, to the open market. She could leave the answerphone on and go shopping. Gerry was due in soon, so the office wouldn't be unattended for long.

The open market traded every day and was one of the sights of Eyot. Stalls, each with a gaily striped canopy stretched overhead, covered the large market place and spilled into nearby narrow streets. Residents jostled with tourists, early lunchers from the local schools wandered by with portions of vinegary chips from the shop on the corner, buskers tootled and sang.

Mimi's spirits rose with the busy scene, and she sauntered along the stalls with a sense of well-being. She bought Edmund a pair of colourful socks, negotiated for a bundle of tea towels and ended up at one of the greengrocery stalls, where she found some unusual ingredients for a salad.

Inspired by the greenery, she decided to be extravagant and

go to Gumbles, the famous Eyot food emporium, for cheese and some Italian and Hungarian salamis and French paté.

'Ah,' said a voice in her ear. 'Are you the mouse or the cat?'

'Hello, Sylvester,' said Mimi. 'Come and have some lunch. Gerry will be there, but not Edmund. He's still in London.'

'Of course he is. That's why I wondered if you were the mouse whooping it up in the cat's absence, or whether Edmund is.'

She laughed. 'Edmund? He's buried in the British Museum. Nothing playful about Edmund.'

'Don't you be too sure.' He relieved her of her heavier bags. 'You can be married to someone for half a lifetime and still not know them. I had a friend who'd been living a double life for the best part of twenty years. He'd had a very close relationship with an Egyptian chap all that time, and his wife knew nothing about it.'

'You aren't suggesting that Edmund . . .'

Sylvester was contrite. 'Good heavens, no. I can say with certainty that that isn't Edmund's scene at all. No, no. And don't be so prosaic, look at the way your mind instantly turns to liaisons of a sexual nature.'

'You started it.'

'Perhaps. There are other secrets, though, that husbands and wives may have, apart from the obvious ones. Secrets of the mind and soul, that's what I'm talking about.'

'I don't think Edmund's secretive. He's not given to cunning and covering his tracks. He's very open about what he's up to.'

'Admirable, if true.'

'Not at all, I sometimes think it's a kind of arrogance, not caring what anybody thinks of his actions.'

'I wonder,' Sylvester said to himself as they walked down the main street before turning off into a narrow passageway which led to the river.

'Where's your car?' she asked, stopping and looking around as though the silver Volvo, big enough to take two cellos in the back, might miraculously appear in the alleyway.

'Parked in the Guillibert Hotel, where I always leave it. I'll get it later.'

They walked along the river path and over the bridge and then along to the bottom of Mimi's street.

'I'll hold those other bags while you dig out your key,' said Sylvester.

'Door's open,' sang out a voice from inside. 'And keep to the newspaper, or you're dead, Mrs Sconce has just done the hall floor.'

'Gerry's here.'

'So I gather.' Sylvester picked his way carefully across the jigsaw of Victorian tiles, which gleamed wetly on either side of the newspaper path.

Gerry was busy in the kitchen. Visitors found it disconcerting to come across him loading the dishwasher or putting plates away, but Mimi was quite used to it. Gerry was like the friendly and helpful brother she'd never had. After college, she and Gerry had kept in close touch. He went off to Milan for a year, and she had visited him there, happy to pick up all kinds of inspirations for her own work.

He'd lived in London when he came back from Italy, but on a weekend visit he'd decided that he liked the look of Eyot and had stayed, giving Mimi a hand when he could and doing freelance work. Then he'd taken the job at the Cathedral School and Mimi's business had developed enough for her to be able to pay him properly.

'Have you bought something for lunch?' he asked. 'Hand it over. I've tidied up in the office, and there was a phone call from a friend of Lady Wray's.'

'Lady Wray?' said Mimi suspiciously.

'One Elvira Winthrop. She said she knew of you through Lady Wray. Isn't that Edmund's aunt?'

'Yes. What did she want?' Mimi was wary; she and Edmund's aunt had never hit it off.

'A fountain.'

'Oh, business.' As long as it wasn't a sociable call. 'There won't be any problem with her, I'll dig up the catalogue of nice garden ornaments for the conventional older woman.'

'I think she wants to commission something special,' said Gerry. 'To commemorate her four husbands.'

'Four?'

Sylvester laughed at Mimi's shocked look. 'Good for Elvira,' he said. 'Forget the conventional older woman, that's not Elvira at all.'

'You know her?'

'I do indeed.'

Gerry was delighted at the prospect of another commission. 'It would be really good if you get this one. Just a bit more work from you, Mimi, I'll be able to give up another day's teaching at the Cathedral School.'

'It's very bad for the youngsters,' complained Sylvester. 'All you highly trained young artists are desperate not to teach.'

'Needs must,' said Gerry unrepentantly. 'It's all right for you, Sylvester, you only teach when and who you want to. You don't rely on it, you command huge fees, prestigious venues, fat recording contracts. It's quite different in the lower reaches of the artistic world where I hang out.'

'Aim high.'

'I am. I know what I want to do. I want to spend all my time designing such delights as fountains and strange items of furniture, and I'd love to make some original doors. Don't you think doors are due for a renaissance? Don't you think doors are terribly dull?'

'No,' said Mimi quickly, seeing his eye resting speculatively on the handsome six-panelled number which led into the sitting-room. 'Hands off.'

'No spirit of adventure,' said Gerry. 'Edmund's much more exciting than you are, I shall have a word with him. When's he back? I must say, it's very quiet here without his overpowering presence.'

'Edmund isn't overpowering,' said Mimi.

'Don't be indignant,' said Gerry, his mouth full of a Bath Oliver smeared with a lump of soft and smelly cheese. 'One knows when Edmund is about, that's all.'

'I had a strange phone call from him this morning,' said Sylvester. 'Asking if I know anyone who's sound on poltergeists.'

'Poltergeists?' said Mimi, puzzled. 'He didn't say anything about poltergeists when I spoke to him. Besides, what would he want with a poltergeist expert? Edmund has no interest in the supernatural; I'm sure he doesn't believe in any of it. I certainly don't.'

'I expect Edmund does, you know,' said Sylvester. 'The Mountjoys have a knack that way. But no doubt it's for research purposes. Isn't he deep in the Cathars and Templars and so forth?'

'That'll be it.' She tucked into a chunk of coarse paté. Inez wouldn't be able to help with anything ghostly; that was clean out of her field. The thought gave her great pleasure, which she tried to suppress. She must pull herself together, she was becoming obsessed with Inez.

Gerry had been thinking. 'Edmund should get in touch with Will Wrackham, a guy who teaches the piano at the Cathedral School. He's a notable ghosthunter.'

'Will, of course, the very man,' said Sylvester. 'Mimi, pass that on to Edmund. Will Wrackham. Gerry will be able to give you his number.'

# 9

The telephone rang and rang.

Mimi stirred in her sleep, then rolled over to prod Edmund into life. He was a morning person, she wasn't. Then she remembered that he was in London. The telephone rang on, and she slithered across the sheets to grope for it.

'Uh?' she said sleepily.

'Elvira Winthrop here,' came a voice so brisk that Mimi blinked and moved the receiver away from her ear. 'Good morning. I rang early, so as to be sure of catching you.'

'Uh,' said Mimi again.

'You didn't ring back yesterday. I spoke to someone at that number who said they'd give you a message.'

'Oh.' She gave her head a shake, as though that might help her to gather her wits together. 'Um, yes.' Then her brain cleared. 'I did return your call, but there was no reply.'

'Then I was out. Quite right, you see, to make a call at this time of day, to be sure of catching people in.'

And asleep, thought Mimi resentfully. She had just caught sight of the clock; ten to seven. This woman was clearly mad.

'I suggest that you come round here at, shall we say, ten thirty?'

It wasn't a question, rather a command. Mimi opened her mouth to say no, that time wouldn't suit her; just on principle. Then she shut it again. Business was business, and commissions not so plentiful that she could afford to offend a potential client. She swallowed her pride. 'Very well. Where?'

Elvira sounded astonished that she should ask. 'Don't you

know? I thought everyone knew where I lived. The Manor House, Hustle.'

'It's a lovely house,' said Gerry. 'I looked it up in Pevsner. What a place to design a fountain for!'

Mimi sat yawning at the breakfast table, still suffering from her abrupt early awakening. Gerry was firm. 'Off you go, or you'll be late. Don't forget to take the portfolio.'

Hustle had once been a village a mile or so beyond the city walls, but had long since been absorbed into the city. Hustle Manor and its gardens, however, stood aloof from the terrace houses which surrounded it; an oasis of green in a sea of redbrick. Eyot people knew the Manor well, and rich citizens coveted the exquisite Queen Anne house with its honey-coloured stone and perfect proportions.

The wrought iron gates stood open, and Mimi drove up the drive, jamming on the brakes as she saw the house, golden in the sunlight. She sat and gazed and gazed, until her attention was caught by a small figure beckoning imperiously at her to come closer. The drive ended in a gravel circle round a small pond, fenced with aromatic hedges; idyllic, thought Mimi as she pulled up on the far side of it.

'Good,' said the small, plump woman. 'On time.' She waved a hand towards the pond. 'You see? Hopeless. I've been meaning to have something done about it for years. There was a dismal Victorian fountain there once, but my second had it taken down, he couldn't stand it. Now I've just had a windfall from some shares I thought were worthless, and I've decided to spend the money on a fountain.'

'I see,' said Mimi.

'Coffee, first,' said Elvira. 'We'll have it on the terrace, and you can show me what you've brought. I don't know what you've done, but I'll know at once whether you'll be suitable for this job. Round the back, it's much quicker than going inside.'

Mimi would rather have gone through the house. Just passing by the front door, she got a glimpse of the beauties within, but the veggie patch was her lot as Elvira led her through the kitchen gardens and through a wide half-panelled door into the kitchen.

A ratty little shape emerged from a basket in front of the Aga, bared its teeth, and flew, in a welter of yaps and growls, at Mimi's ankles.

'Silly dog,' said Elvira, as the creature sank a fine set of sharp teeth into Mimi's leg.

She let out a yelp of pain and kicked out. She should have worn jeans, what a mistake to have put on a summer skirt. She rubbed her leg, keeping a wary eye on the horrid little animal, who was making a renewed series of rushes in her direction.

Elvira picked it up by the scruff of the neck and dumped it unceremoniously back in its basket. 'Stay,' she commanded. And then, to Mimi, 'He must like you, he only bites people he likes. Oh dear, quite a few punctures, I'll get the iodine.'

Bloody dog, thought Mimi savagely. And bloody woman, to keep such a dog. Indignation rose in her. Waking her up at the crack of dawn, giving her orders, letting wild animals loose on her. It was too bad. To hell with it. If she wanted a fountain, she could go elsewhere. Gerry would lose enthusiasm anyway, once he had to start work on some dull Italianate copy.

She bent over to pick up several items which had spilled out from her portfolio during the savage attack.

Elvira pounced. 'Why, this is the very thing,' she cried. 'Exactly what I had in mind.'

Mimi, opening her mouth to make her anger clear before she took her leave, stared at the drawing in Elvira's hand. It was the sketch that Gerry had jokingly done of the naughty nymphs frolicking with the well-endowed and highly excited Tritons.

'Sorry,' she said. 'That shouldn't have been in there, I must have put it in by mistake.' She stretched out a hand to take it back, but Elvira snatched it out of reach.

'Mistake? I love it. Perfect. I'll supply photos of my husbands, and then there can be a likeness, how delightful. Of course, none of them had quite these proportions, more's the pity, but artistic licence, you know, makes it permissible.'

Mimi was all set to argue as she stared at the wild and witty baroque design which Elvira was flapping up and down in her excitement.

Then an image of Gerry's face came into her mind. He would love to do it. He could never hope to find another customer with the will – and, apparently, the funds – to commission such a work. How could she say no? He would never forgive her, and even if she didn't ever tell him, she wouldn't forgive herself for depriving him of such an opportunity.

Besides, the offer of a commission, whether accepted or refused, would get out. This was Eyot. Everything, sooner or later, got out.

'I'd love some coffee,' she said, taking the proffered bottle of iodine and a piece of kitchen towel. 'Then we can talk about details.'

Gerry was hard at work in the office when she got back. 'Any luck?'

Mimi told him.

Gerry was speechless. He stared at her. 'No! I don't believe it. You're having me on.'

'I'm not having you on,' said Mimi shortly, still feeling that she shouldn't have listened to Elvira Winthrop.

'Can we do it? It's going to be a bugger, apart from upsetting the natives. Does she have any idea of how much this is likely to cost?'

'I gave her a rough idea. I'll have to do the costings extremely carefully, because we're talking thousands.'

'I could cut down on the number of figures,' he said, squinting at his artwork. 'I mean, this is just an impression of what it could be like.'

'I get the idea she's thinking lavish.'

'How wonderful to be rich,' said Gerry with a hefty sigh. 'Now, I want to hear all about it. What's she like?'

'Much-married, for a start.' Mimi swung her feet up on to the wide and sumptuous sofa which Edmund had bought for her on their first anniversary. It was where she did most of her thinking.

Gerry, buzzing with excitement and interest, was perched on a strange leather pouffe which Edmund had had since childhood.

'Four husbands. Of whom two are deceased, one missing and one extant and living in India.' She laughed, remembering what Elvira had said. 'She wants you to make the figures in the fountain look like them.'

That startled him, as he had visions of portly colonels or weedy aristocrats desporting themselves in his fountain. 'Help. Do you know any more about them?'

Mimi counted on her fingers. 'Number one was the money-bags. He was much older than she was, and she married him when she was only nineteen. She says she was fond of him, and he was very handsome, but he turned out to have some rather strange habits. She didn't go into those, which is just as well on a first meeting, don't you think?'

Gerry's face showed that he would love to know more about the habits. 'Go on, then.'

'He keeled over with a heart attack while pleasuring a whore in Soho. Bit distasteful, I think, but Elvira said she didn't mind at all. His family hushed it all up, but she thinks it was how he'd have chosen to go. So, there was the money, and the house, and after six years of him, Elvira thought it was time to suit herself.'

'No children?'

'No children. No children by any of them, she told me she can't have children.' Mimi wound the tassel of a fat velvet cushion round her finger as she thought of Elvira's next husband. 'She met him in a supermarket in London, buying spices. He was half-Indian, half-Portuguese, and, she says, the most beautiful man she ever saw.'

'Beautiful?' Gerry was doubtful about that.

'Very, very masculine, so she said. Not a flaw anywhere. She waxed quite lyrical about his anatomy. You'll be able to tell for yourself, for she's got lots of photos of him in the nude. For you to work from.'

'Sounds promising.'

'She says she's going to be fussy about him, since she has so many happy memories of their time together.'

'What happened to him?'

'They didn't have much in common besides bed. He was desperately keen on football, which isn't her cup of tea at all, and what with one thing and another, and him hankering for the bright lights of London, and not altogether settling down in Hustle, they drifted apart. She used to go up to London for a few days of serious delight with him, but then he went back to India, and she never saw him again.'

'Dead?'

'No, they got divorced.'

'How? He doesn't sound the sort to be signing papers and conferring with lawyers. Or did he take her to the cleaners?'

'Not at all. She's very canny with money, and I don't suppose he knew quite how rich she was. She paid him off, I gather.'

'Next?'

'Next was Gustav Greerson.'

'What, the explorer? Good heavens, she does get around. Did he have a good body as well?'

'One imagines so, he must have been very strong and muscular with all those outdoor activities.'

'Did he expire in a welter of snow or white water? I don't remember.'

'He disappeared. Eaten by crocodiles, possibly, although Elvira still dreams about him, thinks he may be holed up in one of the last unknown places on earth, perfectly happy as a member of an ancient tribe.'

'If he just vanished, didn't that make for a problem when number four came on the scene?'

'Not at all. Elvira waited for seven years, not minding much as celibacy, she told me, is not in her nature, and then she had him declared dead. She promptly married Hamish. From Scotland, as you can tell from the name. They were very happy, she said. Only he shot himself last year.'

Gerry tsk-tsked from his pouffe. 'Suicide? A bad business. And messy, to shoot yourself.'

'Accident,' said Mimi, who had unearthed a little bottle of nail polish from under the cushions and had begun to paint her toenails a vivid purple colour. 'He was climbing over a stile, and he hadn't done whatever it is you do to guns to make them safe. He tripped, and that was that. Definitely an accident, so Elvira, who is no slouch when it comes to money matters, I feel, was able to clean up on the insurance.'

Gerry approved of all this. 'Not the sad demises and disappearances, but the back-up info which indicates that Elvira Winthrop is well able to fork out for a major garden ornament. You'll have to go into the question of hardware very carefully, you've never done anything as big as this.'

Mimi was quite confident about her ability to handle pumps and flows. She understood water. Her fears lay in another direction. 'The council commission, and now this,' she said. 'It's going to be very tedious when life returns to normality and pithoi and lion's heads.'

Gerry disagreed. 'I find that once life gets more interesting, then it goes on being so. One ends up on a higher plane, as it were.'

10 ∫

'I'm Will Wrackham. I've come about the haunting.'

Mimi, faced with an unfamiliar but stunning young man, stood at the front door and stared. She had been upstairs in the loft, hunting through old papers in search of an address, when the doorbell rang. Edmund, she thought, as she hurtled downstairs. He must have forgotten his keys. Again.

But it wasn't Edmund, with or without keys. Instead, it was this impossibly handsome man, with dark wavy hair swept back from a noble forehead, and a pair of moody, passionate brown eyes. 'Haunting?' said Mimi feebly.

'This is number 14? This is Guillibert Road? Edmund Mountjoy's house?'

'Yes.'

'He rang me. From London, I think. Explained there was a problem, asked me to call round. I came straight away, always keen to get on to a new haunting. Are you his wife?'

'Yes.' Haunting? Edmund ringing from London? This didn't sound like finding out about poltergeists for his book. 'I think there's been a mistake,' she said. 'A slight misunderstanding. You'd better come in.'

Will bent down and picked up a large square leather case which he carried carefully into the house.

'I thought you were Edmund when I heard the bell,' said Mimi. 'I'm expecting him back from London at any minute.'

Will's face brightened. 'Splendid. Then he can tell me exactly what the problem is, and we can take it from there.' He looked about him, his eyes sparkling. 'Big house,' he said appreciatively. 'Nice.'

'Yes. Do you want to wait? Edmund said he'd be catching the train that gets in at quarter past eleven.'

'It'll be late, I expect,' said Will. 'It always is, that train. Have you noticed any manifestations?'

'Manifestations?' Had she let a madman into the house?

'I was at Sylvester's house a couple of nights ago. He's had some poltergeist problems in the past, and I get a similar feeling here. You know Sylvester Tate, do you? The cellist.'

'Yes, he's an old friend,' she said, leading him into the sitting-room. If this man knew Sylvester well enough to be visiting Midwinter Hall, then he probably wasn't mad. 'Um, was it a professional visit? To Sylvester's?'

'No. He's amused by my ghost-hunting; he says spirits are much better left alone. It was purely a social visit, I and my wife went to dinner there.'

That was a relief. A wife and dinner with Sylvester sounded quite normal.

'I wonder, might I look at his study, where the problem seems to be?'

Where was Edmund? What was he thinking, summoning this very strange man to his house? Especially when he wasn't there.

Then she heard the sound of the front door opening, and the thud as it swung back to hit the chest behind the door. Edmund was back.

His voice rang out. 'Mimi? Mimi, where are you?'

She flew into the hall, to be greeted by a huge bunch of flowers, a passionate kiss, and a breathtaking embrace. Will and his manifestations were quite forgotten, until a slight cough brought her and Edmund back to earth.

'Who's this?' asked Edmund, releasing Mimi and frowning. He wasn't the most noticing of men, but she could see that Will's astonishing looks had made an impression.

'You asked him to come. This is Will Wrackham. He's a friend of Sylvester's. He says he's come about the haunting.'

Edmund looked decidedly shifty. 'Ah,' he said. 'Yes. I hadn't expected . . . that is, I rather thought . . .'

Then he recovered himself. 'I did ask Will to come, quite right, although it isn't a matter of a haunting exactly. Just some advice.'

Will's face fell. 'Are you telling me that there's no haunting?

No poltergeist? No manifestations? What a terrible disappointment.'

Mimi was suspicious. What exactly was Edmund up to?

Meanwhile, he was getting into his stride. 'It's a general question. Not specific. For a book I'm working on. Come into my study, and I'll explain.'

'Oh, my,' said Will with reverence as Edmund opened the door to his study and stood stock-still, amazed and rendered quite speechless. 'What a scene of devastation. Did you leave it like this?'

Mrs Sconce was mystified and inclined to take it all personally. 'I did in here yesterday afternoon,' she said. 'Not a serious clean, mind, just keeping the dust at bay and doing the carpet. No, of course it wasn't like this. I wouldn't leave a room in this state. I'd have come straight to find you, Mrs Mountjoy, and told you to call the police.'

Edmund thanked God that she hadn't done so. He resumed his role of interrogating counsel. 'Now, let's be absolutely clear about this. Everything was in order when you came in here yesterday afternoon?'

Mrs Sconce stepped carefully over a heap of lever arch files, lying open and bereft of their papers, which were doubtless reposing with all the bits and pieces from Edmund's desk in the overflowing wastepaper bin. Mimi was sitting, stunned, in the shabby old armchair by the fire place, clutching a bin liner, but making no move to clear up.

Mrs Sconce stood with her arms akimbo, on her mettle now. 'I'll tell you exactly what it was like. There was a pile of books on your chair. As there so often is; I've said to Mrs Mountjoy time and again I can't think why you leave them there. Why don't you put them on your desk, or, better still, back on the shelf? And all your drawers were open. And your fountain pen was lying without its cap, on a sheet of paper.'

'What did you do?'

Mrs Sconce gave him a contemptuous look, and spoke as to a not-very-bright child. 'I tidied up. I closed the drawers, put the books back on the shelf, capped the pen and put it back in the jar with the other pens and pencils.'

They all looked at the pencil pot, which was lying upside down on the floor, pens and pencils arranged in a corona round it.

'It's a practical joke,' said Mimi finally. 'How did anyone get in? That's what I want to know.'

Edmund knew, before he spoke, that Will was going to spill the beans.

He did so, his eyes on fire with enthusiasm. 'It's simply an escalation. Edmund's told me about the previous happenings in here, his sense of a presence. Now, this spirit, entity, whatever it is, is particularly concerned with Edmund. His room, his possessions. And when he went away, it got angry.'

Mimi let out a squawk of disbelief.

Will gave her a delightful smile. 'It hasn't happened in the rest of the house?'

'No, it hasn't. And what are you talking about? Are you saying there's a poltergeist in the house? I think not. There aren't any teenagers in the house for one thing, it's teenagers who cause things to fly about, everyone knows that. There haven't been any strange noises or bangs or thumps and nowhere else has been disturbed, only this room. And no one's seen anything, which is because there's nothing to see.'

'Edmund's been aware of someone else being in the house at night,' said Will tactlessly.

'Thank you, Will,' said Edmund quickly, as Mimi proceeded to lose her temper with an abandon and completeness not equalled since she had flattened Stephen Horslitt in the fourth form.

# 11

Mimi felt in her bones that Inez was behind it.

Why?

Mimi was pretending to be rational about this deep suspicion. It was a reasonable supposition, she told herself. Opportunity? Inez had a key to the house, from earlier days. Days when she was virtually living with Edmund. Motive? They were days that she was sure Inez would like to experience once more.

A fierce jealousy gnawed at her vitals, however much she told herself that she was looking at this matter dispassionately, simply going for what anyone would agree was the most likely explanation.

No chance.

While she and Mrs Sconce began to restore some order to Edmund's study, and that idiotic Will fiddled about with meters and yards of trailing wires, Edmund had hared off to the university. To make sure there were copies of some key papers, he said.

To see Inez, Mimi was certain.

Gerry wasn't convinced about the Inez theory. 'I've seen some strange things before this,' he said. 'Why, there was a poltergeist in the pub in the village where I grew up. It threw knives about. The landlord came down one morning to find a Sabatier knife plunged twelve inches deep into a stone wall. They had to call a stonemason to get it out.'

'Rowdies drinking in the pub after hours,' said Mimi.

Gerry shook his head. 'The kind of village we lived in, people knew if you turned over in bed at night. It was a poltergeist all right. They got hold of a travelling exorcist, and that did the trick.'

'A clergyman?'

'I don't think so. A more efficient Will Wrackham, from what I remember. Anyhow, after he'd been, the knives stayed where they were meant to. Although it proved all to have been too much for the publican and his wife. They sold up about a year later. He went into a home for alcoholics, and she ran off to Spain with a girlfriend. It just goes to show.'

Mimi got up from her hands and knees and dusted herself down. 'It just goes to show that I don't believe any of it. There's a perfectly natural explanation for all this, and it's one I don't like very much.'

'You've got a bee in your bonnet about Inez. No way could she, or would she, do this.'

Edmund, returning that evening from the university in an abstracted mood, did nothing to help matters, answering Mimi's queries with monosyllables, and staring at her blankly when she made a remark about Inez.

He's not going to bamboozle me, she thought furiously. So much for husbands. She would throw herself into her work, and if he chose to run off with Inez, which is what it would probably come to, then so be it. She wasn't going to give it another thought.

What an insinuating sort the woman was. Pretending to be so concerned about Edmund's work, about his book, about his position at the university. And he lapped it up. He in his turn pretended that Inez was merely a figure in the past, their affair long since over and forgotten.

She should have known how it would be. She should not have married. She knew what men were like. Her lovers before Edmund had taken their ease and pleasure and then left. All right, she had left one or two – but that was a case of getting in first.

Michael's stricken face rose before her eyes. Nonetheless, he was no more to be trusted than the others. And then there was Roger. That was different; she had parted from him on the most amicable of terms when he joined a Trappist monastery.

All in the past.

She was married now. Marriage was different. Especially when you were married to a man with a past he saw every time he went to work. The traitor.

'Inez?' said Edmund, puzzled, when she pushed him away. 'I haven't seen Inez since I went to London. Why do you go on about Inez? How the hell do I know how Inez is? And I don't care, either,' he said, sliding his hands beneath Mimi's silk shirt with a sigh of lustful zest.

And I don't believe a word of it, she thought, deciding nonetheless to live in the moment and giving herself up to further delights.

That had been on the sofa, a pre-dinner flourish. Much later, after a glorious time in bed, Edmund had sunk into a deep sleep, his arms wrapped affectionately round Mimi.

Look at him, she thought, not a whit bothered by the day's startling events, out like a light.

She didn't know that Dr Fuseli had prescribed a one-at-bedtime pill for him, to ensure a restful night's sleep and remove the temptation to wander about the house in the hours of darkness in pursuit of invisible and intangible presences.

Mimi awoke convinced that she was the victim of a conspiracy.

Yesterday she'd been woken at the most ungodly hour by Elvira's phone call, and now there was a peremptory ring on the doorbell. At cockcrow. It must be the post. Go away, she mouthed, covering her ears with the bedclothes. They could put a card through the door, she'd go to the sorting office later. No way was she going to get up.

Another peal on the bell, and then loud rappings on the knocker. Why was Edmund still asleep? Why hadn't he woken up? Exhausted by his efforts the night before? Not if she knew him; he probably just didn't want to get up.

She dragged herself out of bed and padded to the window. She peered out. Goodness, a huge van. She gave a huge yawn. It must be the furniture from her mother's flat, the chair and the desk. She opened the window, shouted down, 'Coming,' and went back to the bed to rouse Edmund.

'Boxes,' he said sleepily, ten minutes later, as a man in overalls staggered through the door. 'Some mistake, I feel. We are expecting two items of furniture. A desk and a chair. No boxes.'

'Sorry, mate,' said overalls. 'The van's full of boxes and a lot more besides. All to this address. No furniture, though. Now, where do you want them all to go?'

Mimi and Edmund looked at each other.

'Vincent,' said Mimi.

'Your wretched brothers,' said Edmund.

Sylvester was vastly amused when he dropped by to catch up on the news about Mimi's visit to Elvira and heard instead all about the early-morning visitation. 'So where did you put the van load?'

'In the old stable-block,' said Edmund. 'And it isn't bloody well staying there. I'm not having a lot of boxes cluttering the place up. Those three can take them away, or the lot's going to the tip. You ring them and tell them so, Mimi, they really are your problem. Tell them I don't care what they've sent here, I'm going to throw everything out.' His face was dark with fury and he was stalking up and down like a panther in a temper.

'They won't believe me,' she protested. 'People are always threatening them with the most terrible things, and they never happen.'

'This will be the first time, then. It's the cunning I can't stand. Never a word to me. Empty flat when I went to hand over to the estate agent. Immaculate, not so much as a note on the board or a forgotten sock.'

'There's more here than they ever had in the flat.' Mimi felt that this ominous piece of news had better be broken to Edmund sooner rather than later. 'They parked their possessions all over London when the house was sold. I think they've gathered everything together and sent it all here to us.'

'They are the limit,' said Edmund. 'You've got to do something once and for all about those brothers of yours.'

'Calm down,' said Sylvester in his jovial way. 'Finella's boys are a force of nature. Always have been. You won't get the better of them, nor will Mimi. You'll simply have to light a candle to St Jude.'

'St Jude?' said Edmund, momentarily distracted.

'The saint who looks after lost causes. Send up a quick prayer that one day they'll meet their match.'

'They have,' said Edmund. 'Me. Now, Mimi, straight on the phone and tell them to arrange for those things to go.'

'Can't,' she said. 'We don't have a phone number for any of them. Nor any addresses. We'll have to wait until they get in touch.'

'Their round, I think, Edmund,' said Sylvester.

Edmund was infuriated by Sylvester's insouciance. 'It's all very well,' he began, only to be interrupted by another loud peal on the doorbell. This time whoever it was didn't wait, but set up a brisk tattoo on the knocker even before the strident clamour of the bell had died away.

'You answer it,' said Edmund to Mimi. 'Probably another load of your brothers' worldly goods.'

'No,' she said, returning as swiftly as she'd gone. 'It *is* the furniture this time.'

'That's something, I suppose,' said Edmund grudgingly. 'Mind now, my chair's to go in my study.'

'It's actually my chair,' said Mimi, feeling that Edmund had been exceptionally bossy about the boys. Although she didn't begrudge him the chair; she had never liked it, and it suited his long-legged frame.

While she escorted the desk and chair to their destinations, she didn't notice another van drawing up behind the dignified green and gold van of the reputable firm of carriers.

This was quite the opposite, utterly disreputable in fact. It gave a loud fart as the driver turned the engine off and climbed out. He was a grubby individual, with a three-day growth of tacky beard, disgusting old jeans and holey T-shirt, with dirty toes poking through a grimy pair of plimsolls. 'You Mimi?' he asked with an ingratiating and truly horrible leer.

'What?' said Mimi, who had been wondering which of her neighbours this type was calling on.

He pulled out a crumpled envelope from his back pocket and slid a black-nailed finger along the address. 14 Guillibert Street. 'You Mimi?' he asked again. 'Ferdie's sis? He said you'd be here, to take this lot in.' He jerked his unsavoury thumb towards the back of the van.

Edmund had joined Mimi on the pavement, a look of disbelief and rage on his face. Sylvester loomed behind him, fascinated and not wanting to miss any of the action.

'What lot?' said Edmund.

'Load in the back. Stuff from his studio. You know, sculptures. Torsos. Works of art. If you like that sort of thing. And there's fifty quid to pay, he said you'd see to that. Yeah, and he said you'd fix me up with a meal, too. I got a long drive back, and this van isn't exactly in the Rolls Royce league on the comfort front.'

# 12

Edmund looked with disbelief at the writhing torsos piling up in his hall.

'I don't think your brother has any talent at all.'

Mimi made a thoughtful clicking noise with her tongue. 'He's very good at muscles. He knows his muscles.'

'No human being ever had muscles like that.'

'Possibly not so many of them and so well developed, no.'

'And why torsos? Why only from neck to bum?'

'That's what interests him. Besides, heads are difficult. And his models are mostly male friends, and Ferdie's male friends are always ugly.'

It was too much for Edmund. The torsos would have to go, things were bad enough with alien visitors to his study; he couldn't have a house full of these terrible torsos. He said so, at some length.

Mimi was as cross as he was, but trying not to show it. He was having to put up with a lot as far as her brothers were concerned. She would have to cope, and at least she could remain calm. The torsos could go, for the time being, into the stable on the other side of the courtyard. At least there no one would have to look at them.

'It's your mother's fault,' Edmund was saying. 'Insisting that all her children were artistic. Why, for heaven's sake?'

'A quirk. And a reaction against *her* mother, who insisted that she train as an engineer, thus promoting women's rights. You go and shut yourself away; I'll see to this lot.'

'I'm off,' said Edmund. 'I shall go and work at the university today. It isn't convenient, but this place is rapidly turning into a madhouse.'

The buildings to the rear of the house were older than the main part, which was one of a terrace of a dozen houses built in the nineteenth century. Their one, though, had been built on the site of a previous, more humble dwelling, which was part of the farm attached to the nearby ruined abbey. So at the back, they had a pleasing cobbled courtyard, the old stables and a small barn which Mimi had converted into an office.

Two old loose boxes remained on the ground floor, and above them were what had been the coachman's quarters, but had been modernized and made habitable by Edmund some years previously. 'They were offering grants for conversions,' he had told Mimi, who felt that the already large house hadn't needed any more rooms. 'I wasn't going to miss a chance to get something back for all the taxes those bastards wring out of us.'

So Mimi rang Gerry, and summoned the services of a willing neighbour, usually garrulous, but stunned into silence by the sight of Ferdie's works.

'Eeh,' he said, dumping the last one to the ground with scant respect, so that several chips flew off. 'Eeh,' he repeated, wiping his brow with his arm. 'Nasty imagination this sculptor has got. You aren't planning to use these as garden ornaments, are you?'

She assured him that she wasn't, and he went off muttering about being fair buggered if he'd ever seen the like of it.

'Nicely put, really,' said Gerry, thankfully closing the door of the stable behind him. 'Does he ever sell any of these?'

'Among his circle.'

'He needs to find himself an honest profession, take his mind off all this. Maybe now your ma's hopped it, he will.'

Mimi didn't think that at all likely, but Gerry was optimistic. 'If she's away for a good long time, he might. She's obviously exerted a lot of influence on your brothers and their artistic careers. On you, too, before you got away; I remember how she used to go on at you.'

She thought of the long hours spent at the piano, the almost unendurable boredom of music college, and felt she couldn't argue the point. 'Come inside, and I'll make us a cold drink.'

'Where's Edmund?'

'Escaped.'

'Mm. Just what he needs, all this upheaval when he's trying to get his book finished.'

'Think of the conditions he used to write in when he was doing his travel pieces.'

Edmund, inheriting an unexpected legacy, had taken off after university and spent several fascinating years in Greece and the surrounding area. He had managed to wangle his way across the border into Albania, only just getting out before the forces of darkness closed in on him.

Then he had made his way to France, where his scholarly instincts surfaced, and he began work on the life and times of an intriguing family at the end of the twelfth century. His travel writing paid for his keep while he was writing the book; his articles were much appreciated by the readers of the highbrow Sundays, who sat in their comfortable cars in traffic jams, and imagined themselves as intrepid travellers in the places so accurately and perceptively described by Edmund.

With a finished book under his arm, he had returned to England. An astonished publisher, who had advanced the lanky new graduate the sum of £50 several years before, in case he felt like writing a book while on his travels, found an untidy pile waiting on his desk one Tuesday morning. A few days later a tall and formidable young man appeared in the publisher's office to enquire whether he liked the book. The rest was publishing history.

'Made a fortune from it, didn't he?' said Gerry, pushing the high stool back from his drawing board and having a good stretch.

'Enough to buy this house, which was a wreck, and do it up. His second book did well, too.' Mimi pulled the large stapler towards her, clamped a pile of invoices together and stuffed them into a file.

'When did that come out? Quite a while ago, wasn't it?'

'Six years.' She carried the file over to the filing drawers. 'Money still comes in from it, but he needs to have the new one out.'

'The university must pay him something.'

'Yes.' Mimi didn't want to say how little it was. Edmund

had a visiting fellowship at Eyot University, which gave him a cubby-hole in the History department and some status in return for not very much money and an agreement to supervise the occasional doctoral student and give two or three lectures a term.

Gerry had caught the note of restraint in Mimi's voice. 'You'll have to build up the business,' he said. 'Nothing like two earners to keep the wolf from the door.'

Edmund was as concerned as Mimi about finishing his new book. What he knew, but she didn't, was just how far it was from being ready. Not even Inez really appreciated that the welter of typewritten pages building up in the files were research notes, not a book.

He walked unenthusiastically up the stairs to the History department and along the corridor to his room. As he opened the door, he noticed the dust on the window shown up as a thick patina by the sun streaming through. He tugged at the Venetian blind, jerking it down to hang at an uneasy angle above the shelf which ran along the wall beneath the window.

Then, turning round to face his desk, he saw the all-too-familiar signs of a visitor. The drawers were opened, the top two half out, the bottom one full out so that it had tipped down on to the floor.

His files here had also been disarranged, he could tell that at a glance, although at least the papers hadn't been strewn about as they had in his study at home. And, once again, a pile of books relating to the thirteenth century were stacked in a pile on his chair.

Edmund stood stock-still. Then his ears caught a distant click-clack. Inez in her high slingbacked sandals, tit-tupping along the corridor towards his room. He judged that she wouldn't yet have turned the corner by the library, and flung himself out of the room, just taking time to lock it behind him before fleeing to the back stairs.

The History department of Eyot University was housed in the Old Admiralty Building. This was a Victorian edifice, built in the neo-classical style. It had splendid views up and down the Eyot, and the way out of the main entrance brought you directly on to one of the city's many bridges.

Edmund walked quickly across Boar Bridge, looking more than once over his shoulder to see that Inez was not coming after him. He couldn't face her today, not with all those endless, well-meant questions and comments on his work. He knew she meant to be helpful; it wasn't her fault that it felt to him like oppression and nagging. And as for the mess in his office, he didn't want to think about it. She'd be full of concern, anxious to help tidy it all up, wanting to call administration and senior staff, telling him he should complain about students taking practical jokes too far.

He grimaced at the thought, imagined, quite erroneously, that he could see Inez's unmistakable head of hair on the other side of the river, and dived for cover, ending up inside the hall of the Music department. A sturdy bassoonist went past, giving him a puzzled glance; two chattering flautists gave him the quick once-over with practised eyes, but clearly decided he was too old, and a cellist pounded past with purposeful steps, sending him backwards into a mobile noticeboard.

Enough was enough. He would go and sit in the Sir Fleury Jenkins concert hall and recover his dignity and calm. He made his way up the stairs leading to the main hall, struggling through a tide of violinists and viola players pouring out of one of the rehearsal rooms. It was with a feeling of relief that he pushed open the doors to the hall and sank into a seat in the back row.

He wasn't alone in there. He looked down the ranks of seating to see an absorbed, solitary figure playing a harpsichord on the central stage below. He knew her slightly, she had been at college with Mimi and was a friend of Gerry's.

He settled down to listen with real appreciation. Bach was just the job for soothing tangled thoughts and troubled spirits, and he was cursed with both just then.

The fugue in B major reached its pleasing conclusion and the harpsichordist relaxed for a moment, her hands in her lap, before she rose and closed the lid of the instrument. Then she looked up in the auditorium to see who was sitting there, recognized Edmund and gave him a friendly wave before disappearing through one of the lower doors. There was a flash of light as the door to the outside opened and shut, and then silence.

He descended to the platform and went across to the lower door. It would be better to go out a back way, just in case Inez should still be lurking in the vicinity. He upbraided himself; what harm was Inez? Why should he be so anxious to avoid her interested queries, her helpful suggestions, her tactful understanding that the book wasn't going as well as it might?

Because he didn't want to admit to himself, let alone to Inez, that the book wasn't going through the doldrums; that it was, in fact, dead on the ground. He didn't want to acknowledge that soon he would have to let his agent, his publisher and everyone else know the truth.

Including Mimi.

He knew that she was worried about money, but she probably didn't realize just how difficult it would be with no new money coming in and a large advance, long since spent, to be repaid to Messrs Brace and Hatchet. His editor there might be understanding but the accountants of the Poseidon Publishing Company, the parent firm of B and H, were well-known for their ruthless treatment of recalcitrant authors.

'Oh, hell,' said Edmund. A bus rumbled past, tooting at him to get out of the way. He jumped back on to the pavement as the bus drew up at a stop a little way along from him.

He gazed, transfixed, at the destination board, which announced that the bus was headed for Midwinter and Mountjoy via Gossiby.

That's it. Edmund broke into a run as the bus began to move away. He would go to Mountjoy Castle and take a chance on Val and Magdalena being there; hadn't Desmond Fuseli mentioned they were coming north for a few weeks?

That would take his mind off poltergeists and penury.

# 13

Mimi pushed her worries about Edmund, the problems over her brothers' possessions and the little matter of the gone-over study to the back of her mind and settled down to work.

She had two smallish fountains to deliver to Grimsley, part of a new line she was importing from Italy. Then she was going to call at a garden centre to discuss a watery display intended to encourage customers to buy more fish for their ponds. She would stop off at Jackals on the way back to see if a faulty pump had been repaired yet.

Gerry was loud in his approval. 'Keep busy, that's the way when there are things on your mind,' he told her as he shut the back of the estate car.

Mimi put her head out of the window. 'What makes you think I've got anything on my mind?'

'My dear,' said Gerry seriously. 'Ghosts in the house, tetchy husband, and three lunatic brothers. That's enough for anyone.'

'Edmund is not tetchy,' she said, revving the car to drown out any further remarks.

Of course, Gerry was right, she had to admit. By the time she returned to the house several hours later, she had everything in perspective. She would cook Edmund a special meal, by which she meant she would have a sortie on the chilled food counter, get him to open a good bottle of wine, and drink a toast to whatever deity looked after troublesome brothers.

Gerry wasn't hard at work in the office as he'd planned, but was instead in the kitchen looking after some visitors.

'Hello, Sylvester,' said Mimi, pleased as always to see her large friend. He was accompanied by a red-haired girl who was sitting rather listlessly on a cushion. 'Hello, Phoebe, have you come to tea?'

The child looks ill, she thought, taking in the green eyes which were too big for her pale face. And her flaming red curls didn't look as bouncy and glossy as normal.

'Quinta's at the hospital for her check-up,' explained Sylvester. 'Phoebe here was due to have a cello lesson after school, but she didn't feel up to it, so I brought her here.'

Mimi had met Quinta soon after coming to live in Eyot, and they had become good friends. They shared a love of music; Quinta was a luthier, who was beginning to make a name for herself making cellos and violins. She was married to Titus Croscombe and they lived in a house they'd bought on the other side of Boar's Bridge just across the river from Guillibert Street.

Phoebe was the daughter Quinta had had as an underage teenager. Mimi knew there was some scandal attached to Phoebe's father, and she had a good idea who the man was, but they had never discussed it. The child now had a happy and settled home, and her stepfather adored her.

'Quite right to bring her here,' said Mimi, who was very fond of Phoebe. 'Have you got a cold?'

'Sort of,' said Phoebe. 'I've had a sore throat for ages.'

'Have you seen a doctor?'

Phoebe nodded. 'He said it was a virus, and it would go away, but it hasn't yet.'

'When's your mum's baby due?' asked Gerry.

'In three months.'

The phone rang, and Mimi answered it. 'Hello, Quinta, we were just talking about you. Yes, Phoebe's here, with Sylvester, did the school give you the message? Oh, Quinta, what a bore. I am sorry.'

Phoebe kept her head down as she played with the straw in her iced chocolate drink. Sylvester and Gerry listened unashamedly to Mimi's conversation.

'Well?' demanded Sylvester when a frowning Mimi finally put the phone down.

She gave Phoebe a quick look. 'Phoebe, they're keeping your mum in for a while. It's nothing to worry about, it's just that she's been getting these very swollen ankles and they're insisting on bed rest.'

Phoebe's face darkened. 'She can rest at home.'

'Only she wouldn't,' said Sylvester genially. 'You know Quinta, she'd be up and about within an hour, wouldn't she?'

'I suppose so.'

'Titus is away, is he?' asked Mimi.

Phoebe nodded. 'He's gone to America for a conference.'

Phoebe's stepfather was a distinguished mathematician, specializing in chaos. 'He won't be back for ages yet. What am I going to do? I can't go to Lydia and Alban, because they're in London.'

'Your mother mentioned Pauline.'

'Out of the question,' said Sylvester, in outraged tones. 'Dreadful woman, you know her, Gerry. Mother from hell.'

Gerry shuddered. 'I do indeed. I have the privilege of teaching her precious son, Peter; my weekly penance, believe me.'

'You can stay here with us,' said Mimi. 'Would you like that, Phoebe?'

'Yes.'

'I tell you what we'll do. We'll take you home and get your things, and pack a bag with the things your mum will need while she's in hospital. Then we'll go up to the hospital and see her.'

Phoebe beamed, and then her face fell. 'I shouldn't go to the hospital, not with this sore throat. I might give it to someone there.'

'We'll ask for a mask. You can't give it to Quinta; if she was going to catch it from you, she already would have. And on the way, we'll stop off and get some fruit for her.'

'She'd like that,' said Phoebe. 'Are you sure you don't mind me staying here? It won't be for long.'

'As long as you like. Edmund will be delighted, he's a great fan of yours.'

Gerry looked at his watch. 'I must be off,' he said. 'I'm depping for Titus at the cathedral. Fifteenth evening, too, what an effort.'

'What's special about that?' said Mimi. She knew Titus was a member of the cathedral choir, and that Gerry, who had a good voice and sang with the Eyot Camerata, occasionally deputized for him. Since she never set foot in the cathedral, she had no idea about services and settings.

'Psalm 78,' said Phoebe knowledgeably. 'It usually takes twenty minutes with Simon Praetorius conducting. Only, last month, one of the lay clerks took the choir and he did it in seventeen and a half. Simon heard the men and boys grumbling about how long he takes, so he says he's going to stretch it out to twenty-five minutes this month.'

Gerry groaned. 'Spare me. And how do you know all this?'

'Simon told me. He teaches me the piano.'

'Of course he does. Let me have another cup of that tea before I go, Mimi. I shall need something to sustain me.'

'Amen,' sang Phoebe in a croaky voice.

On the bus, Edmund's young cousin Thomas was telling him about the fifteenth evening. How, when he was a chorister, he used to time the psalm, and how one of the men ran a book on how long it would take each time.

'I won fifty pence one November.'

Thomas had boarded the bus at the next stop after Edmund. He swung his heavy schoolbag up the step, bid the driver a cheery hello, and surged down the bus looking for a seat.

'It's you. Hi,' said Thomas, dropping down into the seat in front of Edmund. 'What are you doing on a bus?'

A woman sitting further back decided they must be father and son, what with those deep blue eyes and the same dark, almost black hair. Not to mention the size; the youngster was already a big lad, and with more growing to do by the look of him.

Her neighbour leant closer and hissed in her ear. 'Mountjoys.'

'Like the village?'

'They own the castle, only they mostly let it out these days. It's a big expense, a castle.'

'Must be. Draughty, too, I shouldn't be surprised. Is it a ruin?'

'Parts of it. It's just a big house, really, with towers and walls and other remains from when it really was a castle.'

'And that lad lives there?'

'He does that, only not much in school time. He was sent

away to some posh boarding school in the south, but it didn't suit, and he came home. He goes to the Cathedral School, now. Better, really, for a lad to grow up with his family.'

'I don't hold with boarding schools. Well, when you hear what goes on in those places . . .'

They contemplated the horrors of the English public school system with relish for a few minutes, as the bus left the suburbs behind and bucketed along the open road.

'Who's that with the lad, then?' said the woman presently.

'I wouldn't like to say. One of them, though, you can tell.'

'He's a bit of all right. Wouldn't mind a night out on the tiles with him.'

'What would your Dan say to that?'

'Him! Nobody wouldn't want to be caught in a dark place with him.'

Thomas was plying Edmund with questions. Edmund had to rack his brains as to when he'd last got on a bus; it had to be several years ago. 'And when I was abroad,' he admitted. 'Mind you, if people like you travel on buses, then it's probably best to settle for other means of transport.'

Thomas took this in good part. 'I have to travel on a bus, unless I can wangle a lift.'

'I thought you lodged in Eyot. With Lydia and Alban.'

'They're away, so it's back to the castle for me for the rest of this week. Lucky timing, actually, because Val and Magdalena are here, which they usually aren't these days. Are you going to see them, or are you calling on Sylvester?'

'I thought I'd drop in and say hello to Val while he's up here.' He looked at his watch. As he'd thought, not very late. 'How come you're out of school so early?'

'Never ask,' said Thomas. 'Skiving, actually. It's end of year exams, only I haven't got one this afternoon. So I should have gone to games, but I fixed it so that the tennis coach thinks I'm off with the cricket mob, and vice versa.'

'Trouble if you're caught?'

'I'm always in trouble,' said Thomas with perfect good humour. 'I can't get worked up about games. Did you like games at school?'

'Loathed them.'

'There you are, then. I don't suppose it's hindered you in your career, like they tell you it will. "Team spirit, employers look for evidence of team spirit." That's what they say.'

'Quite right.'

'You don't need team spirit, do you? Not to write books. I read that one you wrote about the French family. It was good.'

Edmund was flattered. 'Did you? Hardly set reading at your age.'

'No, I only read it to score a point off the history teacher. I liked the de Maligny family, though. Are you writing another book?'

'Trying to.'

'Writer's block?' asked perceptive Thomas, who had noticed Edmund's jaw tense when he mentioned his book.

'Historians don't get writer's block,' said Edmund lightly. Liar, he said inwardly.

'What's your new book about?'

Edmund knew persistence when he met it; easier to answer than to try and change the subject. 'It's about the Templars,' he said.

'The knights? With white tunics and the big red cross? And all that burning and so on?'

'My book is about Templar finances,' said Edmund repressively. 'The Templars were great bankers.'

Thomas thought about that for a while. 'Sounds dull,' he said finally. 'I mean, reading about those de Malignys is like reading a novel. All those interesting people.'

'There are interesting Templars.'

'I bet there aren't when you're writing about the money-bags.'


'That wasn't the hospital, was it?' said Phoebe anxiously, as Mimi put the phone down.

'No, not the hospital. Why should it be?'

'You looked kind of stricken. I thought it might be bad news, about Q.'

'No, I promise you, it was nothing to do with your mum. That was Edmund. He's turned up at Mountjoy Castle for some reason he can't explain, he said he just hopped on a bus which was going there. On a whim. He's staying to dinner there, and someone's bringing him back to Eyot later. Maria somebody.'

'Maria Luthier?'

'That's the one. Do you know her?'

'Her daughter used to be my best friend, but she goes around with someone else now.'

Daughter. What a relief. Not that marriage lines and family kept you from straying, but still, a married woman would be complicated, and Edmund had never been one for a complicated life. Mimi felt as unreasonably elated as she had been downcast minutes before.

'I know what, Phoebe. We'll go out and have a pizza. And when you get back, you can ring the hospital and say good night to Quinta. And don't worry, I thought she looked fine, and when I had a word with the sister, she told me they were only keeping her in as a precaution.'

Just going out of the house did Mimi's spirits good. It was May, when it was light in those northern parts until far into the night, and the town hummed with life. They decided it was warm enough to go to de Laurio's, where you could eat outside and watch the river flow sluggishly by, bearing its load of pleasure cruisers, narrow-boats, the occasional barge and a flotilla of rowers out from the schools and the university.

'Better than eating at Mountjoy Castle, with Val creating,' said Phoebe, wise beyond her years.

'Do you know the Mountjoys?'

'I go there with Sylvester sometimes. Val's a violent sort of man, isn't he? I don't mean he goes round biffing people, it's just that he's a bit fierce. I think it must be horrid for Magdalena. When I grow up, if I get married, it won't be to anyone bossy like Val. Is Edmund bossy? He's a cousin of Val's, isn't he?'

'Yes, he is, and he can be firm about things, but no, he's not a steam-roller like Val, I'm glad to say.'

Phoebe toyed with her fruit salad and ice cream. 'Then I expect you don't mind having married him. Lots of people were after him.'

Mimi stiffened. 'What?' How absurd the child was, where did she pick up all this gossip?

'Everybody knew about it. He nearly married Maria Luthier, the one who's there tonight, after she got divorced. She poured cold cucumber soup over her husband, you know. At a restaurant. She's terribly attractive to men. Very flamboyant, Quinta says.'

The icy fingers of jealousy began to tighten round Mimi's vitals. 'Edmund had lots of girlfriends before he met me,' she said in what she hoped was a light-hearted way. 'People do. I went out with plenty of men when I was single.'

'He was really, really serious about Maria, though,' said Phoebe, wiping an indiscreet finger round the bowl to catch the last traces of the ice cream, and then quickly licking her finger before Mimi said anything.

Mimi wasn't worrying about table manners. 'And of course, he went out with Inez, who's at the university.'

'He lived with her. That was after Maria went off with her toy boy.'

'Toy boy?'

'He wasn't exactly young enough to be her son, but he was only twenty.'

'Oh,' was all Mimi could find to say. Still, a woman who was installed with a toy boy wouldn't be casting covetous eyes in Edmund's direction.

'It didn't last,' went on Phoebe. She sat back with a fat sigh. 'That was good. Thank you very much for bringing me here.'

'Who's Maria with now?' Mimi held her breath, as Phoebe thought. 'Nobody,' she said. 'She did go out with one of the masters from school, but then he went to America.'

'She's probably on the lookout for a new husband, then.' Mimi caught the waitress's eye and asked for the bill.

'I think she likes to play the field,' said Phoebe daringly. 'Like her friend Angela. Angela's always got a new man in her life. She went out with Edmund too, before he took up with Inez. Of course, Edmund and Inez were together for ages, everybody thought they'd get married. Then Edmund went to stay in London, and came back married to you.'

'Yes, that was lucky for me, wasn't it?' said Mimi, inwardly churning.

'You sound as though you're gritting your teeth,' said Phoebe. 'Have you got indigestion?'

Mimi woke from an uneasy doze, and rolled over to look at the clock. Ten past one. The bed beside her was empty, the house silent.

She sat up and ran worried fingers through her hair, blinking as she turned the light on. Of course, it was clear what had happened.

1) Edmund had succumbed to long pent-up passionate feelings for Maria Luthier, and, having left the castle hours ago, they were locked in a ferocious and lascivious embrace in her house.

God, what a slut the woman must be.

Or, 2) Maria L wasn't only a slut, but a drunkard. Filled with far too much of the excellent Mountjoy wine, she had run into a tree on the way back to Eyot, and Edmund was now lying dead or maimed in a ditch.

Or, 3) Maria was so tanked up, and Edmund so clearly in a lustful state, that Val, a born adulterer himself, had amusedly offered them a room for the night in the castle.

Even as she thought the last of these evil thoughts, it did cross Mimi's mind that Magdalena might have something to say about items 2 or 3. But there was nothing she could do about 1, which was by far the most likely scenario. And not one that would surprise Magdalena in the least; she would probably shrug and say, what do you expect when you've got a Mountjoy for a husband? After all, look at Val's crashing infidelities over the years, although people did say that now, with his family responsibilities, he had calmed down a bit.

What was that? Had she heard something? She sat rigid in bed, listening hard. 'Is that you, Edmund?'

It was.

'Sorry to be so late,' he said. 'Val and I got talking, and didn't notice what time it was. Poor Maria was yawning her head off.'

A likely story.

'And then I wanted to stop at the chapel for a moment.'

'Chapel?'

'The Mountjoy chapel. To see that crusader Mountjoy who

lies in there. Val and I were arguing about which crusade he was on.'

Crusade? You'd have to have been born yesterday to believe that his mind had been on crusaders.

Edmund padded into the bathroom. Mimi slid down beneath the sheets, her mind a positive swarm of stinging thoughts. He emerged, shook a pill out of the bottle he held in his hand and took a swig of water from the glass beside his bed.

'What's that?'

'Just something Dr Fuseli gave me,' said Edmund, getting into bed and turning the light out.

'Sinuses again?'

Grunt.

Mimi moved nearer. Edmund gave another grunt and hunched the quilt over his shoulders. Then, with a violent jerking movement, he sat up, and leapt out of bed.

'Whatever is it?'

'I heard a noise. This time I heard him. Quite definitely. Ha, now we'll see what he's up to.'

'Are you mad? What are you on about? That's just Phoebe going to the loo, I told you she was staying for a few days. You know that lavatory always makes those clanking noises. I've had a go at it myself, and called the plumber in, but there's no cure for it.'

Edmund paused by the door, listening hard. There was the sound of a door shutting, the unmistakable pad of slippered feet.

'It is Phoebe,' he said. 'You were quite right.'

And with that he sank back into bed, and within half a minute was fast asleep.

# 14

Mimi collected Gerry the next morning on her way to Hustle.

'Have you remembered the tape measure?' he asked as he slid into the passenger seat.

She gave him a look, and pointed to the stout leather case resting on the shelf under the windscreen. Gerry was unabashed; his mind was already running on other lines. 'What have you done with Phoebe?'

'I dropped her off at school.'

'How's Quinta?'

'Still up at the hospital. The consultant's seeing her this morning. Phoebe hopes she'll be home today, but I think Quinta's in for the duration. Phoebe doesn't know it, but she had a miscarriage last year. So they're being ultra cautious.'

'That'll be hard on the kid.'

'Yes, and she's a bit down, with this virus. I've never seen her so muted.'

'Is it being ill? Or is she unhappy?'

'I don't think so.' Mimi tapped her fingers impatiently on the steering-wheel, her green and gold nails glinting in the sunlight, as she watched the car in front begin a lengthy parking manoeuvre to fit into a tiny space.

'He'll never get it in there,' said Gerry.

Mimi's mind was still on Phoebe. 'She's missing Quinta, naturally, and she worries about her, but I think it's mostly that she's just not feeling well. Titus will have to come back and look after her.'

'Titus has got a lot on. Frenzy bursting out in the world of chaos, so my university friends tell me. Not the best time for him to be tied to home and hearth. He asked me back in the spring if I could cover for him in the choir for several weeks around now.'

'Too bad,' said Mimi unfeelingly.

'Now, now, work's work. You wouldn't ask Edmund to drop everything and take up domesticity, would you?'

That would be the day, she thought, cutting recklessly in front of a bus and just making it through the traffic lights by the stadium.

'I reckon Phoebe's got glandular fever,' he said after a while. 'Do you think they tested her for it?'

'They must have.'

'I'd ask.'

'It's none of my business, really.'

'With her father away and her mother in hospital, maybe it should be your business.'

'I can hardly take her to the doctor.'

'She can take herself.'

'Yes, but I'd have to nag her into going, she's that kind of child. I know, I was one myself. And I'm too busy and have got too much on my mind to take on a tough-minded twelve-year-old.'

'Just wait until you've got kids of your own, then you won't be able to sidestep like this.'

Mimi hated it when people made remarks like that.

*'You'll feel quite differently then, everybody does.'*

*'It isn't the same when it's your own.'*

*'Wouldn't be without them, would we?'*

Even her own mother, wrapped up as she was in her writing and her tiresome sons, had taken time at Christmas to remark that Mimi and Edmund must have been married for three years now, were they ever going to have children? And Edmund, past forty . . . You don't want to wait too long, darling, children need lively parents, and it's so tiring when you're older.

Tiring when they're older, too, thought Mimi savagely, her brothers springing to mind as a handy example.

She accelerated, overtaking two monks on bicycles and then braking hard to avoid a car which had heedlessly hurled itself out of a side road.

'Two monks,' said Gerry. 'Is it a convention, do you think?'
'They'll be from the monastery on the other side of Hustle.'
'Dominicans, from their robes.'

Mimi was constantly surprised at what Gerry knew. He said
it came from drawing anything and everything from early childhood; you acquired all kinds of knowledge just by finding out
what you had drawn.

'I know about monks from that working trip I did all round
Italy after I finished at college in Milan. There were priests and
monks and nuns everywhere, especially in Rome. I've got a
notebook full of drawings of them. I met a very jolly nun in a
bar, who told me what all the orders were. I did a few cardinals,
too, I shall put them into a painting one day. All that glorious
red, and the general sleekness of them . . .'

She slowed down for the turn into Hustle Manor. 'You will
behave, Gerry, won't you?'

'Haven't you noticed I'm wearing my best pair of trousers?
It's not every day I mingle with the nobs.'

Elvira was waiting for them on the steps of the house. 'I heard
your car turn in at the gates. Take it round to the back, down that
driveway there. We can't look at the setting with that spoiling
the landscape.'

Gerry hopped out, and Mimi drove off. Very peremptory Elvira
was, in her way. Brusque, you might say.

Gerry didn't mind. He had wandered over to the pond and
was eyeing the house and the gardens; terraces to one side of the
house, woodland to the other. In the distance, forming a back-
drop to the view from the front of the house, were the majestic
fells, purple and dusky green in the midsummer sunlight.

'Nice,' he said at last.

Elvira had been watching him. Now, as Mimi came round the
house, she asked who the young man was.

She told her.

Elvira's whole being radiated approval of Gerry. Mimi was
astonished at the vitality which crackled out of her. She had
seemed quite lively before, but this was different. Bloody sex,
that's what it is, she told herself.

Gerry wasn't Mimi's type, not at all. She liked rangy, dark-
visaged men. She appreciated Gerry's wiry masculinity, but only

in her mind, it brought no stirring of her senses. But he was clearly very much to Elvira's taste. Mimi was philosophical. If her client got a frisson from working with Gerry, she would be more enthusiastic about the project, more expansive, less liable to haggle over costs.

Apart from her visible appreciation of Gerry, Elvira was behaving in a model way. She quite understood the need to scale down his original inspiration. She could perfectly well see that the elegant circle in front of her Queen Anne house was hardly on the same scale as a Roman square or a formal palace garden.

She installed Gerry under an umbrella at a table on the terrace, brought coffee and chilled exotic juices, spoke of lunch.

He drew and planned.

Mimi prowled, her mind on the prosaic. On cabling and pumps and water flows and other such fascinating matters, which demanded her whole attention, and took her mind away from its pointless worries and presentiments.

An hour later, she was finished. She stuffed her notebook into her bag, and went over to the terrace to gather Gerry up for the return to Eyot.

Elvira was having none of it. 'We've hardly started. I have all kinds of photos to show Gerry. We have to discuss features.'

He swept his heap of drawings to one side and showed Mimi a sketch. 'This is what Elvira wants.'

Elvira? It hadn't taken Gerry long to get on first-name terms. Then she blinked. His original sketch had been wild in its detail, and she was startled to see that, while he had reduced the scale and size of the fountain, he had retained much of the priapic fervour of its figures.

'It's quite a public thing, a fountain,' she ventured.

Elvira was amused. 'If the neighbours are offended by these fine fellows, that's their lookout. They won't see anything from their windows, and if they come visiting, why, they must put up with my ways.'

'Noble, nude and antique, I feel,' said Gerry, watching Mimi with a laughing eye. 'And this plump nymph, a look of expectant relish on her face, don't you think?'

Mimi didn't think that at all. Fun was all very well, but this design was toppling into the obscene.

'Nonsense,' cried Elvira. 'Don't be so fuddy-duddy. The pleasures of the flesh have always been important to me. Still are,' she added, giving Gerry a very saucy look.

Damn it, thought Mimi. Past fifty, you'd think her mind would be running on different lines. Or at least on men nearer her own age.

'I'll bring Gerry back later,' said Elvira. 'For you won't be able to give me a price until he knows what he has to do, will you? Best for him to work on while he's here, and in the mood. I do know about the artistic temperament, you see; I have always mixed with artists.'

'I can wait,' said Mimi, who didn't in the least want to spend hours at the manor, but felt that Gerry might need support, or even rescuing.

He gave her a dark look. 'I can look after myself, thanks all the same.' And he returned to his pad, building up detail with swift and assured strokes of his pencil.

# 15

Edmund was lurking.

His rangy figure wasn't designed for the minute tables and spindly chairs of the little coffee bar at the corner of their road. He was sitting uncomfortably in the window, the *Financial Times* held firmly in front of him, pretending to turn the pages over so that he could have a quick look at who was coming past.

Edmund and Mimi's house was in a cul-de-sac, one of the many Eyot streets which ran down to the river and ended in a cobbled stretch of riverside parking. In their case, there was no road along to the next street at the river end, only the river footpath. From where he was, Edmund could see any car coming up the street. It would be impossible to miss Mimi in her red car.

He hadn't missed her; there she was. She was driving much too fast as usual. He watched nervously as she nipped into the heavy stream of traffic heading into the city centre. Phoebe was with her, he had caught a glimpse of her pale face through the windscreen. That child wasn't well, probably shouldn't be going to school.

But he had no time to worry about Phoebe's health. The question was, what would Mimi do? Might she drop Phoebe near the cathedral precinct to walk across the green to school, and then return home? He thought not. Mimi was never very communicative in the mornings and she'd been like a bear with a sore head today. But after a cup of coffee her mood had lifted slightly and while she struggled through a bowl of Choccy-pops, she'd mentioned that she and Gerry were going out to Hustle Manor.

Hustle was the other side of Eyot. That should give him an hour or two, more than enough time for what he had in mind. Rising from his table, he edged round the counter and squashed himself into the narrow space where the payphone lived.

'All clear. No, I'm not in the house right now, I'm in the bar at the corner. I'm on my way back now. Listening in? The poltergeist? I never heard such nonsense. You've known it happen? Hell, bloody ghosts keeping up with technology, it's enough to turn you to drink.'

Will arrived on his bike a few minutes later. Looking so dramatically handsome that he caused the milklady to run her float into the side of the road, he dismounted and began unpacking his panniers.

Edmund was waiting for him. Will handed Edmund a heavy black box. 'If anyone asks, say I'm the electrician,' he said conspiratorially.

'Why should they ask?'

They went inside the house. Will advanced purposefully along the hall, opening doors and glancing round each room. 'Perfectly quiet, no feeling of any unwelcome visitors. Unwelcome to you, that is; personally, I always hope for that tingle one feels in the presence of the beyond.'

Tingle, indeed, thought Edmund irritably. Any tingles Will felt were much more likely to be the result of a particularly lively night with his wife. They were a couple well-known for their mutual enjoyment of pain, and were frequently seen sporting the resultant bruises. And as for the beyond, he'd rather not know.

'Is there anyone else in the house at the moment?' asked Will, looking around.

'Mimi's out, there's no one else in, although Mrs Sconce, who cleans, will be in later.'

Will turned his mind to less corporeal beings than Mrs Sconce, and once satisfied that there were no entities or spiritual beings floating round the house, he homed in on the study.

'No trouble last night?' he enquired.

'No.'

'Anything different in your routine last night? It does seem from what you've said that this presence is attuned, as it were, to your movements.'

'What?'

Will gave him a brooding look. 'While you were in London, the presence suffered what seems to have been a panic attack. While you are here, about your normal daily doings, the presence merely repeats the pattern of drawer opening and book removal. What was different about last night?'

'Maybe it – whatever it is – has got fed up. If it's practical jokesters, they've got bored, or think they're going to get caught. Maybe all this is unnecessary, and there'll be no more trouble.'

Will shook his head. 'No, no, that isn't the way these things work. Take it from me, what's happened so far is just the beginning.'

Edmund flung himself into Finella's wing chair and hoped Will was wrong. The whole business was ridiculous, and Dr Fuseli was a charlatan, suggesting he call in a ghost expert instead of investigating allergies or his digestion. And he was sure Will wasn't what Dr F had had in mind. Some bearded type with little round glasses and the attitude of a train spotter, or a Germanic professor of linguistics, that's what ghost seekers should be like.

Not preposterously handsome musicians. Inez had drooled when he mentioned Will's name, and said that when he'd given a recital at the Music department last term, none of the women had been able to take their eyes off him. Edmund wondered if Will wreaked havoc among the hearts of susceptible sixth-formers, or whether they were only interested in thin and stubbly youths. How could he be sure that Mimi wasn't as bowled over as Inez was? One look from her in that direction, he told himself, and Will and all his wires and black boxes are out.

God, all he wanted was life to go back to normal. No happenings in the night, no need for sleeping pills, which didn't work all that well and, he had a nasty suspicion, were starting to wreak havoc on his libido. He would go off sex, or horrors, be unable to do anything at all, limp and wan in bed. Mimi and he would become estranged; where might that not lead?

And meanwhile his bloody book wasn't getting written. He

knew what his colleagues were saying behind his back. Caustic Dr Cara Sicilienne, a senior historian in the department, feared throughout the university for the sharpness of her tongue and the clarity of her mind, had kindly passed on various comments from fellow academics.

'Hasn't published for some time, has he?'

That was Fanshawe, an evil little man with a hundred and twenty pointless papers to his name.

'Flash in the pan, those two books.'

That was according to Tompkins, who had published a one-volume work in a popular paperback series which instantly bombed due to its total unreadability.

Muriel was dismissive. 'In my opinion, those early books weren't worth the fuss that was made of them. Not the type of books you expect a scholar to write.'

Muriel's books might be called scholarly, if endless footnotes and tens of pages of bibliography made for scholarship. They were also dull, tendentious and inaccurate.

'He's out of touch. The narrative approach to history is dead. All that personalization – fundamentally unsound.'

That would be Gramson, the coming man on human waste, carefully sorted and quantified from vast heaps of statistics provided by sites and contemporary references. Doubtless a worthy field of study, but as far as Edmund was concerned, a man who spent his time poking his nose into shit was not an historian worthy of attention.

'Must be getting short of money. Made a packet on those books of his, but sales don't go on for ever. You have to come up with a new product, otherwise it's backwater time.'

Street-smart Jessica, with a new biography every other year and an endless stream of useful contacts from the literary pages and the publishing world trooping through her bed.

Edmund yanked himself up out of the chair with a grunt. 'I'll put on some coffee,' he said. It was very boring sitting here watching this glowing specimen of perfection fooling round with meters and little electrical gadgets.

'Peppermint tea for me please, if you have it,' said Will, absorbed in his work. 'And you don't happen to have any arnica cream about the place, do you? I've got a nasty bruise coming up.'

'I bet you have,' Edmund muttered, making for the kitchen.

He looked up at the clock, wondering how long Mimi was likely to spend out at Hustle Manor. Then he prowled backwards and forwards, waiting for the coffee to brew. He had rummaged in every cupboard and finally unearthed an ancient peppermint teabag. It looked thoroughly unpleasant, but Will would have to put up with it. Did peppermint tea go off? This one looked as if it had passed through that stage some time ago and moved on to higher things.

Edmund dropped it in a mug, added boiling water. He watched with distaste as the liquid turned a nasty shade of green, and gratefully poured himself out a strong black coffee. Feeling his strength needed building up, he stirred in a spoonful of brown sugar and helped himself to a biscuit. Then he took Will's tea into the study.

'They say,' Will announced from under the desk, 'that if you have a vexed spirit in your house, you should leave out a glass of brandy.'

'What on earth for? What a waste of good drink. Unless you mean cooking brandy, and even that's a waste.'

'It soothes them. I wouldn't advise it, however. In my experience it has the contrary effect and stirs them up. Although I am quite sure that in this case we aren't dealing with a normal spirit. I feel this one is quite out of the usual run of phenomena.'

Phenomena. In his study.

It was too much.


Alone in the house once Will had departed, Edmund felt at a loose end. He knew that he should go to his study, sit down and get on with some work. Or go to the university and put in some hours there. The trouble was that he didn't feel inclined to work either at home or at the university; he didn't want to work at all.

The phone rang, making him jump. It was Quinta, calling from the hospital, in, Edmund could tell at once, something of a panic. He was fond of Quinta, with her merry ways and her stalwart spirit in the face of adversity.

Quinta was bothered to hear that Mimi was out. 'Back at lunchtime,' Edmund hazarded. 'I just came in to collect some papers,' he lied, 'and heard the phone ringing. Can I help? Is it something to do with Phoebe?'

He listened to what Quinta had to say. He told her not to fret, and thankfully abandoned all idea of work to take up being a Good Samaritan. He thought for a few moments, decided that troubles shared were troubles halved, and called Sylvester's number. Sylvester's housekeeper answered, and he told her Quinta's news.

'I'm not surprised,' said Lily. 'She was looking dreadful last time I saw her, she's been trying to do too much. Rest is what she needs, with someone trained keeping an eye on her. She doesn't want to lose another one. I'll be going into Eyot later, and I'll take her in some provisions, the hospital food will drive her mad. Is Titus still away?'

Edmund told her that he was, and that Quinta wasn't sure exactly where. He was moving about apparently, catching up with colleagues while he was there, and visiting several colleges. He'd thought it would be a good time before he would be back, although he planned to return well before the baby was due.

'Trust a man to get it wrong,' said Lily unreasonably. 'I'll get Sylvester, you'll be wanting to talk about what's best to be done with young Phoebe.'

'Mind-reader,' he murmured, well-used to Lily's witchy ways.

Sylvester boomed into the house, full of organizing spirit and carrying an enormous bunch of flowers.

'For Quinta,' he said as Edmund backed away from the vast and fragrant floral offering. 'Lilies, and orchids, do you see? She can scatter them around to cheer herself up, and you know how hospitals smell. I got them on the way, to save time. We can head off there straight away and pick up the key to her house en route.'

'Good thinking,' said Edmund, looking around for his car keys.

'Don't bother,' said Sylvester. 'We'll go in mine.'

Sylvester was extremely tall and built like a tank. Edmund was also tall but of a more athletic build; the two of them together caused quite a stir as they surged into the maternity wing of Eyot General Hospital.

Nurses flickered interested glances at them, although Sylvester could have told them to save their powder as far as he was concerned. Doctors eyed them with professional interest, the hospital chaplain flattened himself against the wall on encountering a glare from Sylvester as he strode toward the lifts. He did not like clergymen.

'Just what you don't need when you aren't feeling a hundred per cent,' he said. 'Some weed in a dog collar uttering platitudes from the end of your bed. And no way of escape.'

'He's probably here for baptisms and so on,' said Edmund, not very well up on baby procedure.

'Only in extremis,' said Sylvester. 'Poor things. Otherwise, it's the font and clucking family all round; have you never been a godfather?'

'All too often,' said Edmund, giving the Up button a few good thumps to encourage some action.

'You did say she was in the Plunkett Ward, didn't you?' said Sylvester, squeezing his bulk in beside a vastly pregnant woman in a wheelchair. 'Sorry,' he said genially.

'Don't worry,' she replied. 'I'm just as big as you are.'

'What have you got in there?' asked Sylvester, eyeing her huge bump with respect. 'Twins, is it?'

'Triplets,' she said mournfully. 'Not what I'd bargained for.'

Sylvester rolled off at the third floor, followed by an expostulating Edmund. 'Really, Sylvester, you shouldn't ask personal questions like that.'

'Nonsense, pregnant ladies like someone to take a bit of interest. I like babies, so it's quite genuine, and she will have sensed this. Now, where do we go?'

Edmund did a quick recce, although he found the multitude of arrows pointing in all directions rather confusing. 'Through those swing doors there, and to the left. I think.'

Glowing with virtue after their visit to Quinta and feeling a trifle worn by their sortie to the maternity wing, Edmund and Sylvester decided to call in at the Mountjoy Arms for lunch before attacking the next phase of their good deeds.

Edmund tucked into shepherd's pie while Sylvester ate chicken curry with gusto. 'Lettuce leaf and a banana back at Midwinter Hall,' he said with satisfaction.

'No good thinking you've got away with it. Lily will know, and you'll find the lettuce leaf on your plate for dinner.'

Sylvester winced, wiped his mouth and got down to business. 'Off to Quinta's house, find everything on her list, deliver same to hospital.'

'Collect Phoebe from school,' continued Edmund. 'Do you think they'll let us whisk her off? We won't be arrested for abduction or anything troublesome like that?'

'Good gracious, no. They know me.'

'Of course they do. I was forgetting.'

'You're going to have a word with the university, see if we can find out where Titus is at the moment.'

'Mrs Snuffe, the departmental secretary, is our woman for that. There's nothing she can't find out, given time and a phone.' Edmund got out his wallet, had a brief squabble with Sylvester about the bill, and paid for their lunches.

Sylvester led the way out to his car. 'Excellent. There only remains the task of soothing Phoebe. That's going to be the tough one, telling her that Quinta's in Plunkett for the duration.'

'Nearly three months, Quinta said.'

'I don't know how Titus is going to manage, and Phoebe isn't going to like it one bit. Not feeling the way she is.'

'You told Quinta she was better.'

'Tact, Edmund, tact.'

Edmund wrestled with his seat-belt and finally pushed the twisted strap into its holder with a firm click. 'We'll leave all that to Mimi to sort out.'

# 16

It was peaceful, lying there against Edmund.

He seemed relaxed, too, which was unusual these days. He had an arm wrapped round her, his corduroy-trousered legs stretched out along the length of the sofa, a book propped on her shoulder.

Mimi wasn't thinking, just musing, watching the pattern of the leaves stirring outside the window in the evening breeze. Phoebe, calm now after a scene of despair about her mother, was fast asleep upstairs.

'Should you have given her whatever it was?' said Edmund.

'It's only a mixture of aspirin and codeine, not very strong. It'll help her throat and she'll sleep, which is what she needs to do.'

'I thought I heard a noise upstairs.'

'It's only the window rattling on the landing. It's loose, and the wind is rising. I think it's going to rain, there's a smell of wetness in the air.'

'Very unscientific,' said Edmund. 'Never trust your instincts, they're always wrong.'

She wriggled her way round so that she lay looking up at him. 'I trusted my instincts when I married you. Everyone said, don't do it, you've only known him for three weeks. He may be Bluebeard. Or worse. My mother said you came from a wild line, my brothers mocked me and said it was lust, why not just take you to bed and be done with it.'

'You'd already done that. What was it, two days after we met?'

'*I* took *you* to bed? If you remember, *we* fell into bed thirty-six hours after we met. You see my instincts were right.'

'I do remember falling into bed,' he said, giving her an affectionate stroke with his free hand. 'But was that instinct, or lust?'

'Both, but it was instinct that told me I wanted to marry you. That happened the very second I saw you.'

Edmund's mind was turning to gloom. 'I wish my instincts would buck up and tell me how to finish this book of mine.'

'Is that what's worrying you? Is that all?'

'All?'

'It's a practical matter. You've done it before, why shouldn't you do it now?'

'Good question.'

'Is it really going so badly?' Mimi was sceptical. More likely too much time chatting to Inez, not enough time tapping the keys.

'I have been working at it, if that's what you mean. It's a technical problem, though, just a lot of material to handle, and it's got to be right. Nothing that a bit of concentrated effort won't sort out.'

His voice was reassuring, and she was deceived. She didn't think that work was worrying Edmund. Work, for him, came from his rational mind. He wasn't a Gerry, having to dig deep to get anywhere near what he wanted to achieve, endlessly frustrated and cast down, starting again, chasing the elusive dream which had stirred his imagination.

And whatever was bugging Edmund, and something was, it was emotional. Ergo, it wasn't work. A woman; she knew it in her bones.

The peaceful moment had gone, and before there was any chance of drifting back into oneness on the sofa, the doorbell rang.

'I'll go,' said Edmund, heaving himself to his feet. 'Probably Sylvester, he said he might look in later.'

He crossed the hall and opened the door, and a whirl of wind and rain rushed in. Mimi's instincts had been right, and the summer's day was giving way to a stormy night.

'Come in,' said Edmund, before he realized who his visitor was.

'Thank you, I'm soaked. What a trek from the station, and not a taxi to be had.'

'Who is it?' Mimi called from the sitting-room.

'Guess what,' said Edmund grimly. 'It's your brother.'

Silence.

'Which one?'

'Vincent,' said the visitor, divesting himself of his dripping jacket. 'Don't rush out to show your delight, Mimi dear.'

'Vincent!' she said, coming into the hall. 'What are you doing here?'

'Passing through,' said Vincent airily. 'There's a big sale near here tomorrow, and I knew you'd give me a bed for the night.' He leant forward and gave his sister a cool peck on her cheek. 'I haven't eaten, so if there's any food in the house, I won't refuse. Otherwise, I'll borrow a brolly if I may, and find a pub. Edmund might care to join me.'

'We've eaten,' said Mimi flatly. 'Of course there's food. Edmund, take Vincent upstairs.'

'I wouldn't dream of putting you to the trouble,' said Vincent. 'I know the way, second door on the right, isn't it?'

'No, it isn't,' she said. 'We have another visitor, so you'll have to go into the small spare room.'

Vincent raised an elegant eyebrow. 'Another visitor?' He looked around. 'Am I to be introduced?'

'No. She's asleep.'

'Asleep! What a strange guest.'

'She's twelve,' said Edmund. 'And not very well.'

'How tiresome,' said Vincent. 'Very well, I'll go into the big room on the second floor; your small spare room is so cramped.'

'The rooms on the second floor aren't habitable; we had some work done recently, and we haven't got them straight. It's the small room or nothing.'

Vincent's face showed clearly what he thought of that, but Edmund took no notice. 'Come on, and I'll dig out some sheets for you while Mimi sees if there's any food you might like.'

Mimi couldn't help laughing as she opened the fridge and took out some ham and a couple of eggs. Vincent clearly didn't care for being deprived of a big and comfortable room for the sake of a sleeping Phoebe.

She was quite right. Vincent, who never gave up, was urging

Edmund to swap Phoebe into the other room. 'Much more suitable for a child, she'll be alarmed by all the space in that lovely room. And it has its own bathroom, hardly necessary for a twelve-year-old, one would have thought.'

'In here, Vincent,' said Edmund, ignoring his remarks and opening the door into a modestly sized room on the other side of the passage. 'Quite comfortable, and it's only for a night. Phoebe may be staying with us for some time.'

Vincent's sharp eyes took in the sage green and white striped curtains, the thick white bedspread, the fat green and gold cushions dotted on the bed, the Lloyd Loom chair.

He sighed. 'Very provincial. I see my dear sister is adapting well to life outside the capital.'

Edmund yanked open the door of the airing cupboard on the landing and pulled out sheets, pillowcases and a towel. Vincent watched him, asked for a small towel as well as a big one, took it with a murmured thank-you, and disappeared into the bathroom.

An enraged Edmund made a messy bed for his brother-in-law and thundered back downstairs again to shout at Mimi.

She was unperturbed. Vincent always had this effect on people: friends, family, strangers, they all ground their teeth at his little ways. In a while, he would make his languorous way down to join them, and would set about soothing them into happy acceptance of his next outrageous demand.

Not me, however, Mimi decided rebelliously. He had oppressed her for too long. She was in her own house, with support in the shape of an annoyed husband. Vincent simply wasn't going to get away with it.

'A whisky, Edmund? How kind, what excellent taste, if I may say so.'

There followed a learned discussion about single malts from extremely obscure Scottish islands.

'Ham and eggs, Mimi? How delicious, I can't tell you how much I've missed home cooking since Ma left so abruptly.'

Must have been quite difficult for him after all these years of creature comforts, Edmund found himself thinking. Then he felt Mimi's sardonic eye upon him and he scowled terribly.

'If you'll excuse me, I've got some work to finish.'

'Of course,' said Vincent, rising courteously to his feet. 'A great writer beckoned by Clio can hardly refuse the summons.'

'Clio? Who's Clio?' asked Mimi, instantly suspicious.

'Clio, the muse of history,' said Edmund as he departed. 'You should know that.'

'We didn't do muses at music college,' she said to the door which had banged behind him.

'Nor much else, one gathers,' said Vincent, reaching out for the fruit bowl and selecting the best of the peaches. 'Italian? A little early for really good peaches, but let us see.'

Mimi clashed Vincent's plates together. She was certain that Vincent had been living out of a baked bean tin as was his idle and uncivilized way. 'I wouldn't have thought any sale up in these parts would attract you, Vincent,' she said sharply. 'Peasant furniture, surely, rustic tables and so forth.'

'If so, very valuable,' said Vincent, unruffled. 'However, I doubt it. Good Victorian mahogany is what I expect, quite fashionable in London just now. Perhaps, if I'm lucky, one or two eighteenth-century pieces at sensible prices.'

'And what are you going to do with any pieces you buy?'

'Sell them on, I have to, with nowhere to store them.'

'You managed in London.'

'There was usually room at a friend's, or even at home for one or two small items.'

She remembered his small items. The huge carved fire surround which had blocked Finella's tiny hall for three weeks. The Italian marble statue which Vincent had squeezed into the bathroom so that it was impossible to take a bath. The six seventeenth-century chairs in desperate need of upholstery, which had dribbled their insides all over the flat. 'A find,' he had declared. 'Very valuable, they'll sell in no time.'

Well, that was over now. Vincent would have to get himself together, shell out some of the cash he undoubtedly had, and was so reluctant to part with, to get himself premises of some kind. And a van, he couldn't go on asking friends for favours, and their mother's car had vanished with her, whether to a buyer or to be stowed away somewhere against her return, they didn't know.

Either way, it was out of Vincent's greedy grasp. 'And don't get any ideas about bringing things here,' she warned. 'Edmund's furious about all those boxes from London. They're in the stable now, but they'll have to go.'

'Go? Where to?'

'That's your problem.'

Edmund stayed in his study until late. Mimi went in at midnight, but Edmund was deep in a book, and merely muttered a good-night and gave her an absent-minded kiss. 'Don't wait up for me,' he said. 'I'll be late, there's something I want to finish.'

Her fears, forgotten in the warmth of being with Edmund that evening, and by Vincent's unexpected arrival, came flooding back. Why was he becoming more and more distant? Why had his habits changed? He used to be a man glad to get to bed, to make love with her, to chat, to read, to sleep the sound sleep of the just. Now he came to bed late, slept badly, prowled, had even lost some of his vigour as a lover, and that had never happened before. Not even when he'd hurt his back, or was suffering from a dreadful cold.

To Mimi it all added up to an Outside Interest. And, she felt more and more sure, one with dark, come-hither eyes and a gross bosom.

Yes, and what was a woman like that doing at a university? There was no way a university department was her natural habitat. She should be working in the lingerie department at Kings and Wallup. Or posing for a porn magazine, or serving drinks in a sleazy club, thought Mimi nastily.

Then she rebuked herself. Brains and intellectual ability had nothing to do with looks. Just because so many university women had minds above clothes and make-up didn't mean that they all did. Or that the basic material wasn't there, only, unlike Inez, few of them chose to make much of their assets.

Why couldn't Inez fall in love with some dull professor and settle down?

Mimi laughed to herself, thinking of the professors she knew, and imagining them with Inez. But once in bed, she couldn't sleep. She tossed and turned, then rolled over and looked at the clock ticking irritatingly on her bedside table. Ten to three, and still no Edmund. No, she wasn't going to go downstairs, ask what he was doing, coax him up to bed.

She turned the clock face away from her, humped the covers over her shoulder and settled down for some more tossing. Outside the window, an owl hooted. There was a distant squeal of brakes, as some late-night reveller made his or her reckless way home.

The great bell of the cathedral donged the hour; one, two, three.

She could stand it no longer. She sat up and leapt out of bed. She had a brief fight with her dressing-gown, finally disentangling the sleeves and wrapping it round her. Then, barefoot, she went out into the darkness of the passage, and quietly down the stairs, anxious not to wake up either of her sleeping guests.

The study door was ajar, and a sliver of light showed through into the hall. Mimi went soundlessly across the hall, and pushed the door open.

A scene of total disarray met her startled eyes, and she let out a sharp cry before clapping her hand over her mouth to stop herself.

The window was flung up, and the curtains billowed in the wind, half in and half out of the room. Papers lay damply on the window sill, and one, caught in the tree outside, flapped like a trapped creature.

Every single book was off the shelves. They lay open on the floor, the desk, the chair. The china mug in which Edmund kept his pens was smashed to pieces. And, strangest of all, there were wires, looking as though they had been pulled out of something. An unrecognizable piece of electrical equipment balanced precariously on the edge of the desk, its face smashed, the dials twisted off.

Mimi saw all this without really taking it in. Her chest was tight, she couldn't breathe.

Edmund. Where was Edmund? He had been attacked, injured, dragged away.

Only he hadn't. He sat, legs on the fender, relaxed and blissfully asleep in his wing chair. His breathing was even, his hand, when she grabbed it, relaxed.

'Wake up,' she said. 'Edmund, wake up.'

He gave a pleased grunt, and, without opening his eyes,

groped with a hand to catch hold of Mimi and pull her down to him.

'Edmund,' she said, right in his ear.

He opened a sleepy eye. 'Mimi, darling,' he said indistinctly, and then sank back into his slumbers.

It was as though he was drugged, she thought, but he seemed to be quite unharmed. A bottle stood in solitary splendour on the ravaged shelf beside the fireplace. She picked it up and read the label. 'One to be taken on retiring.'

Sleeping pills! Edmund had been taking sleeping pills. But why? And why hadn't he said anything to her about them? He adored taking medicine, discussing any pills or potions the doctor was unwise enough to prescribe, watching out for all the listed side-effects, wondering whether he was on the right dose, sharing every twinge with Mimi.

She looked more closely at the label. A London pharmacy, and a recent date. He must have got them while he was in London. Perhaps he had trouble sleeping, the traffic, the general hubbub of life in London . . .

Oh, nonsense, her reason told her. Edmund was quite used to London, and it wasn't exactly quiet where they lived now. Thirty tablets, it said on the bottle. She tipped them into her hand and counted. There were twenty-five. Well, he'd hardly taken an overdose.

She looked down at Edmund, and then round the room again. She felt out of her depth, uncertain what to do about the room, about him, about anything.

'First,' said a languid voice behind her, 'we should close the window.'

Vincent. Bloody Vincent had woken up, and naturally would have come downstairs to investigate any sounds; there was no one in the world nosier than Vincent.

He leant over the desk and wrestled with the window, finally yanking it down. He pulled the catch over. 'Burglars?' he said almost to himself. 'Hm, I think not.' Then he bent over Edmund. 'Too much whisky?' he enquired.

Mimi had found her voice. 'Don't be silly,' she said, nonetheless snatching a glance at the bottle of Glenfocharty which had rolled across the floor to lodge by the chair leg. She bent down and picked it up. He had perhaps had one more glass after she and Vincent had gone upstairs. Hardly enough to turn him into a maniac, or to cause this oppressive sleep.

'We'll get him upstairs,' said Vincent. 'There's nothing else you can do now. Unless you want to call the police, and frankly, I don't think they'd be very interested. Only Edmund can tell us if anything's missing, but I doubt it.'

'How can you be so sure?'

'If it's a break-in, why leave his wallet, look, with quite a sum in it? And the tape recorder, an expensive one, I can see that. And the silver paperweight, which is now reposing behind the door. No, this is something quite else, Mimi dear. A poltergeist, perhaps? An uneasy spirit abroad?'

'Oh, balls,' said Mim crossly. She wasn't going to tell him what she suspected, which was that the sleeping pills had had a strange effect on Edmund, as such pills could in some cases.

'Whatever it is, the best thing is to get Edmund to his bed, and then you and I can make the most of such sleep as is left to us tonight.'

# 17

Gerry arrived early, at about half past eight, and let himself in. He was planning to put in a serious morning's work.

The house was quiet, which was unusual at that time. The kitchen was dark and empty and the kettle cold. Lazy lot, thought Gerry, who had risen at six and prepared his next week's lessons for school. He plugged in the kettle, pulled up the blinds in the kitchen, and went through into the sitting-room.

That, too, had an undisturbed and night-before look which bothered his sense of order. He drew back the curtains, picked up a book which was lying open on the sofa, had a punch-up with the cushions, kicked a rug back into place and collected an empty glass to take back into the kitchen.

In the hall, he listened for signs of life.

Nothing.

He noticed that the door to Edmund's study was open. He put the empty glass down on the small hall table, and went in to see if Edmund was up after all. He often rose early and settled down to work in his study. He might like a strong cup of tea, his preferred brew first thing.

Oh, hell.

Gerry stared, his eyes going slowly round the room. What a mess! Shit, what was going on in this place? No wonder they were all in bed; this must have happened in the middle of the night.

There was a ring at the doorbell. That would be the postman.

It wasn't.

'Hello. I thought you were the postman,' said Gerry, as

Sylvester bounced through the door and swung his cello case down on its side.

'No. Where's Phoebe? I said I'd drop in and give her a lesson before school, they said she doesn't have to be in until ten this morning.'

'No one's up yet.'

Sylvester frowned. He was an easy-going man, but anything to do with music he took seriously.

'Naughty of her,' he said. 'Run up and tell her I want her down here in five minutes, there's a good chap. I don't care if she's in her pyjamas, a lesson's a lesson. Is her cello still in the sitting-room?'

'Yes,' said Gerry, who had nearly tripped over it.

'I shall go and get it out and tune for her, you get her up.'

Before he reached the sitting-room, a thin, croaky voice called his name, and he looked up to see a woebegone face looking over the bannisters. Red-haired Phoebe had a naturally pale skin, but just now she didn't look pale so much as green.

'I'm dreadfully sorry, Sylvester,' she began.

'You look terrible,' said Sylvester, in much more kindly tones. 'Has your sore throat come back again?'

'Yes, and I feel all hot and dry.'

'Temperature,' said Gerry at once. 'You hop back into bed, Phoebe. You aren't playing anything this morning. Is Mimi up?'

Phoebe shook her head and vanished, but the voices had woken Mimi from an exhausted and troubled sleep. She emerged, yawning and pushing the hair out of her eyes, and stared down into the hall. 'Hello, Sylvester. What are you doing here? What time is it?'

Sylvester explained. Mimi gave a whoop of concern when she heard it was nearly nine, and shot back into her bedroom.

'I'll make coffee,' said Gerry, giving up thoughts of getting down to his morning's work for the time being. 'Mimi looks like she needs it.'

Sylvester followed him into the kitchen. 'What's up with Phoebe? She seems worse.'

'She's worrying about Quinta,' said Mimi, coming into the

kitchen. She had showered and dressed at lightning speed. 'Gerry, have you seen the study?'

'I have, and I can tell you right away that you'd better not ask Mrs Sconce to clear it up. Not again. Besides, there's no point; much better to leave it as it is.'

Mimi was shocked. 'Gerry, we can't.'

Sylvester, ever curious, had gone to see and he came back looking surprised and saying that, whatever it was, it had to be stopped.

She said that Will had supposedly got matters in hand, but with no very great success. She kept her views about Edmund to herself.

'That's probably his equipment all chewed up in there,' said Sylvester. 'He won't be pleased.'

Mimi put bowls on the table and a pile of spoons beside them, Gerry frowned, he liked things to be exact. 'Too many,' he said. 'Phoebe won't be down, she's feeling poorly.'

'But Vincent will be,' she said wearily.

'Vincent?'

'My brother. From London. On a visit.'

Sylvester couldn't help laughing, although he knew Mimi wouldn't find Vincent remotely funny. 'Sorry, Mimi. Just what you need, your supercilious brother trolling about the place. How long is he inflicting himself on you for?'

'He's come for a sale, he only needed a bed for last night.'

'Believe that and you'll believe the moon's made of purple cheese,' said Sylvester brutally. 'And don't give me that quelling look, Mimi; you know what your brother's like as well as I do.'

'If this were London, maybe. But stay in the north for more than twenty-four hours? I think not. Besides, he was appalled at the scene of destruction in Edmund's room, he won't feel that it's safe here.'

She noticed that Gerry had shrugged himself into his jacket and was looking as though he was about to depart. 'You aren't going, are you?'

'Rat deserting the sinking ship, eh?' said Sylvester.

'I won't be long. Just popping back to my house.' Gerry lived with several friends in a house on the other side of the main road. It was in an area close to the football stadium, with streets of big

Victorian houses, which for years had been considered likely to rise in status and property values. The inhabitants, a motley assortment of old-timers, students, staff from the more esoteric university departments and wilder spirits like Gerry, were still waiting, but they liked the slightly scruffy atmosphere of their terraced streets and were quite happy not to have the smart types moving in. 'I've got a neighbour who might be able to help you, I'll see if she'll come.'

'Gerry, no,' called Mimi, but it was too late; the door had shut behind him, and they could hear his shoes scrunching on the gravel surface and then the tinkle of his bicycle bell as he swung out into the road.

When Edmund came downstairs some forty-five minutes later, it was to find a witch in his study.

He didn't at once recognize her for a witch. As he said afterwards to Mimi, it wasn't the first thing that sprang to mind, and she didn't have the traditional tools of her calling with her.

'What did you expect? A besom at the door and a pointy hat?'

Edmund glared at the ash blonde woman with spiky hair and orange fingernails which she was waving dramatically above his desk.

'I don't like the look of her at all,' he said to Mimi, in what she thought was an unnecessarily loud voice. 'Who dredged her up?'

'She's called Jemima. She teaches Magical Studies at the tech, and lives with the Professor of Contemporary Theology. You know him, from the university,' she whispered.

'To hell with it,' said Edmund. 'I don't care if she lives with a goat. What I mind is her chanting away in my study.'

He shot the witch a look full of suspicion and dislike. 'I don't want to interrupt,' he said untruthfully.

She ignored him, reached the end of her chant, and then spun herself neatly round, like a trained ballet dancer. Three times in one direction, and then three times in the other. Her twirls completed, she stopped and opened her eyes again.

'It isn't a normal spirit,' she said with great authority. 'I can tell you that for certain. Not a spirit trapped in the material world; this isn't a haunting in the usual sense.'

'It's a poltergeist,' said Edmund.

'It's no such thing.' The witch sounded sharp, she wasn't used to having her judgement questioned. 'I've worked with Will, and his paraphernalia can be quite useful. It's no good here at all, a complete waste of time. No, we're dealing here with something totally different. It's very interesting.'

'It isn't in the slightest bit interesting.' He was getting more annoyed by the minute. 'It's tiresome, and time-consuming, and very distressing for the whole household.'

'It's a presence. Not an elemental, no, it's the wrong feeling for an elemental. It comes from the world beyond, but not the customary one. This comes from a part of the spirit world that I have had very little to do with. I'm going to have to give this some thought.'

Thought? Edmund was incredulous. The last thing this witch woman was capable of doing was thinking, he'd never heard such a heap of twaddle in his life.

The witch Jemima tapped her cheeks with her long, beringed fingers. 'Of course, someone in this house must have summoned it.' She advanced on him, fixing his eyes with her own disturbingly pale and unblinking ones. 'You are the channel. It is through you, from within you, by means of you that this force of destruction has been let loose.'

Mimi gave a strangled protest; the witch took no notice.

'It is not a spirit of mischief, or of evil. It is simply trying to gain attention.'

'Very successfully,' said Sylvester, who was watching the whole scene with much interest and amusement. 'Look at us all.'

The witch was silent, her eyes were shut. They all watched her intently. Mimi suddenly realized that she was holding her breath, and let it out with a noisy whoosh. Sylvester winked at her.

'You've seen nothing, is that correct?' The witch snapped the question at Edmund.

'No.'

'Nor heard anything?'

'No.'

'You are never present when the upheaval occurs?'

Upheaval? He supposed that was one way of describing what happened. 'I was in here last night. But I fell asleep. I heard and saw nothing.'

'What were you thinking about?'

Bloody woman, asking all these pointless questions.

Mimi's voice, anxious. 'Do answer, Edmund. It might help.'

'What the hell do you suppose I was thinking about? Here, in my study? Work of course.'

'Which is?'

He shut his eyes for a moment. 'Writing. I'm writing a book.'

The witch's pale eyes flickered in interest, her mouth moved as she muttered inscrutably. Then she spoke again. 'What kind of book?'

'History. An academic work.'

'What subject? What period?'

'Thirteenth century. The finances of the Templar order in England and in France.'

She shook her head. 'You are dealing with powers beyond your control, with forces we do not understand in our modern age. You must give up your studies in the arcane world of the Templars. The mysteries of the Orders . . .'

Later, Mimi and Sylvester relived every moment.

'Sylvester, she hissed.'

'No, no, you exaggerate. She merely drew in a sharp breath.'

'I count it a hiss. And she is a snaky person. That little tongue which kept flicking out to moisten her lips. Those eyes.'

'Yes, and a tail and fangs, I dare say. Now you're being fanciful, Mimi.'

'You look properly at her next time you see her.'

'That is a pleasure I will happily postpone,' said Sylvester with a dramatic shudder. He hadn't taken to the witch. 'She certainly treated Edmund to a spot or two of venom, though, I will grant you that.'

'I've never known him so cross,' she said thoughtfully. 'I know he can be loud and assertive . . .'

'That's the Mountjoy side,' said Sylvester, nodding.

'. . . but mostly, as you know, he keeps his temper with people he doesn't know. To fly into a passion like that, and threaten to throw the woman out of the house, it isn't like him.'

'No, I've never seen him react so strongly,' Sylvester agreed. 'Do you think Gerry will ever forgive him?'

'Gerry's not one to bear a grudge. I think he realized that his friend went too far. Any fool could see that Edmund felt he was being goaded, and there are limits to what anyone can take. Particularly when you're under the kind of pressure he is.'

'Pressure? What pressure?'

Sylvester was surprised at her vehemence. 'Come on, having your study turned over isn't much fun. And then he's got to get the book finished, that's a lot of pressure. You must be used to that, with a writer for a mother.'

'Edmund's writing is quite different. It's intellectual, scholarly work, that's not nearly as fraught as writing fiction.'

Mimi knew what she was talking about. Her childhood and adolescence had been dominated by her mother's writing. The early, orderly days of each book, with hours put in while Mimi was at school, the writing put aside for the evening. Then the phase of temper and tantrums, when the book faltered, to be followed by days, weeks, even, of the blackest depression.

Those were the times when she and her brothers could do nothing right, and when friends were banished from the house, which used to take on some of the horrific gloom which characterized the highly successful works of Finella Ostiman, Queen of Crime.

Then, without any warning, her mother would be up at six one morning, in and out of the bathroom, through the kitchen like a mini-hurricane, leaving dirty cups and open packs of cereal behind her. She would lock herself into her study for eighteen hours at a stretch. When her children pleaded with her, she would open the door to snatch a plate of food. As bedtime came, and she was still good for another six or eight hours, she would demand gin and Benzedrine.

And once it was all over, the pages immaculate in a precise pile, stacked into a box ready for delivery, Finella would stumble out, have an hour-long bath, and then sleep the clock round.

'Quite different from Edmund,' said Mimi.

'Maybe,' said Sylvester.

Drs Cara Sicilienne and Daphne Whitgift, members of the departments of History and English respectively, had met for breakfast in the university cafeteria, a place they both despised, but which they found convenient. Also, it gave them a chance to look around and see how their fellow-academics were facing the day. They were quick to spot a hangover, an unshaven face, blurry eyes and other signs of dissipation.

'More trouble at Edmund's last night, I hear,' said Cara, spreading her toast with a thin film of butter and then tapping some marmalade on to it.

Daphne pursed her lips. 'He'll have to do something about it, sooner or later. It's going to get out of control, otherwise, and then he'll be sorry. Some people just can't take a hint. It's time he thought about his future, what kind of a book he's trying to write. He has to change, of course, he needs to move on, work in new fields.'

'It's hard on his wife.'

'I couldn't care less about his wife. But I do care about Edmund, I could kick him when I see him pottering on in his financial wastelands, year in, year out, getting nowhere.'

'Disheartening, such an able man,' agreed Cara. 'I must go, I have to give a lecture on the causes of civil rebellion in late-republican Rome.'

'Julius Caesar, an example to us all,' said Daphne, giving up on her breakfast. 'There was a man who knew what he wanted and let nothing stand in his way.'

'Yes, well, he never worked in a university.'

# 18

Mimi had wanted to catch Vincent before he left in the morning. She was planning to have a further word with him about the various brotherly possessions overflowing out of the stables at the back.

Vincent was too wily for that. He had slipped out of the house while the witch was about her business, storing up such delights as had caught his ear in a few minutes' eavesdropping. It would make an entertaining story for his cronies when he was back in London. That couldn't be too soon, he told himself as he closed the front door gently behind him and went quietly out of the gate.

The mild days of early summer had been chased away by unseasonal north-easterly winds, and Vincent wrapped his coat about him, wondering why anybody dreamt of living in the north. Even the dogs being walked along the chilly pavements looked blue with cold.

He hadn't rung for a taxi from the house, not wishing to draw attention to himself. It wasn't only that. Certainly, he wanted to avoid the inevitable interrogation by Mimi, but also he was by nature secretive. He would rather nobody knew where he was.

He walked up to the main road where, he remembered, there was a taxi rank. Three taxis were drawn up at the kerbside. Their drivers, each wearing a flat cap, made a picturesque trio on the pavement as they exchanged pleasantries and blew on cold fingers. Vincent sauntered to the first car, got in, gave the driver the address, and sat back to survey the passing scene with his customary cynical eye.

The sale was a few miles to the north of the city. It was being held to dispose of the contents of a large country house, now on the market after an acrimonious divorce. As Vincent had expected, there were quite a few Eyotshire dealers, a throng of keen amateurs, looky loos from the local village dying to see just how their richer neighbours had lived, and a smattering of buyers from further afield. Vincent nodded to one or two acquaintances and wandered over to view the contents of the stables, in which he had no interest whatsoever.

There was time enough before the sale to have a look at what did interest him; meanwhile, he would bore any snooping dealers into getting back to their own business. He investigated a mangle, several Belfast sinks and a butter churner before moving on to such items of gracious living as a collection of flowered china money-pigs, all slightly chipped, ten plain white chamber pots, ditto, and an old leather hat-box.

He found himself standing next to a well-rounded middle-aged woman. Good clothes, if a trifle eccentric. Expensive shoes, a very classy watch; she was probably at the sale to spend money. No way was she interested in chamber pots. A local dealer? Perhaps she was the owner of a nearby antique shop.

She looked Vincent up and down with a practised eye. Tallish, thin, but would grow portly when he was older. Must be in his thirties; a noticeable man with that dark hair and arched brows against a pale skin.

'I quite like the pigs,' he ventured.

'More fool you.'

'Perhaps you're after the mangle,' said Vincent, nettled. His charm rarely failed him, but this woman had a sharper eye than he liked.

'No, I'm here for the furniture,' she said. 'There's a tallboy in the sitting-room that would be exactly right in my house. I came out here to get away from a silly woman who knows me and wants to natter.'

'Tallboy?'

'Early Georgian. No point in hiding it from you, you'll notice it soon enough.' She tapped the back of her hand with the programme. 'It's all in here. Are you a professional?'

'In a way,' said Vincent.

'I'm off,' the woman said abruptly. 'I can see Millie coming this way. Perhaps you can interest her in the potties.'

Vincent met up with her again in the sitting-room. She was chatting to a sleek, pink-faced man in tweeds, a young representative of the auctioneers, Vincent thought at once. The man was extolling the virtues of the tallboy, and sounding very knowledgeable.

Vincent drifted nearer, and stood waiting to speak to the woman, a clear look of dismissal on his face as he eyed the auctioneer. The man broke off and slid away.

'It's you,' said the woman without enthusiasm.

'Don't buy it,' said Vincent.

'Why ever not? I like it.'

'It's a fudge. The top and bottom are from two separate pieces.'

'What? Nonsense. Oh, I suppose you want to talk it down so I won't bid against you.'

'I wouldn't dream of bidding for this piece, my clients rely on me. I can't palm them off with rubbish.'

'Rubbish?'

Vincent moved closer to the tallboy. 'See for yourself. The top isn't an exact fit for the bottom half, you can see how it's been taken down. And the detailing, look, that's been redone to match the other half.'

'I'm not convinced. Besides, it says in the catalogue that it's a fine example of a George II tallboy. And look at the price guide. They'd never dare to put that for anything that wasn't pukka.'

'Oh, yes, they would. They do it all the time. I assure you, more than half of what you see in the salerooms isn't what it's made out to be. From time to time it's much better than it's been described, but this isn't one of them. I wouldn't have that as a present, and I'd advise you not to bid for it.'

'It's perfect for my house.'

'There's plenty of genuine stuff around if you know where to look for it. You'd never be happy with this, knowing it wasn't right.'

'Only because you've come creeping up to me making insidious remarks about it.'

'It's your money.' Annoyed, Vincent bowed and went out of the room to look at a mahogany side table in the dining-room.

An hour later he bid for it, successfully, and for a pair of matching Italian seventeenth-century chairs which had stood in the hall. They were battered; they looked as though the children of the household, their dogs, the kitchen cat and, for all he knew, the parrot had all been allowed to climb over them and use them as though they were common stools. Disgraceful. However, they would look quite different after some attention, and then would be eminently saleable.

The tallboy came up, and went for something above its guide price. To his amusement, the woman didn't bid for it, although she seemed on the verge of doing so, and had several enquiring looks cast in her direction by the auctioneer. It went to one of those Vincent had ranked as amateurs; some uninformed northerner with more money than sense, he thought contemptuously.

The woman accosted him on the way out. 'I'm sure you're wrong. If it had been what you said, it would never have fetched that price.'

'It did,' said Vincent simply. 'Did you notice that none of the professionals bid for it?'

'How do you know who the people bidding were? You aren't from these parts, I'm sure.'

'It's my business to know.'

The woman looked at him. 'Where are you from?'

'London. I go back this afternoon.'

'Are you driving?'

'No, I came by taxi. As soon as I've made the necessary arrangements with the auctioneers, I'll ring for one to take me back to Eyot, where I'll catch a train.'

'I'll give you a lift,' the woman said.

She listened and watched unashamedly as Vincent wrote a cheque and discussed delivery.

'How come you have an Eyot delivery address for what you've bought? Is it a customer?'

'No, my sister lives in Eyot. Very handy, although I'm not sure how pleased she'll be when this lot appears on her doorstep.' He looked at the woman's ancient jeep very doubtfully. 'Do you drive this?'

'I do indeed, no time for all these shiny new numbers. I prefer a jeep; down-to-earth, practical, never goes wrong, and I can set the whole thing against tax.'

Vincent hesitated. A strong instinct told him this woman was worth cultivating, and he was torn between the convenience of a lift and a reluctance to travel in such a decrepit and grubby vehicle.

'Suit yourself,' the woman said, starting the jeep and revving the engine with much farty popping from the rear. A bilious cloud of smoke came out from the exhaust, but she didn't seem bothered. 'I'm off then,' she said, letting in the clutch.

'No, wait,' said Vincent, wrenching open the door and clambering in; how irritating high vehicles were.

'Watch out for the dog,' said the woman, starting with a jerk. 'He doesn't like strangers.'

Vincent craned his head round and found himself face to face with a small white dog, which was growling ferociously. 'Shut *up*,' the woman said.

Vincent turned his head back, ignoring the dog, which seemed nonplused at this weak response. It growled more loudly, then broke into a series of shrill yaps before sitting down, defeated, on the back seat.

While Vincent was being driven at breakneck speed along the winding Eyotshire lanes, Mimi was sitting in a traffic jam. In the car beside her was Councillor Henthorpe, gloomily bringing her up to date on the meanderings of the Civic Fountain Sub-committee.

'They're a spineless bunch,' he grumbled. 'Nowt but bread-crumbs between their ears if you ask me.'

'What's the problem? Is it the design, or the cost, or what?'

'Everything. One or two like the boar. Even the gummocks can recognize a boar, and they know it represents the city. Then there's Mrs Elgin, she thinks a wild animal is most inappropriate, however symbolic. And she reckons that your boar is particularly wild in its appearance, by which she means masculine, let's not mince matters, and she's surprised that a young woman would dare to offer such a design.'

'Bother Mrs Elgin.'

'Aye, I agree with you. I've often thought, to hell with her, but there's no denying she carries a powerful voice in the chamber. Then there are the old guard who quite fancy a nice martyr or two, and the hard lefties, who say not to spend a penny on such rubbish. No one listens to them, but there is some support for the member who wonders if a nice heap of pebbles with a dribble in the middle wouldn't do just as well.'

Philistines, thought Mimi, venting her temper by jabbing her horn and giving the van driver in front a nasty shock.

'Of course, it does count for a lot yours being an Eyotshire firm, and Gerry living locally. Anything else, they'd have to go to Leeds or Manchester, maybe, and they're none too keen on that. We'll just have to hope for the best.'

There was doubt in Councillor Henthorpe's voice. Then he cheered up. 'Well, I like a bit of a fight, and I'm fed up with all those southerners sneering at us for our lack of taste. We need something out of the usual way, and that's what I asked for, and that's what you've come up with. You just leave it to me. Now, I'll hop out here, and many thanks for the lift.'

Mr Henthorpe leapt nimbly into the Eyot traffic. Mimi edged forward another foot or two. She shouldn't have cut through the centre, she might have known she'd be held up. Never mind, it was a bit of luck spotting Councillor Henthorpe standing at the bus stop; much easier to have a chat in the car than to call on him at his office on a formal visit.

She looked at her watch, and wondered when Vincent would be back. She must catch him before he flitted back to London, get it into his obstinate head that she was serious about the stuff in the stables; it all had to go. And he must tell Ferdie that the torsos would go to the dump if he didn't make some arrangement about them. For some reason, those torsos really got up Edmund's nose, and he was jumpy enough without worrying about writhing statuary.

The latest train he'd want to catch would probably be the nine minutes past eight. How long did country sales go on for? It could be quite late, she thought, remembering Vincent's excursions in the past, but of course there was no knowing whether he had come straight back from those, or even gone at all. You believed what Vincent told you at your peril.

She spotted a gap in the traffic and made a dive through it, hurtling down a one-way street which ran parallel to hers, but several along. Like hers, it led down to the river and ended in a cul-de-sac. She would leave the car down there, and walk home by the river; she could collect it later in the evening, when the rush hour was over.

A thin and icy drizzle had started, blown into neck and eyes and hands by the wind. She didn't have far to walk, but she was wet through by the time she got home. To her surprise, Gerry opened the door as she stood damply on the porch, hunting for her key.

'Still here?' she said, surprised.

'I stayed to keep Phoebe company. There was a call from the hospital and Edmund went over there.'

'Quinta? Oh dear, what's up?'

'Nothing serious, except that she's beside herself with boredom. Edmund's gone up with tapes and books. We didn't know when you'd be back, and he said he could do with a walk. And he's right, it's a relief to have him out of the house, if you don't mind me saying so. I've never seen him in such a fret. All this is getting him down, Mimi, you'll have to take him off on a holiday.'

She hung up her dripping jacket, and shook her hair. 'Do you think he'd go? And besides, I can't go away now. We're too busy, and I can't lose business, we need the money.'

'I'll look after things if you want to go. A week isn't going to harm the business, and it might make all the difference to Edmund.'

'I can try,' said Mimi doubtfully. 'How's Phoebe?'

'Asleep, and not too well. I took her round to the doctor's this afternoon. No, it's all right, I rang the hospital and asked Quinta if I might. Not to worry her, you know, just said that I thought Phoebe needed a stronger cough medicine than you can get at the chemist.'

'Is she coughing now? That was thoughtful of you, Gerry, but I'm sure there's something in the house I could give her.'

'Don't be dim, that was just for Quinta. Listen, that kid is seriously down, it's time she had a few tests done. I pretended I was her brother, which she thought was very funny and a good wheeze. I think the doctor was a bit suspicious, it was one of those tough women with a bun, but once she'd got a good look at young Phoebe, she just said she was glad someone had brought her in.'

'Oh dear.'

'Not to worry. She's fairly sure it's glandular fever, like I suspected, because I had it when I was at college, and I felt just like Phoebe does. There's no cure for it, supposedly, except rest and time. Mind you, homoeopathic remedies can work; I'll ask Quinta if she'll let a chum of mine suggest something.'

'What sort of a chum?'

'Oh, he's a doctor, but into natural cures and things. He spent a year training in Germany, they're very hot on that kind of thing over there. Don't look so concerned, I'm not proposing to poison Phoebe. It can't do any harm, and it may do some good.'

'Where does this doctor hang out? No, don't tell me, he lodges with Jemima.'

'He does, actually.'

'What a surprise.'

## 19

Never had Mimi felt so oppressed or found life so complicated.

For a start, there was Vincent.

Of course, he hadn't caught the 20.09, nor the trains an hour or two hours later. He hadn't got back to Eyot until half past ten; far too late to go to London, Mimi must see that. And besides, he thought he'd stay on for a few days, there were some remarkable bargains to be had, he'd spotted some art deco pieces at ridiculous prices, and she wouldn't want to stand in the way of her brother making a humble crust, now would she?

Yes, she would.

It was a vain stand; nothing had ever been known to sway Vincent. She couldn't plead the stress in Edmund's life, he would merely be delighted to hear about it; he knew the marriage was doomed from the start.

Mimi had tried to pretend that Phoebe was contagious. Vincent was unimpressed, Phoebe almost certainly had glandular fever, which he'd had a few years back, and you didn't get it twice.

'You can,' said Mimi defiantly.

'Not me.'

Then there was the constant, nagging worry about Edmund, and Phoebe herself. She wasn't well, and there was no one else to look after her. She must feel very insecure with Quinta in hospital for the indefinite future, and however much everyone reassured her, Mimi was sure that Phoebe didn't quite believe that her mother was going to be fine. She wouldn't have done in her place.

She sighed, wondering how best to break the news to

Edmund about Vincent. You didn't have to be an ultra-perceptive wife to know that he wasn't going to be pleased.

Edmund was furious.

'That's it,' he said, when she finally told him that not only had Vincent not left, he wasn't proposing to. 'I will not have your unspeakable brother staying in my house. I shall throw him out.'

'Edmund!'

'Now. This very instant.'

He started up from the bed, and Mimi, alarmed, pushed him back on the pillows. 'Stop it. You can't make a fracas at this time of night; no and not at any other time, either.'

'I shall make a fracas in my own house as and when I like. Anything is better than having that limpet installed for the duration.'

Mimi wrapped a shocking pink satin robe round herself, and sat down at the dressing-table. She took up a hair brush and started to give her hair firm, even strokes.

'What are you doing?'

'Brushing my hair.'

'You never do it. At least, not like that. You look like something out of an old film. A not very good film.'

'It's soothing to the nerves.'

'It isn't your nerves that are the problem. You're used to Vincent, I'm not.'

She put the brush down and pouted at her reflection in the mirror. This latest colour was too pale, she decided. She'd make an appointment at the hairdresser tomorrow, change it to a richer, deeper hue. 'Nobody is used to Vincent. I wish to God he'd get married.'

Edmund shook his head. 'No woman on earth could be mad enough to take on Vincent.'

His temper was subsiding, and he felt tired. Everything got him worked up at the moment, he was overreacting. But there was no question about it. Vincent had to go.

Vincent was up and out of the house long before anybody else was up. Naturally an early riser, it was no hardship for him.

Best to be out of the way of the family, he felt; a considerate guest never liked to interrupt the household routine.

'Sneaked out, has he?' Edmund had no illusions about his brother-in-law. 'Well, when he comes back, it's down to the station with him.'

Stirring words, only Vincent had had the foresight to remove a set of keys from the hall table, and he didn't return until the early hours. By then Mimi had fretted herself into a restless sleep, full of imaginings of terrible things that might have befallen him, and how she was going to break the news to her mother, and how she could even begin to find her mother to tell her . . .

Edmund grimly took one of his pills, and fell asleep hoping that something terrible *had* befallen Vincent . . . Nothing fatal, perhaps, but bad enough to make him shake the dust of Eyot from his feet and vow never to return . . .

Meanwhile, Vincent slid in through the front door, removed his shoes and tiptoed silently up the stairs to his room. In no time at all, he was sleeping the deep and peaceful sleep of the just.

Mrs Sconce was the only one to see Vincent leave the house the following morning, when he rose betimes again. She had come in bright and early, especially to do Edmund's study; she couldn't stand it looking like that for another day.

'And if I don't tidy it,' she had told her husband as he set off for the early shift at the railway works, 'who knows what that evil sprite mightn't do? Better he should turn it topsy-turvy again than set it alight or some other mischief.'

'I don't like you working in a house where that kind of thing's going on.' Pete Sconce took his lunch box from his wife's hand, and stuffed it into the big pocket of the stout jacket he wore to work. He gave her a peck on the cheek and opened the front door. 'Mind you wear that cross I gave you, and keep the Lord's words in your mind.'

Mrs Sconce wasn't the enthusiast for the Lord's words that her husband was, although she duly accompanied him every Sunday to the hall where his Pentecostal sect held their worship.

God and that lot were all very well on Sundays, if you felt the call, but she believed strongly that for the rest of the week she could choose what words she would have in her mind, and they wouldn't have much to do with the scriptures.

Phoebe was awake. Bored with being in bed, she had got up and dressed. 'I can always go and lie down if I feel tired,' she told Mrs Sconce, who was hunting in the kitchen for all the implements she needed for her onslaught on the study. 'I don't actually have to be in bed. I'm not that kind of ill.'

Mrs Sconce paused to make Phoebe a drink of hot chocolate, and coaxed her into having a piece of toast. Phoebe did her best, but, as she said, it was amazing how un-hungry a person could feel. 'Do you think it's too early to ring the hospital?' she asked Mrs Sconce when she had managed to eat half her toast.

'Best leave it a bit. If you want something to do, come and help me in the study.'

'Okay,' said Phoebe. She liked Edmund's study; at least, she did when it wasn't in a state of disarray. There were lots of books, and a lamp that twisted itself into the strangest positions, and a Turkish rug on the floor. Not to mention Edmund's old wooden swivel-chair, which swung round and round so delightfully.

Mrs Sconce handed Phoebe a tin of spray polish and a duster, and advanced towards the study, the gleam of battle in her eye. 'You can help me straighten his papers,' said Mrs Sconce. 'I know what these writers are like, fuss, fuss about some missing page. Still, I reckon there's nothing I can do in there to make matters worse.'

'How strange,' said Phoebe, as she pushed open the study door. 'Edmund must have been in here himself, because all the papers have been picked up, and look, they're all sorted on his desk. They've been done very neatly, too; they're much neater than he usually has them.'

Mrs Sconce clicked her tongue. 'Mimi told me that Edmund wouldn't set foot in here. Cunning, that's what he is. It comes of having an imagination. You mark my words, Phoebe, never marry a man with imagination. It always leads to trouble.'

Phoebe had started to pick up books and restore them, after

careful thought, to the shelves. 'Hasn't your husband got any imagination, then?'

'Certainly not.' Mrs Sconce was shocked. 'I won't have any of that sort of nonsense in my house.'

'My stepfather's got a lot of imagination,' said Phoebe thoughtfully. 'But I'm not sure that my real father has.'

'And who's he when he's at home?' said Mrs Sconce, wrestling with the lamp, which seemed to have tied a knot in itself.

'Oh, someone,' said Phoebe. 'If he'd had any imagination, he'd have known that I might come along and been more careful. Lucky for me he didn't.' She carefully tucked an errant page back in its place in a battered paperback. '*History of the Crusades* by Runciman. We've got this at home. This is Vol. 2, I wonder where the others are?'

Edmund's stomach tightened when he saw the study door standing open. Then he heard the voices, Mrs Sconce's rather deep one – she sang a good alto in the Oratorio Society – and Phoebe's higher, lighter one.

He looked in. His eyes fell on the papers on the desk, and uttering imprecations which sent Mrs Sconce off into a chorus of disapproving clucks, bounded across the room. 'Who's been at these? Phoebe, you must realize . . .'

Mrs Sconce was having none of that. 'You leave Phoebe alone, she hasn't done anything to your pesky papers, and no more have I. They were like that when we came in here this morning, weren't they, Phoebe?'

Phoebe nodded.

'I said to Phoebe, now look, Edmund's been in here after all, and sorted his papers, when he said he wasn't going to.'

Edmund wasn't listening. He was staring at the pages, turning them over, bending down as though to read something difficult. 'I don't understand,' he said at last. 'These have been completely rearranged. Very well, but quite a different order from the way they were. The notes on banking . . .' His voice tailed off as he did some more riffling through the pages. 'And look, annotated, in brown ink.' He peered at the squiggles which had appeared in the margins of his pages.

'What does it say?' asked Phoebe, much interested in this new development.

'It's all quite illegible.' Edmund sat down in his swivel chair, and sunk his head in his hands. Phoebe and Mrs Sconce heard him mumbling something to himself. Then he pulled his head up and stared in front of him out of the window.

'I think I'm going mad.'

'What?' said Mimi, putting her head round the door and smothering a prodigious yawn. 'Where's Vincent?'

'Gone out. Early,' said Mrs Sconce. 'And Phoebe and I came in here to tidy up a bit, and the papers have been sorted out and tidied up, and put ever so neatly on the desk. And now Edmund says he didn't do it, and someone's written notes on the pages, and he's losing his wits.'

All on one breath, thought Edmund, a flash of admiration lightening his doomed feelings for a moment. 'Mimi, did you do this?'

'No,' said Mimi. 'I never touch your work.'

'Then who on earth . . . ? What is going on? Someone, and someone with quite a lot of brains, is making free of my room, one night running amok, another putting my work into much better order than it was before. Who?'

'Not who,' said Mrs Sconce. 'What.'

Ranulf sat watching them, a stocky if invisible figure in the winged chair. Ha, that had given Edmund something to think about. It was the first time he'd seen Edmund clearly, everything was becoming clearer now. He'd been on a visit to Mountjoy Castle, well, he wouldn't have recognized it, although Sir Hugo's place in the chapel was just as it used to be.

He'd have known Edmund for a Mountjoy anywhere, that hawkish face and aquiline nose. Many was the time he'd seen Sir Hugo looking down his own nose, and it never boded well.

Who was the child? Almost, he thought, she could see him. Perhaps she could. Children's minds were different.

He uncrossed his legs and left as Mrs Sconce started work with her can of polish. He wasn't at all keen on the spray.

'Neat the room may be,' she was saying, 'but that's not

the same as clean. I shall give it a good going over, just in case.'

'That's right,' said Phoebe, setting to work with a will and a duster. 'We'll polish all traces of the other world away.'

# 20

Edmund had gone off for a long, long walk.

He stalked along the riverbank, down as far as the forest, where the riverside path ended in a tangle of barbed wire and a scrawled 'Keep Out' notice. If you got that far, then you could clamber up the bank, catching hold of roots to help you, and walk along the edge of the forest to the village of Watby.

Where, Mimi knew, there was an excellent pub, famed for its lunches. 'I'll meet you there, and we'll have lunch,' she had suggested.

'No,' said Edmund abruptly. 'I want to be alone, I've got a lot of thinking to do. This rearrangement of my papers has given me an idea, and I want to get it all clear in my head. No interruptions.'

She could see how troubled he was, but he had withdrawn, he wasn't reaching out to her or anyone else.

She looked at the pile in her action tray; it never seemed to get any smaller. Well, there wasn't much she could do about it this morning; she and Gerry were due at Hustle Manor to see Elvira Winthrop.

Gerry appeared, whistling tunelessly, carrying a large portfolio under his arm. 'Elvira said she'd like to look at some of the rest of my work,' he explained.

'I can't stay very long at the Manor. I've got a pile of paperwork.'

Gerry had advised Mimi more than once to get someone to help in the office. Even a part-timer would make a difference. But she was adamant that the business didn't justify it; she insisted that she could handle that side of things as she'd always done.

'Difficult when you've got a houseful, and you're worried about Edmund and so forth. It means you can't put the hours in.'

'Oh, shut up, Gerry,' said Mimi. 'Off into the fray. We've got a short walk; some idiot blocked our entrance last night, and the car is in the next street.'

'In that case, you'll need a coat. This wind comes to your area courtesy of the Arctic and Siberia. Forget summer; it's woolly underwear time again.'

When they reached the manor, they found that Elvira was not alone.

Mimi and Gerry had parked the car at the back, and got out of the car into the teeth of a vicious north wind which was sending angry black clouds scudding across the sky.

They tumbled into the kitchen, where Elvira welcomed them with glad cries. A man stood by the coffee pot, ready to dispense cups to the new arrivals.

'Oh, no,' said Mimi.

'Christ, it's Vincent,' said Gerry.

'Do you know each other?' said Elvira, looking from one to the other.

Dr Cara Sicilienne and Dr Daphne Whitgift had watched Edmund's lonely figure set off along the river path. He had called in at the university to let them know that he wouldn't be taking his scheduled lecture that morning, and then set off, shoulders hunched against the wind, head down, a stalwart and lonely figure.

'Kind of you to take his lecture for him,' said Daphne. She was standing at the large window of her colleague's office, which looked out across river to the line of fells, almost invisible on this grey day.

'It's hardly difficult, Philip IV of France and his attitude to the Templar order.'

'What was his attitude?'

'Greed.'

'Very enjoyable,' said Daphne. 'I wish we tackled such straightforward subjects in my department.'

'He's starting to crack,' said Cara, watching the speck which was Edmund. 'It won't be long now.'

'You don't have any sympathy for him at all, do you?'

Cara shrugged. 'None. It isn't in my nature to be sympathetic. Besides, he doesn't need sympathy, he just needs to get on with it, make up his mind, haul himself on to the right path.'

'He's having trouble with his brother-in-law, I hear.'

'The one called Vincent?'

'Yes, and I suppose the other two are on their way.'

'Good. That'll irk Edmund. Disruption, upset, pressure, anything to shake him out of his rut.'

Mimi stalked into the hairdressers, causing the luscious lips of the receptionist to suck into a silent O of disapproval. She put a tick beside Mimi's name in the appointment book, after pretending that there was some mistake; claiming that no Mimi Mountjoy was booked. Then she rose and, heels clicking defiantly on the polished parquet floor, led her to a robe and a basin.

Tilly was the colourist. She was only about five feet tall, with an hour-glass figure and a bundle of perfectly natural dark blonde curls piled up on her head to give her height.

'Shocking condition,' she said, running friendly fingers through Mimi's hair. 'Have you been overdoing it? Still, don't worry, I've got a new conditioner on trial, super. Same shade?'

'No. I want something a bit more lively. A plummy colour.'

'Victoria, Spanish or greengage?'

'Dark, velvety burgundian red.'

Tilly looked at Mimi's purple skirt and top. 'That'd look very vivid with those clothes.'

'I like bright colours, it'll be fine with purple.'

And strangely enough, it was. Mimi sailed out of the salon two hours later to a chorus of admiration. Even the polished sourpuss at the desk uttered one or two cool words of appreciation for Tilly's skill.

She felt much better for her self-indulgence. Feeling that she was more than a match even for evil Inez, she stopped at Gumbles to buy Edmund one or two of his favourite things. Sharp herrings from Denmark and aquavit to go with them, tubs of Italian and Spanish salads and a spicy roast chicken from the spit. Madeira cake was something else he was very partial to, and a box of amaretti.

It had been an expensive afternoon, but worth it, felt Mimi. She had a twinge of guilt about Phoebe, left in the care of Mrs Sconce for the morning, with Sylvester promising to be there in the afternoon.

'I'd take her back to Midwinter for the day,' he'd said, 'but I suspect maximum peace and minimum moving about is best for her at the moment. She can come and spend some days when she's feeling better. When the weather returns to something more appropriate for the time of year, and there's no danger of frostbite.'

Mimi decided to buy something for Phoebe. She was too old for toys or crayons, so she bought her a new paperback and a kaleidoscope of sparkling beauty. Even if Phoebe didn't like it, Mimi was going to get a lot of pleasure out of it.

She needn't have worried. Phoebe greeted the book with cries of delight as being by one of her favourite authors, and carried the kaleidoscope off in triumph to show Sylvester, who was puzzling over an accompaniment at the piano.

'I'm feeling perfectly all right,' Phoebe said, 'but I think I'll just go upstairs for a bit and read this book on my bed.'

With the book under one arm, and the kaleidoscope balanced on a tray with a jug of orange juice and a glass, Phoebe went carefully upstairs.

'She's feeling rotten,' said Sylvester, following Mimi into the kitchen. 'What's that delicious smell?'

'Chicken from Gumbles. For Edmund's supper. Do stay, there'll be plenty, because Phoebe hardly eats anything.'

'You've got Vincent to feed.'

'I have not. Vincent! I could wring his neck,' she said ferociously, the morning's encounter coming back to her. 'Listen, do you realize he's making up to Elvira Winthrop? That's why he's so keen to stay in Eyot.'

'Nonsense,' said Sylvester. 'He wants to stay because he has a comfortable bed, a civilized base, and he doesn't have to worry about any household expenses.'

'There is that, but he's always had a rich older woman on the go, and Elvira fits the bill exactly. It's too bad, he's taking her off furniture buying, giving her tips on decorating her house and even telling her gardener what to do with her hedges. Elvira has lots of hedges.'

'It keeps him out of the house.'

'Huh. Not out enough. Edmund's fuming about his staying on in Eyot, and Vincent's been at Phoebe, who is often awake in the early hours when he comes in, trying to bribe her to swap rooms. No, it isn't funny.'

Sylvester thought it was. 'Have you spoken to him about all the belongings and works of art which the three of them landed you with?'

'I never get the chance. Vincent is very slippery when he wants to be, like now. I've left notes in his room, but he just throws them in the bin. I don't suppose he even reads them, and he certainly won't take any notice of them. We never see him, he sneaks in late and slides out at the crack. I set my alarm this morning to catch him, but both Edmund and I slept through it.'

Sylvester shook his head. 'You'd have to do better than that. Any more news on the ghost front?'

'We do not have a ghost. It's more of an occurrence.'

Sylvester made a cynical noise. 'We shall see. Well, I'll hand Phoebe over to you, and be off.'

'I'm going to put in a bit of time in the office, give Phoebe a chance to have a rest, and then I'll take her up to the hospital for visiting hours.'

Phoebe was exhausted by the time they got back from the hospital. Edmund had got in from his long walk, and was flat out on the sofa, similarly worn out. 'My legs,' he said dramatically. 'My feet! My back!'

Phoebe gave him a scornful look and trudged off to bed, quite uninterested in the promise of a tray of supper. 'Must I?'

'Just something light,' begged Mimi. 'A bowl of cereal?'

'I suppose so.'

Mimi bent over Edmund and gave him a quick kiss. 'I bought you lots of lovely things to eat today.'

'Oh, good,' he said, lying back and closing his eyes.

He was woken by a terrible shriek from the kitchen, which galvanized even his tired limbs into action.

'Mimi! Whatever is it? Are you hurt?'

A speechless Mimi was making keening noises, and pointing to the fridge. There, neatly laid out on a shelf, were the remains of her careful shopping.

'Barely a quarter of the chicken left! Practically no salads. All the herrings gone, and the cake. Oh, oh!'

Edmund had spotted a note. 'Thanks for the food. Will be away two or three days. Have taken aquavit and amaretti; knew you wouldn't mind, Vincent.'

Mimi kicked the fridge door shut, and gave it two or three more hearty kicks. Then she banged the table with her fists.

'Calm down,' said Edmund, concerned. 'Mimi, darling, it doesn't matter.'

She threw herself into Edmund's arms. 'It does, it does matter. I chose everything so carefully for you, at Gumbles, I spent a fortune, and beastly, sadistic Vincent has spoiled it all.'

'It's all right. I'll go out and get us a takeaway, and a bottle of wine. Please don't take on so.'

'How could he do it? He must have known it wasn't for him.'

Edmund reckoned that Vincent knew perfectly well that it was a special supper, bought by Mimi. Trust him to wade in and spoil it; that man was a menace.

'Tell me,' he said, still holding a sobbing Mimi. 'Is this Elvira a tough cookie?'

She hiccuped inelegantly. 'I would have thought so, but she can't be, if she's been taken in by Vincent.'

'Maybe Vincent's met his match.'

'Oh, dear God, I do hope so.'

# 21

Footsteps in the hall.

Phoebe reached for her watch and squinted at the luminous dial. Half-past three in the morning! It must be Vincent coming in. Then she remembered that Mimi had told her that he was going to be away for a couple of nights. So it couldn't be him.

It was some other sound, then, that had woken her from a particularly vivid dream. She had been setting off on a journey overseas, in the company of knights on horseback. Everywhere banners were fluttering in a brisk wind, and she could see stubby sailing ships with pennants flying from endless masts. And there were noises, and smells, and people; masses of people milling about, seemingly with no purpose, but all apparently having a good time.

She had been roused out of this interesting dream by creakings and sounds of people moving around; what bad luck. She snuggled down in bed, clasping a childish owl which still had rights of residence by her pillow, and tried to slip back into that other, more colourful world.

It was no good.

Someone was up and about, and she needed to know who. Had the hospital rung, was there bad news about her mother? Phoebe jumped out of bed and put on her dressing-gown. Her feet were bare and silent as she padded out of her room and along the landing.

All the lights were off, and the house seemed quiet. Aha, no. There was a pale light coming out of Edmund's study. Was he down there working? Or could it be the wrecker at work? Emboldened by the thought that at least there probably hadn't been any awful telephone calls, she crept down the stairs. Halfway down, she paused. If she sat down, she could see into the study through the banisters.

Someone was in there.

Quite definitely. She could hear rustlings, and mutterings, as though someone was grumbling. A man, thought Phoebe; it was a deepish grumble. Then he crossed in front of the door, and she saw him quite clearly. A neat and not very tall man, dressed in very strange clothes. He held a book in one hand and a cassette in the other. He was holding the cassette up to the light as though trying to read the title.

Strangely, she didn't feel in the slightest bit frightened. Curious, yes, alarmed, no. It was like watching a film: intriguing and gripping, but ultimately happening up there on the screen while you were safe in your seat. Nonetheless, she didn't feel inclined to go on down the stairs, push open the door and ask who he was, what he was doing, how he had got in.

She looked over to the front door. It was firmly shut, with the big bolts drawn top and bottom; Vincent wouldn't be coming back in tonight, even if he wanted to.

Then a sudden wave of utter sleepiness overtook her and, with a vast yawn, she went back upstairs and along the landing to her room. She cast off her dressing-gown, still yawning, when her attention was caught by another noise.

This was different.

She listened, frozen.

This was a real sound. This wasn't part of any dream. This was a sound from outside. Several sounds, in fact. A gate or door opening and shutting, with a loud squeak. Footsteps. Another door opening, and what sounded like a window being raised.

Phoebe slid to her own window, and flattening herself to one side, peered out. It was a moonlit night, with the nearly full moon riding high above and casting its usual unreal shadows in the courtyard below. She tensed. That was a figure. That was someone up to no good, going through the stable door. That was furtive.

Quick as a flash, she ran to her door, wrenched it open, and hurled herself along the landing. She pounded, panic-stricken, on Mimi and Edmund's door. 'Wake up, wake up! Burglars!'

Edmund, naturally, went on sleeping. Mimi, stunned from being woken so abruptly, struggled to the door. 'Phoebe, what is it, a nightmare?'

'No, I saw a man. There's someone outside, in the stables.'

Mimi shot into Phoebe's room, telling herself the child had been dreaming, but needing to have a look, just in case.

Dear God, she was right. There was someone down there. 'Get back into bed, Phoebe. Lock your door first, and don't open it, unless it's me. Don't worry, I'm calling the police right now.'

She hurtled back to her bedroom, and tried to wake Edmund. Useless. All the shakings and shoutings in his ear had no effect besides a mumbled 'eh?' He turned over and sank back into his druggy slumbers.

Hell. And so typical. When you needed a man to be up and doing manly things, what did they do? Sleep. On reflection, though, did she want him dashing out to the yard, accosting what might be a dangerous intruder with who knew what consequences? She shuddered and picked up the phone to dial 999.

Stay where you are, they'd said. All very well, but she was desperately trying to remember if she'd locked and bolted the back door. If not . . . Off she went downstairs, her heart thumping in her mouth, tiptoeing to the door. Help; just as she'd feared, neither locked nor bolted. That was soon remedied.

She paused in the hall, uncertain what to do. Should she open the front door to let the police in? Or might the lurker whiz round to the front of the house, called by some burglarious sixth instinct, and come in?

Better leave it. The police would ring the doorbell. Best to get upstairs and get dressed, you couldn't face anyone in your nightclothes, however dashing your green silk pyjamas were.

As she hustled herself into trousers and a jumper, she heard a car draw up at the back, and the engine cut out. Then another car, and another silenced engine. She flew out of her room and knocked at Phoebe's door. It opened immediately, and the girl stood there, with bright, excited eyes. 'The police are here,' she said. 'I've been watching.'

There were shouts and cries from outside. A bright light flashed on; in the distance a siren wailed, and there was a sudden crackle of sound from a walkie-talkie.

'They've got him,' said Phoebe. 'It's a shortish man with very tight curly hair. He looks very indignant, and he's shouting at the police. What a nerve!'

Tight, curly hair? Shortish? A dreadful suspicion struck Mimi. No, it couldn't be.

She flung open the window and looked down into the yard on to a ring of upturned faces.

'It's all right,' said a helmeted man. 'We've got him.'

The burglar was handcuffed to one of the officers, and dancing with fury. Now he looked up. 'Mimi,' he cried. 'What on earth's going on? Tell these idiots who I am, and make them let me go.'

'Do you know him?' said Phoebe, eyes like saucers.

'Unfortunately, yes, I do. It's my brother, Ferdie.'

# 22

Mimi dressed in red, the colour of danger and intent. The frenzy of the night before had vanished, and she was now full of steely purpose.

Then she thought of Ferdie, no doubt serenely asleep in Vincent's bed. She looked across at Edmund, himself still soundly asleep. Soon, she would have to wake him up and tell him about the night's drama. She would have to tell him about Phoebe's fright, and the police coming. She would have to break the news that Ferdie was here.

Not feeling quite so steely, she decided to leave him to sleep a little longer. Fortified with a cup of coffee, she would be more alert, readier to face the day – and Edmund.

The unfortunate consequence of her decision was that he woke up by himself about half an hour later. He pottered backwards and forwards as he normally did, taking his time under the shower, always a good place for thinking, he found. Then a leisurely shave, a mull over what clothes to wear, a pause to read an article in a magazine which he'd brought upstairs the night before.

He was filled with a sense of well-being. He had sorted several knotty points out in his head while walking yesterday. He and Mimi had had a delicious time in bed, dispelling any worries either of them might have had about the effect of the sleeping pills and/or his incipient psychological breakdown. And, best of all, Vincent had shoved off. Even if only for two days; a lot could happen in two days in the way of schemes and plots to be rid of a tiresome brother-in-law.

Of course, in bygone and more lawless days, it would have

been easy enough to dispose of a troublesome relative. In renaissance Italy it was quite the custom, and look at how the Tudors removed anyone who bothered them.

Musing on those happier and better-ordered times, he emerged from the bedroom, his mind on a substantial breakfast.

And there, standing outside his door was another brother. A brother clad in a pair of very tight lime green underpants and nothing else.

'Ferdie!' He couldn't believe his eyes. 'Ferdie! What the hell are you doing here?'

'Oh, hello, Edmund. I want to borrow a tie. I left all mine behind, and I can't wear this shirt without one.'

He held up a pink paisley creation.

Why in God's name did anyone built along the lines of a discus thrower, or possibly a lightweight shot-putter, feel he had to wear pink paisley shirts? Edmund ignored the shirt and his request. 'When did you get here? How did you get in?'

Ferdie made a tsking sound. 'Don't snarl like that, it's very bad for my nerves. It was an extremely traumatic incident last night, and I do hope you don't make a habit of treating visitors like that. If you weren't family, I might sue, you do realize that. My friend Lester, who's a very eminent barrister in London, would almost force me to sue if he heard about it.'

'I don't know what you're talking about. Anyway, you aren't a visitor. You aren't staying here with us, let me make that quite clear.'

'You can hardly throw me out, not your own brother-in-law.' He held the shirt against himself. 'Darkish wine shades, I think, if you've got such a tie. I don't suppose for a moment that yours are at all my style, one despairs of the provinces, but I'm sure you've got something which will do me until I can get out to the shops. I can't think how I came to be so careless.'

He sailed into Edmund's room. Edmund, beside himself, was about to leap after him and drag him back. Then he thought better of it. Ferdie, once his mind was set on anything, was relentless. Let him find a tie, he'd deal with him later. Meanwhile, where was Mimi?

Mimi took one look at his face and knew that he'd encountered Ferdie.

'No, don't say anything,' he said. 'I don't want to hear sixteen reasons why Ferdie has to stay for just a day or two. He isn't staying even for an hour. He's going, and all that sordid torso work with him. I can't think why you let him in last night.'

'Let him in? Let him in? Now, listen, while you were snoring your head off . . .'

Dr Daphne Whitgift strolled into Edmund's office at the university. He wasn't there, but a disconsolate Inez was sitting at his desk.

Daphne perched on the corner of his desk. 'No Edmund?'

'No. He's gone away for a few days, according to Mimi, although I don't think you can believe a word she says. She's the most unsuitable wife for a scholar; no interest in his subject, and not enough sense to look after him while he's hard at work on a book, a substantial piece of scholarship. Doesn't she realize what a privilege it is to be married to him?'

'I imagine he's a handful,' said Daphne. 'But of course you'd know all about that.'

'Edmund did a lot of good work when he was with me. Three chapters of this book were drafted when we were together, and now, more than three years later, he isn't halfway through it. In fact,' she went on, picking up a wodge of paper and waving it dramatically, 'I think he's even decided to rewrite all the earlier section.'

'Ah, but the three chapters he did three years ago were as dull as ditchwater.'

'Dull?' Inez couldn't believe her ears. 'Those chapters were the most impeccable scholarship.'

'His publishers don't pay him for impeccable scholarship. They take that as read. They pay him because he turns in a thumping good read. Or did, until this book.'

Inez's lip curled. 'I don't think you altogether understand the mind of an historian. One can perhaps acquire a distorted view of a fellow academic's work when one is in such a totally different area oneself. Such as fiction.'

The way she said 'fiction' summoned up a seedy world of pot-boilers and hack work, with torrid romances and tacky porn lurking in the shadows. 'Personally, I never read fiction.'

'You should. It's the key to understanding the human heart and soul. Perhaps if you'd known more about that side of Edmund, he wouldn't have gone off and married Mimi, and, moreover, you might begin to understand what his writing is – or could be – all about. I hope he takes a good long time off, and comes back feeling more at peace with himself and the world.'

Inez sniffed. 'He needs sympathy and warmth and loving care.'

'Does he now?' Daphne's voice was full of cynicism. 'Such as he finds while reposing on your sumptuous bosom?'

Inez's eyes grew dreamy. 'He's very much a breast man,' she said with satisfaction.

Sylvester called in to enquire about Phoebe's well-being, and was astonished to be met by a raging Mimi.

'Calm down,' he said annoyingly. 'Dear me, this house is always in an uproar these days. Where's Edmund?'

'Gone.'

'Gone where?'

'*I* don't know. I'm only his wife, why should he tell me? He's run off to fall into Inez's arms; I'm sure he has.'

'Oh, I doubt that. Inez's charms are obvious to all, and I think he'd tired of them even before he met you. What drove him out? Did you have a quarrel?'

'Yes, but it's not what you think. It wasn't that kind of quarrel. Ferdie's turned up.'

'Ah.' He pursed his lips and made infuriating whistling noises. 'Bad. Just now, very bad. Where is Benedict, by the way? Are you expecting him, too?'

'I wasn't expecting any of them, as you know perfectly well. Benedict's up with those monks he's so keen on, in the wilds of Scotland. Thank God he won't be landing up on our doorstep; he always goes for at least a month.'

'That's something. And how's Phoebe taking all this?'

'Oh, Phoebe.'

'You don't sound terribly happy about her. Is she getting on your nerves? I thought you'd rather like having her to stay.'

'I do. But now she's been having hallucinations, she insists she saw a man in the study last night. Of course, there was no one there, it was all imagination.'

'There is a rumour flying about Eyot that the police were called out to this address in the wee hours. Was that to do with Phoebe and her hallucinations?'

'Oh, no. That was just Ferdie ill-timing his arrival and creeping in the back way. No, I expect she was sleepwalking and having one of those strange dreams you have when you're ill, nothing more than that. It's just one more problem, that's all, and if it goes on, I'll have to take her to the doctor again for some pills. I don't want Quinta worrying about it, though, so don't mention it if you're visiting.'

'Not a word. So where's Ferdie now?'

'Gone to buy a tie at Kings and Wallup.'

'He has his mind on essentials, as ever. Let's hope he doesn't get the gentlemanly sales assistant with a face like a monkfish.'

She stared at him in horror. 'What a dreadful thought. Is there really one who looks like that?'

'Oh, yes. I thought I'd just mention it, knowing Ferdie's taste. It's best to be prepared.'

Mimi pulled her mind back to the immediate situation. 'Gerry's in the yard, moving Ferdie's sculptures. They get up Edmund's nose in a big way, so Gerry's borrowed the van we use for big deliveries. He has a chum with space in his warehouse, and they're going there.'

'Does Ferdie know?'

'He doesn't, but he soon will. Then Mrs Sconce is going to strip the bed in the little spare room. I shall lock the door and secrete the key in a place so secure that not even the cunning of my brothers will discover it.'

'Supposing you manage to get rid of Ferdie, what about Vincent?'

Her fury returned. 'Do you know, he's gone to Ireland to buy some Georgian furniture for Elvira Winthrop? It's much cheaper over there apparently. But he rang Ferdie before he caught the ferry, telling him how to get into the house through the back, and saying that he could use the room he's been sleeping in.'

'Vincent's a card.'

'Vincent's a menace. Oh, God, I do wish my mother hadn't gone off. It's her fault that they're like this; why should I reap what she's sown? And while I'm lumbered with Vincent and Ferdie, she's sitting on deck savouring the sea air, not a care in the world. It's too bad.'

'Finella should have got them sorted out years ago.'

'She tried. Endless girls to dinner and outings. Useless. Especially in Ferdie's case, of course, but you would have thought Vincent would have been picked up by *someone*. Then he could have provided a nice home for his brothers.'

'Difficult for Vincent to find anyone who feels as fond of him as he does of himself.'

She wasn't listening. 'And now Edmund's done a bunk. I might as well pack up and go as well, only what about the fountains?'

'No particular problem with the fountains, is there?'

'Oh, yes, there is. With all this going on, I never manage to catch up with invoicing, and there are bills to pay, goods to order, queries to answer, customers to get back to and deliveries to see to.'

'Sounds like you need some help on the admin side.'

'Gerry's a tower of strength, but he's going to be spending a lot of time at Hustle Manor. Elvira's asked him to restore the plasterwork in her sitting-room. It was covered with paint in the fifties and badly damaged in the process.'

Mimi didn't begrudge Gerry the work; far from it, she was delighted for him. Only just now, she felt she needed helping hands around her, not out at Hustle.

'And there's Phoebe,' she added dolefully. 'I'm fond of her, but she needs time and attention.'

'Tell you what,' said Sylvester. 'Call an agency, ask for a nice efficient girl to come and give you a hand. A level-headed person, used to working in irregular households.'

'What do you mean, irregular? You make it sound as though we had a red lamp hanging outside the front door.'

'No, no, you know what I mean. Not every temp wants to put up with hauntings and brothers and the police arriving at odd hours and Edmund's temper; you have to admit that it could be difficult for someone of a nervous temperament.

If you can find someone to get on top of all that paperwork, it'll leave you free to concentrate on the things only you can do, and you'll still have the time and energy to cope with the family crises.'

Mimi didn't want family crises. She wanted Edmund, and a normal home life and a smooth-running business, with no attendant brothers, and no poltergeist in the study, and no sirens like Inez lurking in the woodwork.

'Listen, I'm fairly sure where Edmund will be, if it's any help.'

'Where?'

'At the castle.'

'Of course,' she said bitterly. 'Like a homing pigeon, back to the Mountjoy base. For his cousin Valdemar to fill his head full of wicked thoughts, and for him to think how good life is there compared to here.'

'Right now, he has a point.'

Sylvester was right. Edmund was at Mountjoy Castle. When he flung out of the house, his possessions carelessly tossed into a big leather bag which had belonged to his father, he pretended to himself that he had no idea where he was going to go.

London, he told himself.

Then visions of busy streets, traffic, the buzz and rumble of a great city filled his mind. No, that wasn't what he wanted. Not now. And besides, he usually stayed with Virginia when he went to London, and she would be ruthless and contemptuous.

He could find a country hotel, pleasantly anonymous, by a lake . . .

No.

People tried to talk to you in hotels, staff asked if you were comfortable, the bedrooms were always too hot or too cold.

This was all hogwash. He knew exactly where he was going. To Mountjoy, for Magdalena's civilized conversation, for Valdemar's bracing personality, for the delightful silliness of the twins.

For a moment he hesitated, an evil impulse willing him to take the car. No, Mimi needed it for her work. Although she'd better watch it, her brothers were more than capable of commandeering it. On which sour thought, he went quickly out of the gate and towards the main road. He would walk into the centre, visit the bookshop to treat himself to some detective stories, he needed something to relax with. It was a great strain thinking about Templars all the time. Then he'd take a taxi out to Mountjoy.

'Stay as long as you like, of course,' said Magdalena, giving him an affectionate hug. 'We're up in my sitting-room, leave your bag here for now and we'll go up and find Val.' She led the way across the courtyard and up the stone spiral staircase which led to one of the towers. 'Is Mimi going to be joining you?' she asked, as she handed him a cup of tea.

That brought a cynical laugh from Valdemar. 'Can't you see he's left home?' he said acutely. 'Domestic life getting a bit too much for you, Edmund? I hear those remarkable brothers of Mimi's are turning up one by one.'

'Oh, poor Mimi,' said Magdalena.

'Poor me.'

'You've escaped. I dare say Mimi feels she can't. Isn't little Phoebe staying with you?'

Edmund had the grace to blush. 'It's a very unruly household at the moment,' he said defensively. 'I find it difficult to work.'

'Cara and Daphne came over at the weekend,' said Valdemar. 'Full of praise for your brain and your knowledge and your previous successes. I noticed they didn't have much to say about the present opus.'

Perhaps it hadn't been such a good idea to come here.

'Val, leave him alone. Can't you see he's shell-shocked? Haven't you been troubled by a ghost of some kind? Sylvester was telling us about it.'

Good Lord, the gossip in this place. 'Some kind of poltergeist.'

'Sell up,' was Valdemar's callous advice. 'Quickly, before word gets around that your house is haunted, that can drop the price a lot. And before the Ostiman mob acquire squatters' rights. No one will buy the house with them installed.'

Magdalena took Edmund off, well aware that a little of Valdemar's stirring ways went a long way if you weren't feeling strong. And Edmund must be troubled, he wasn't his normal self at all. Usually he gave as good as he got; he too was a Mountjoy, and they were a savage and resilient breed.

# 23

Sylvester arrived at Mimi's house just as a car was drawing up. A graceful and slender young man with red-setter hair got out. He deposited a fat, brown-leather Gladstone bag and a knobbly canvas kit-bag affair on the pavement. Then he leant through the car window and kissed the shadowy occupant a fond farewell. The window went up and the car drove away.

The new arrival picked up his bags and looked dreamily up and down the street.

'Good morning, Benedict. This is Mimi's house, in case you're wondering,' said Sylvester.

'Hello, Sylvester.' Benedict turned his startling blue eyes on Sylvester, and gave him a charming and very sweet smile. He showed no surprise at finding him standing there. 'Is Mimi in, do you think? I couldn't get her on the phone, it was forever engaged, so I didn't say what time I'd be here. I couldn't have anyway, because I was hitching, and one never knows how long that may take. Still, I'm here now, and it's probably for the best, I know Mimi doesn't think it's safe, my taking lifts. She might have worried about me.'

'I doubt it,' said Sylvester, ringing a merry peal on the doorbell. 'Was that a friend of yours dropping you off?'

'No, I never saw her before this morning, she gave me a lift from Edinburgh. Terrifically kind, and she wants to meet me in London.'

'Your fatal charm, again, I dare say. So Mimi doesn't know you're coming, eh?'

'I'm sure she knew I'd be here sooner or later.'

'I'm sure she did.'

'I left the monastery earlier than I'd intended, you see. My agent rang me there about a commission. An entire range of stationery, paper, vignettes on the envelope flaps, address-book covers, notebooks, you know the kind of thing. I couldn't turn it down, since money is very tight just at present. A shame, though, because one does need four weeks to really cast off everyday life and focus on the spiritual side. Brother Gregory was truly sorry to see me leave; he feels I have made real progress over this last year.'

'Brother Gregory? Hm,' said Sylvester unenthusiastically as he rang the doorbell again. Monks ranked very little above more worldly clerics in his estimation. They were marginally less bothersome than many of the others out doing mischief in the world, of course, since they at least had the grace to shut themselves away for most of the time, but even so, in his experience they were essentially untrustworthy.

'We'll go round the back,' he told Benedict. 'Leave your things here.'

Benedict obediently followed him to the end of the row of houses, down the narrow alley at the side, and along the wider walkway which ran between the gardens of the houses in Mimi's road and the one next to it. The gardens were walled, with doors or iron gates for access. One or two dustbins stood outside each house; cats surveyed the scene from the roofs of the invariable rear extensions, with some bolder spirits lurking on the walls.

A handsome Siamese twitched its tail as they approached. 'This must be the back of Mimi's house,' said Sylvester. 'I know that cat, it lives next door. Got the devil of a yowl, let me tell you.' He stopped outside a door painted dark blue and gave it a few hefty bangs.

'It might not be locked,' said Benedict, stepping forward and turning the handle.

It wasn't, and it was as well that he had thought of trying the handle, because no one on the other side was paying the least attention to any noises from outside. Sylvester stepped through the door, delighted to have arrived in the middle of what was clearly a promising row.

Mimi was standing in the doorway of the flat above the old

stable, hurling abuse down in the direction of Ferdie, who, puce with rage, was jumping up and down and waving his arms about in a most dramatic fashion.

A stocky man in his fifties, whom Sylvester recognized as the owner of the yowling cat, sat phlegmatically on an old mounting block. Beside him was an old-fashioned wooden wheelbarrow containing one of Ferdie's livelier works of art. Gerry stood silently between the handles, clearly unwilling to take part in the dispute.

Benedict made a beeline for the wheelbarrow and its contents. 'Goodness,' he said. 'It's Charlie. I always wondered what he'd look like without his clothes on. Heavens, is he really that size? No wonder you were so keen on him.'

A shocked look came over the stocky man's face, and the frenzied shouts of brother and sister faded into silence as they stopped arguing and gazed at Benedict.

'Benedict, good,' said Ferdie furiously. 'Perhaps you can explain to Mimi, who seems to have lost any wits she ever had, that she can't just heave my works out like this. And in a wheelbarrow, it's too bad.'

Magdalena found Edmund in the chapel, gazing morosely at the crusader tomb.

'Edmund, in here again, what has come over you, all this communing with relics and bones of the past? It isn't good for you.'

'Just thinking,' he said, getting up from the narrow and uncomfortable pew on which he had perched himself and dusting his trousers down. 'Bones of the past, that's just the trouble. How the hell do you breathe life into them? And why can't I now, when I've done it before?'

'Come along,' she said, in just the tone of voice she used with the twins when they were being difficult. 'I expect the trouble is exactly that you've done it before. Too many trips to the well, and it's dried up. Time to try something new, I dare say.'

Edmund grimaced and fell in beside her. 'Let me help you with those,' he offered, noticing that her arms were full of branches.

'Thank you, but if you pull one out, they'll all tumble down.'

'Flower arranging?'

'No, whippy pieces of willow for some scheme of the twins. I shall deliver it and then run for cover to Eyot before I get roped in to help.'

'It's all very well to talk in that easy fashion about something new,' he went on, his mind reverting to himself and his problems. 'But when you've got a publisher in daily expectation of a thick typescript landing on his desk, and a fat cheque for an advance already banked and spent, and no way to pay it back, let alone to manage without the next tranche, then new is difficult.'

'Better new and difficult than nothing at all, which is what seems to be the alternative.'

He winced. 'I've done quite a bit,' he said, defensive now.

Magdalena said nothing, rather to his relief. People who weren't writers never understood, of course, how much work went into a book. And as she hadn't read it, she could hardly comment on it. He wasn't to know that since he'd left his manuscript lying about in piles in the library, she had in fact looked at it, as had Valdemar.

Magdalena had chosen to spare him her opinion of what he'd written so far, but Valdemar had no scruples about speaking his mind. Dinner that evening was not a meal that Edmund was likely to forget.

'Have some cheese,' said Valdemar, sliding the board towards his cousin.

Magdalena rose; she could see the glint in Valdemar's eye and thought she would remove herself before he gave Edmund the benefit of his advice. 'I'm going to say good night to the twins,' she said. 'I promised them a bedtime story. I'll make coffee when I come back.'

'Not for me,' said Edmund. 'It keeps me awake.'

'You're becoming an old woman,' said Valdemar as the door closed behind her. 'Good God, how old are you? Younger than I am, and I don't bore on about whether I'm sleeping or not.'

Edmund kept his temper. 'Dr Fuseli gave me some pills, but they don't work if I have coffee.'

'Pills? What pills? Sleeping pills? I never heard such nonsense. I tell you what, you've let that old quack Desmond pull the wool over your eyes. I'm surprised at you. What did you go to see him for?'

'None of your business.'

'No, it isn't, but you brought the subject up, moaning about not sleeping. There's nothing wrong with you, I can see that at a glance. You haven't got enough to do, that's your trouble. Faffing about at the university, no wonder you can't sleep, all those frights who hang about there, they'd give anyone the shudders. Get yourself a proper job. You'll have to soon, if you go on turning out much more of that stuff you're writing at the moment.'

'You know nothing about what I'm writing.'

'Oh, yes I do. I read a great chunk of it yesterday. Who needs sleeping pills? I was yawning away after ten minutes of it.'

Edmund was annoyed. 'You had no business to read my work.'

'You left it lying about on the library table. What do you expect?'

'Even so.'

Valdemar looked surprised. He crunched a Bath Oliver topped with a chunk of Stilton, and reached out to pour Edmund another glass of wine.

'No, thanks.'

Valdemar took no notice at all, but filled his glass. 'No coffee, sipping your wine, which is an insult, it's good, and going all prissy because I cast my eyes over your boring book. I can't think what's got into you, midlife crisis, I suppose, although I don't know why that should make you so dreary. Mimi isn't dreary, full of get up and go, lively woman like that should keep you on your toes during the day and busy in bed at night.'

'For Christ's sake, Val, shut up.'

'No, I won't. You come running to Mountjoy, mooch around the place like you've lost your soul and think I'm not going to speak my mind? The truth never hurts.'

'You still shouldn't have read my book. I don't like anyone to look at it until it's finished.' Edmund fiddled with the heavily chased handle of an unused silver spoon. It appeared to be decorated with foliage, but a closer look revealed the grinning face of a satyr. Even the spoon mocks me, he thought, bugger it all.

'Don't worry, this is going to be one of those books which people put down a lot faster than they pick it up. Oh, no doubt it's good scholarship, accurate, perceptive, all that. Pity that it's so crashingly dull, that's all.'

Magdalena soothed Edmund's bruised spirits after dinner, setting in front of him a bowl of the mint chocolates to which he was particularly partial, offering to make him a cup of camomile tea.

'No, thank you, it sounds revolting.'

'Val said you were having trouble sleeping. A glass of port, then?'

Port was a much better idea.

'Mimi rang.'

That jolted him out of what was turning into a promising doze. 'When?'

'While you were talking to Val. She said not to bother you if you were working.'

'I wasn't.'

'I thought it might be best if she didn't hear that you were relaxing in the dining-room.'

Relaxing? With Val? Fat chance.

'What did she want? I'll give her a ring, I suppose.'

He was missing Mimi very much, and was longing to go home, but after he'd walked out in that determined way, it would be very feeble just to go back. He couldn't stay at Mountjoy much longer, though. New tenants would be taking over soon, and Val and Magdalena would be back in London. There was abroad, but what fun would that be without Mimi?

It isn't a matter of fun, he told himself sternly. It was a matter of getting the book finished.

'I'll ring her,' he said, putting down his glass and getting to his feet.

'Are you going back?' asked Magdalena, who had the paper folded on her knee and was working through the day's crossword at demonic speed.

'I can't work in such a disturbed household.'

'Don't be so pompous. How about Mimi? Doesn't she have to work?'

'Her work is different. She can do that however she's feeling. I have to be in the right frame of mind.'

'And that's what you were before her brothers arrived? Working at full throttle, pages rattling off your fingers?'

Edmund gave her a very uncousinly look, but she simply made a few squiggles on the side of the puzzle and took no notice.

'I may as well tell you that her third brother has turned up. Benedict.' Magdalena filled in the last entry of the crossword and put the paper down on the table beside her.

Edmund wasn't surprised. It had only been a matter of time before he joined his brothers. 'They hunt in packs,' he said. 'That settles it, I'm not going home.' He sank back into his comfortable armchair, 'Not until Mimi gets rid of them.'

'She's trying to.'

'She's feeble. They walk all over her, do exactly as they please. Lock the doors and throw away the keys, that's what I told her to do.'

'She did. Ferdie is, apparently, very good at picking locks. Benedict's ventured into the attics and made himself a nest up there, blissfully happy, Mimi reports, and quite immovable. Titus is back from America, and she's been reduced to begging him to leave Phoebe with her so that there isn't another free room.'

Edmund didn't feel quite so comfortable. He got up from his chair and went over to the window.

'Titus is doubtful about that,' Magdalena went on, 'because he says he'll figure as an ogre-stepfather, which is, I must admit, very unfair, because he adores Phoebe and couldn't be kinder to her.'

'Ferdie will just move into the stable flat.'

'Mimi's hauled some things up there from your basement, she thinks it'll be too uncomfortable even for Ferdie.'

Edmund took his gaze from the spreading chestnuts, just coming into their summer beauty despite the inclement weather, and gave Magdalena an unenthusiastic look. Then he shrugged. 'Well, she must sort it out. They're her brothers.'

'That's just why it's so difficult for her. There are all kinds of emotional ties and guilt about what her mother would say and so forth which you don't have. Much easier for you to be firm and tell them to go.'

'Huh. You don't know them. Nothing short of dynamite will dislodge them, mark my words.'

'Mimi needs your help. And support, after all she doesn't want them there any more than you do. She told me that Vincent, who is back from somewhere strange, oh, I know, Ireland, is making up to Elvira Winthrop, and causing no end of trouble with a prestigious and valuable job Mimi and Gerry were doing for her. I tell you, Edmund, she's at her wit's end, and you should be there, not fretting here at Mountjoy Castle.'

'I'm sorry to have been so tedious.'

'You aren't tedious, well, not precisely tedious, but you do have a lot on your mind. Why don't you leave your book for a while, throw yourself into getting the better of the Ostiman brothers and then, when you come back to it, it may all have clarified and practically write itself?'

For a moment he was tempted, but he knew quite well that a break from the book wasn't the answer.

The answer was the bin, and to hell with chasing the will of the wisp that was scholarly respectability. This thought drifting up from his unconscious so startled him that he took a big gulp of port and choked.

Valdemar came into the room just then and gave him a hearty thump on the back. 'Shouldn't be so greedy, it's a fine wine, take it slowly, savour it.'

Valdemar had a few more words to say, almost as though he was in league with Edmund's buried self. 'Do you really want to moulder in that university department for the rest of your life? Are you aiming for ladder-climbing, readership here, chair there? Surely not, what a dead end for someone with a lively mind like yours. At least it used to be lively, I'm not so sure now I've read your latest effort.'

'Shut up, Val. You've already given me your opinion, unasked for, I may add, now just drop it.'

'Have some more port,' said Valdemar, not in the least suppressed. 'Only don't gulp it down this time. No, I was thinking about you while I did the rounds.'

When Valdemar was in residence at the castle, he stalked round the walls every evening, going up and down each of the towers and checking all the many doors, even sometimes sending the one remaining portcullis rattling up and down to test the mechanism.

Invigorated by these seigneurial activities, he was more than a match for sleepy Edmund. 'Finance and money is fine, but you aren't the man to make it interesting. Wrong field, I'd say, and the wrong approach. How many copies of your next book does your publisher hope to sell?'

Edmund slid further down into his chair and a sulk. Damn Val, going on at him like this. And there was no stopping him when he was in this mood, what a mistake to think he would find solace at Mountjoy.

'Tens of thousands, I'd guess. Paperback edition, foreign rights, they're rubbing their hands at the prospect. I know Junius Paxley is, because I bumped into him at the club and he told me so. You can't go giving them a nasty fright like this.'

Edmund roused himself for a moment. 'You don't understand about scholarship. About the tiny building blocks which gradually grow into a wall of knowledge.'

Valdemar let out a crack of laughter. 'Very good. Where did you pick up that one? Do grow up, there's a good chap. Leave all that to those earnest types sweating over their theses, no point you wanking over something you do so badly. Now, that's enough of that. Mimi rang, so Magdalena said, time you were back home. Bustle about, send those brothers packing, take her off for a few days. It's no way to treat your wife. Your whingeing and brooding here at the castle isn't going to solve anything.'

Whingeing?

Whether it was the port or the bracing conversation, Edmund fell asleep almost at once that night. He slept heavily and then began to dream, chasing Saracens through dusty streets, praying in hot chapels filled with strange smells, always accompanied by a burly, silent man who, in his dreams, he seemed to have known all his life.

Then the sights and sounds and smells of Outremer faded and a pair of winsome women in robes, with not a little resemblance to Inez and Mimi, beckoned him, wove round him in a bewildering dance, teasing, taunting, provoking him before they vanished into a moonlit forest, leaving him to slip back gratefully into a deeper sleep.

He woke up well past dawn to find a cup of tea beside his bed and the sun streaming in through the window, and his thoughts as confused as ever.

# 24

Every time Mimi heard a ring at the door, her heart lifted.

It must be Edmund.

Only it wasn't.

She knew that he would have to ring the bell when he came back; she'd found his keys in the pocket of his jacket hanging on one of the hooks in the hall. So she was in a constant state of alert as bell-ringers came and went: the postman, the milkman, a florist's girl – her hopes had risen at the sight of her, but no, she had got the wrong address – Gerry, who had forgotten his key, the man to read the gas, her neighbour, a delivery of furniture for Vincent, which she had sent furiously away, a middle-aged woman doing a survey and, to cap it all, Inez.

'I must speak to Edmund. I'm sorry to bother you and all that, but it's desperately important.'

'Edmund isn't in,' said Mimi, forgetting herself and shutting the door firmly in Inez's face. She watched from the little window in the downstairs cloakroom as Inez went muttering back to the gate.

Another ring.

No, still not Edmund. It was Sylvester, however, who was bound to cheer her up. But who was this fubsy-faced girl standing beside him?

Sylvester was terribly pleased with himself. 'Stroke of genius, Mimi, I bumped into Henrietta here, found she was between jobs, exactly the person for you, I thought, and brought her along.'

The plain girl smiled. Not so plain after all, thought Mimi

warily, detecting the charm in her smile and in her lively eyes. But why had Sylvester brought her?

He was explaining. 'Henrietta's a whiz at office work. Letters, figures, phone calls, appointments, do anything, Henrietta can. Visiting those shops you have to keep track of, nothing to her. She helped me finish my book when Cleo left, would never have got it done without her. And she works for the festival every summer, they wouldn't know what to do if she weren't there.'

'I've just finished at the theatre, doing a stint in the box office,' said Henrietta. 'I shall be looking for another job, and when I bumped into Sylvester he said you might be wanting someone.'

Mimi was torn. She didn't want anyone else in the house just now, it was far too full as it was. On the other hand, Gerry was in so much less than usual, fighting with Vincent out at Hustle, and spending hours working on the ceiling there, quite apart from the fountains and his teaching job. All that left no time for helping with the admin, and it wasn't easy for her to concentrate on the backlog which was mounting up daily; not in the present circumstances.

'Show me what there is to do,' said Henrietta, 'and I'll tell you if I think I'd be of any use.'

'There,' said Sylvester an hour later as they left Henrietta installed at a desk. She had already done a lightning sort-out and tidy-up; she seemed to know what was needed almost before Mimi had said anything, and was clearly quite capable of running the whole business single-handed. 'I knew she'd be just the ticket. Now you can stop thinking about the business side, except for the big things like the council fountain and Elvira's job, and have lots of time to worry and fret about your brothers and Edmund.'

'Thank you,' said Mimi bitterly.

Unknown to Mimi, Edmund had a spare key, the one which was supposed to be kept by a neighbour in case of lockouts; he was always forgetting his keys. Since he rarely remembered to take the key back to the neighbour after using it, it was a far from foolproof system.

This time, however, it worked in his favour. He let himself

in as quietly as he could, and tiptoed to his study. Once there, he closed the door stealthily behind him, and collapsed into his favourite chair. It was awkward, this coming back when you'd walked out in dudgeon. He'd never left like that before. Would Mimi fall on his neck, begging forgiveness? So happy to see him that there would be no remonstrating, no huff? Or would she be distant? Icy, full of disdain? Uninterested? Cross? Depressed?

How the hell did he know? He'd find out soon enough, what a gloomy thought. Meanwhile, his silently effected entry had given him a time of grace. Time to settle down at his desk again, arrange things as he liked them. At least his turbulent visitor of the night seemed to have kept off while he was away. Perhaps that dreadful witch-woman had done the trick after all.

He had made up his mind about one thing: he was not going back to the university. Valdemar's contemptuous words had stung him, and though he would never admit it to Val, he was right. The university was no place for him, and it was there that his work had gone wrong, taken on a more scholarly and reputable tone, yes, but with the result that it had withered and died.

Start again?

No way. Press on. Finish it. Then go back and tackle those opening chapters again. That was the way to do it.

Oh, no. The door gave a familiar squeak and began to open, very slowly.

He braced himself. Mimi, it had to be Mimi. Or Gerry? Just as bad, he'd call out at once that he, Edmund was back. No tact, that man. Ferdie, maybe, or Vincent; yes, he was sure it was Vincent. Very well, if so . . .

His fingers curled round a likely book. He wasn't in the habit of flinging books about, but this one had been in the wars anyhow, thanks to the office-wrecker. And there was no other weapon to hand, and these were desperate times.

'Vincent,' he hissed, letting fly as the door opened wide enough to admit a person.

'Oh,' said Phoebe, surprised, as the book flew harmlessly over her head and landed in the hall outside with a rustle of pages and a dull thunk. She bent down and gathered it up, nipping into the study and closing the door behind her in one neat movement. 'Why did you throw a book at me?'

'Sorry, I thought you might be Vincent.'

'Him! Well, I'm not.'

'Phoebe, be a good girl, don't mention I'm here just for the moment.'

'No, I won't,' she said. 'I saw you slinking in, so I reckoned you didn't want to announce your return to the world.'

Slinking?

'Although you'll have to face up to Mimi at some point. It's not a bad day for it actually, because efficient Henrietta has come in off the street, and Mimi's thrilled.'

'What?'

'She's some kind of super secretary that Sylvester knows. Come to help Mimi with her work.'

'Oh.' A pause to adjust his thoughts. He rustled a few papers about on his desk to hide his surprise. Employing an efficient secretary, that didn't sound as though Mimi was pining. Not that he wanted her to pine, of course not.

'She's quite old, not as old as you, but getting on, perhaps twenty-fiveish, and a demon at the keys, I can tell you.'

Old? He wasn't old.

'So I thought I'd sneak in and bring you up to date on the Presence.'

'He hasn't been, I can see that.'

'Not here, no, but I overheard Mimi talking on the phone, to someone called Cara, I think. Your office at the university there has been done over good and proper.'

'Ah.' He noticed that some books on the shelves weren't in quite the right order and went over to rearrange them.

'But he's been here as well, because,' and she lowered her voice dramatically, 'I've seen him.'

'Seen who?' Edmund abandoned his books and swung round. 'What are you talking about?'

'I've seen the man who comes in here,' she said, impatient at his denseness. 'Twice, actually. I think he comes here most nights.'

'When you saw him, did you call the police?'

'Police! Not likely. They can't deal with the beyond, everyone knows that.'

'The beyond! Pull yourself together. Have you been sleepwalking again? Hallucinating?'

'I have not.' Phoebe was affronted. 'That's what Mimi said, the first time, when I told her what I'd seen. She said it was me having hallucinations, because of being ill. Only it wasn't, of course. Then it happened again. The night after you buzzed off I woke up in the middle of the night with a horrible sore throat. I didn't have any water, and no glass. It's all very well drinking from the tap in the bathroom, but then you have to get up again if you want another drink. So I came downstairs to get a glass from the kitchen.'

'And?'

'And, there was a light on in your room, as there usually is, these troubled nights. I could see someone moving about, and I thought it was you, creeping back in the dead of night, you know, so as no one would notice.'

Edmund sat down hard in his winged chair. 'How unjust.'

'You've crept back now.'

'Never mind that. Who was in here? You were dreaming, you know.'

She shrugged. 'Have it your own way. As far as I'm concerned, he was here, sitting in that chair, just like you. Nearly as grumpy as you are, I may say.'

'Who was?' Grumpy, indeed. He wasn't grumpy.

'This man. Dressed in very funny clothes, sort of historical but not silks and velvets, more like a leather jerkin over granny's knitting.'

'Granny's knitting?' The child really had taken leave of her senses. 'You're ill, your wits are wandering.'

'Pooh, I am not ill, and my wits are all where they should be, thank you very much. Look, I met the guy who's been giving you grief in here, okay? We had a long chat. About you, and your writing and the crusades, and all sorts of interesting things.'

He was now speechless. Not only did he have three unwanted brothers-in-law and an edgy wife, he also had a deranged child to cope with. Good heavens, no wonder he couldn't get on with his writing.

Phoebe looked at him with a steady and contemptuous regard. 'Hang around tonight, and maybe you'll see him.'

'Are you telling me he's a ghost?'

'No, not exactly. He exists in your head, he's called Ranulf, and you sort of conjured him up.'

Edmund stared.

'He showed me a piece of paper, look, it's there, on your in-tray.'

He picked up the rather tatty piece of paper which lay on top of a pile of pink and green folders. Funny, he hadn't noticed it before. *Ranulf*, it said. It was in his writing, no doubt about it. His doodling writing, the kind of scribble he did when his mind was wandering. *Templar servant, could have gone with Mountjoy in 1293 or 4??? Check dates.*

'This is nonsense. What's this got to do with anything?'

'He's Ranulf. He says you called him, and he came. Ever since, he's been hanging around waiting for you to use him, only you never do.'

Edmund stared for a moment at Phoebe's intense face, slightly flushed and utterly sincere. Then he sat back and laughed, not very convincingly. 'It's a footnote. I found the name Ranulf in a footnote. The name stuck in my head, as names do. I must have written it down without thinking. That's all. And you claim that this Ranulf has tipped up here, out of nowhere? A being from the past? To do all that flinging about in here, and then sit chatting to you? Come *on*.'

'If he didn't, then who did? And he isn't a footnote, he's a figment.'

'A figment, oh really.'

'Yes, a figment of your imagination. You read about him and thought about him, and that made him real again. Now you've got to do something about him. And I tell you what, you don't deserve to have any imagination at all.'

'Good, because historians don't need imagination. Facts, ducky, are what we historians deal in.'

'And when there's a fact staring you in the face, what do you do? Sneer.'

With a sharp bang of the door, she was gone.

Edmund looked at the crumpled piece of paper on his desk.

He picked it up, screwed it into a ball and tossed it into the bin. Ranulf. There was no Ranulf that he remembered coming across in his research; whoever he was, he had nothing to do with the finances and wheeler-dealing of the Templars.

Phoebe must go. He'd have a word with Titus, warn him about her condition, advise a visit to a child psychiatrist or psychologist or whoever you took dotty children to these days. Meanwhile, he would settle down to some peaceful work on a loan made by the Templars to the French king in return for lands in Burgundy, Anjou and Brittany.

Dr Cara Sicilienne yawned loudly as she unlocked the car. 'Get in,' she said to Daphne, tossing the books on the front seat into the back of the car. 'What an exhausting day. And not over yet.'

'Why not?'

'I'm going to drop some letters in for Edmund on my way home.'

'Surfaced, has he? You can stop by the cathedral, I'll walk from there. Rather you than me, I bet he'll be in a bad mood.'

'I won't need to see him, and he won't want to see me, I'm sure. He'll soon be your problem, not mine. He's bound to end up with you, in Eng. Lit., one of these days.'

'I'm not holding my breath, he's got a long way to go yet.'

'Not so long; I've heard there's a nasty letter on its way to him from his publishers. That'll put the wind up him.' She looked into her wing mirror. 'Anything coming on your side?'

Daphne peered forward. 'A bus, and then there's a gap.'

Cara swung out into the stream of traffic. 'I hope Edmund's passport is in order.'

'Passport?'

'Oh, I think he's going to do a flit, don't you?'

'I would, in his shoes. France, that's where he should go. That's where he feels at home, and it's just the place to write his book.'

'It should be delightful at this time of year. I envy him.'

# 25 ♪

'You've made everything twice as bad.'

Mimi was furious with Edmund. There she'd been, longing and longing for him to come back, and now look what he'd done. Sent Phoebe into a frenzy of enraged weeping, so that Titus, visiting with thank-offerings for their looking after his stepdaughter in his absence, had felt obliged to carry her off. No sooner had his car drawn away than Vincent was whipping across the landing to install himself in her room.

Then Ferdie appeared, just like a ferret, thought Mimi uncharitably, flicking up the stairs and slithering into Vincent's ex-room.

Benedict peered down over the banisters of the top landing. 'What's going on? When's dinner, Mimi?'

Edmund took charge. 'You'll have to look after yourselves. Mimi and I are going out.'

'There's very little in the fridge,' said Ferdie, popping out of his room at the mention of food. 'You'll have to go to the supermarket first, stock up, there are all kinds of things you need.'

'We are not going to the supermarket.' Edmund, looking at Mimi's frozen face, had had enough. 'You lot want food, you go and get it.'

Mimi was relieved to feel that she and Edmund were on the same side, however briefly, and she was so glad to have him back she decided she would forgive him almost anything. Lovely dinner, lovely walk along by the river, lovely to be wrapped up naked in bed with him once more, his hand curved sleepily round her; the familiar scent of him, the delight of making love with him again.

'He'll get his own back for this,' she said, as she tucked her head comfortably against him on his pillow.

'Who will?'

'Vincent. He hates to be thwarted.'

'Let him try, that's all.'


'Who was that?' Mimi was in the hall and heading for the front door when the phone rang and Vincent answered it.

'Wrong number,' he said evasively.

Liar, she said to herself, and thought no more about it.

So she was still out when, about an hour later, Fran Coxcombe of the *Eyot Evening Post*, the daily paper read by all true Eyot citizens, turned up on the doorstep.

'So sorry,' said Vincent, full of insincerity, leading her into the sitting-room. 'Mimi is out just now, but she asked me to talk to you.'

'Oh. Are you her business partner? Or,' she consulted her notes, 'Gerry Wilkins?'

'No, I'm her brother, I help her out from time to time, when things get busy. As they are now.'

'She's busy, then?' Scribble, scribble.

'Yes, so many commissions, so many exciting new opportunities.'

'How does she have time for the council fountain in that case? I would have thought it would take priority, Mr . . . ?'

'Call me Vincent. Of course, you won't mention me at all in anything you write, you do understand that this is entirely Mimi's show, I am but a spokesman in her unfortunate absence.'

'Yes, yes.' Her nose quivered as she took in the room, the old brocade cushions, the big Knole sofa, the rugs. Hardly a starving artist, she thought. Posh, she wrote in her notebook as she looked expectantly at Vincent; here was a man ready to spill the beans if ever she saw one. Was he really Mimi's brother? No love lost there, she decided.

'Now, as to time, naturally, she devotes herself to all her work, but of course, when there are exciting offers from London . . . you can see that she has to give priority to her most important customers. And London is London.'

More scribble, scribble; beady little eyes alight with malice. 'I see. Now, would it be possible to just have a wee look at the sketches for the council fountain? If they aren't at the bottom of some pile of more important works, of course.'

Vincent smiled graciously at her sarcastic tone. 'Just wait here, and I'll see what I can find. Of course, they are confidential.'

'Mr Henthorpe told me that there were some delightful drawings available.'

'Mr Henthorpe?'

'Councillor Henthorpe.'

'Councillor? Well, of course, in that case . . .'

Vincent whisked himself out of the room. That blasted Henrietta would no doubt be guarding everything, women like that were always inclined to ask so many questions; she'd be bound to sit on Mimi's portfolio and tell him to wait until she got back.

What luck, she must have gone to the loo, who would have imagined that such a paragon would need to attend to mere bodily functions. He sailed towards the table, his eyes on the portfolio, his face full of satisfaction. He knew that was where all the designs were, because he'd had a good snoop round before Henrietta was installed.

In the distance he heard the loo flushing. In a second he'd snatched the portfolio and was back, calm and smiling, in the sitting-room. He laid the black plastic case at the reporter's feet, and flipped it open as she crouched down to have a look.

There on top was the original design for the fountain, the one which had caught Elvira's eye. This was the detailed, unexpurgated version born of a drunken and bawdy artistic moment. The reporter's eyes widened, and she let out a little cry of surprise.

Beneath this extravaganza were the final drawings of the fountain for Elvira, smaller, and so less startling. Under those were, no doubt, the designs for the boar fountain, but Vincent had no intention of letting Fran Coxcombe look any further. Really, his luck was in today. This would suit his purpose admirably.

She had taken out a little camera, and was adjusting the focus. 'May I?' she asked as she snapped away, her head bent over the drawing.

'Feel free,' said Vincent, his lean mouth curving into a mean smile.

Sylvester drove to Hustle to see for himself how the land lay. He found the front door open, so with a bellow to announce his arrival he walked into the hall. Nearly as handsome as the black and white chequerboard floor of his own house, he always felt. A more subdued answering cry summoned him to the back of the house, where Gerry and Elvira were flirting over their coffee.

Elvira greeted him with affectionate enthusiasm, enquiring after concerts and recordings with real interest. 'And how's that witch, Lily?' she enquired, pushing a plate of cinnamon biscuits towards Sylvester.

'Witch? Now, now, Elvira.'

'Witch. But a first-rate housekeeper, you're very lucky to have her, Sylvester. I'd bribe her to leave you and come to the Manor if I thought I could.'

'Lily prefers to work in more masculine households.'

Gerry gave a guffaw, quickly checked, but Sylvester didn't mind. 'Quiet, young Gerry. Whatever our habits, my and Gabriel's house is not a feminine one.'

They settled down for a good gossip, while Gerry listened and contributed his own mite when it came to school and cathedral matters.

'They say the new Dean is very weak. All that trouble at the school, and he simply waffles.'

'So typical of the senior clergy. Ignore anything unpleasant in the hope that it will go away, dither if it looks as though it won't, and finally, move in for the big cover-up. They've been doing it for centuries, practice makes perfect, you know.' Sylvester's views on the Anglican hierarchy were famously critical.

'Don't the parents mind?' Elvira was fascinated. 'I've never been a parent myself, but I think I would have noticed what was going on and made a fuss.'

'They all know about it,' asserted Gerry. 'Or all those who aren't half-witted or too naïve to live know about it. Mostly, they think that if it doesn't directly involve them, they can simply pretend nothing's wrong. Some do make a fuss; well, the school has ways of getting rid of them and their interesting offspring. A few find it too much to stomach and take their darlings away, very wisely in my opinion.'

'I hope Phoebe isn't affected by all this,' said Sylvester, frowning. 'Or young Thomas.'

'Wrong age, wrong sex in both cases,' said Gerry cheerfully. 'Now, if Thomas were a delicious teenage girl, and Phoebe a smooth-cheeked and pretty young boy, then they might be in the thick of it.'

'Disgraceful,' said Elvira, her eyes shining with gossipy delight. 'And the Dean turns into an ostrich about it all, how wonderful.'

'Hard on the kids,' said Gerry. 'Still, their parents reckon there isn't anywhere else for the little preciouses to be educated, all nonsense of course. So it's on with the merry-go-round. Some jump off, others hop on, and I always have a class to teach, which is what concerns me.'

The conversation turned to the doings of the Mayor, who had bought that lovely Georgian house in the centre of town and installed two very attractive young women in it, and whether the Professor of Chemistry at Eyot University really was a lesbian or did she just like dressing in that style.

The glow of gossip and camaraderie was dispersed very suddenly by the arrival of Vincent. The three in the kitchen stopped in mid-sentence as he breezed in, assured and looking for mischief.

'Back to work,' said Gerry, gulping down the last of his coffee, giving Vincent a dagger-glance and sliding out of the room.

'Been at the cream, Vincent?' enquired Elvira.

'Isn't it rash for you to leave Eyot?' said Sylvester nastily. 'I'd be afraid of returning to find all my possessions on the pavement.'

Elvira was intrigued. 'Why?'

Vincent looked bored. 'Sylvester is making an unfunny joke about my sister, whose tedious husband is not exactly a willing host. He has no manners, and virtually no family feeling.'

'Do tell,' she said.

# 26

Edmund was the first of them to see the paper. He had set out for a walk, and stopped to buy a copy from the man at the corner.

He glanced casually at the front page, stopped in his tracks, turned round, and headed with long strides back towards the house.

Phoebe was hanging round the Maths department at the university, bored and fed up, waiting for Titus to finish, longing to go home. She read all the notices on the board for the third time, and wandered over to the window. She'd brought a book with her, but had finished it; could she be bothered to start it again? No way.

She aimed a desultory kick at the metal waste bin parked by the porter's cabin and noticed that there was a copy of the paper in it; the porter must have chucked it in as he went past just now. She plucked it out, turned it back from the sports page, saw the headline and clapped her hand over her mouth in amazement.

Gerry saw the headlines when he went into his local newsagent to buy some cigarettes. 'Good God,' he said, rushing out, quite forgetting to pay.

'Shall I go after him?' said another customer, a keen member of Neighbourhood Watch, bouncing on his toes.

'No,' said Mrs Gale comfortably. 'Gerry'll be in again, he can pay then. What did you say you wanted?' she added in a carrying voice. '*Escort* magazine, was it?'

Sylvester had the *Evening Post* delivered to Midwinter Hall. 'Lily likes it,' he claimed, but of course he read it avidly himself. That day, Lily took it in as usual from young Jamie, who skidded up the drive on his bike, pretending, as was his custom, to be driving a formula one car past the checked flag. She took one look, gave a shout of laughter, and flew to find Sylvester.

'It isn't funny,' said Sylvester, when he had recovered his calm. 'Not for Mimi, at any rate; good heavens, this is going to cause a heap of trouble for her.' He looked at the picture again, and shook his head. 'Why didn't she ever show me this? I do wonder what the lower part of the fountain is like, must be quite something if the *Post* isn't printing it.'

'The article says it leaves nothing to the imagination.'

Sylvester gave another loud guffaw. 'Attaboy, Gerry.'

'It won't rebound on Mimi, surely; it's a ridiculous mistake, this was never offered to the council.'

He shook his head. 'There's more to it than that. That bunch in the council have been after Henthorpe for a while; just think of Mrs Elgin, that dreadful woman who set up the Morality Committee. She hates Henthorpe with a deep and venomous hatred.'

'Yes, but Henthorpe didn't commission this.' Lily tapped the newspaper with a forthright finger.

'That's not the point. The point is that Henthorpe did commission a fountain from Mimi. She is responsible for this piece of frivolous naughtiness, ergo, she herself must be base and immoral and quite unfit to pollute the pure realms of the council offices.'

'I'll give Susie Elgin pollute. If it comes to that, I know a few fruity details of Susie's far from blameless past.'

'No!' said Sylvester, entranced. 'Spit it out, Lily, this could be useful.'

Councillor Henthorpe was in his office. His secretary came in without knocking and wordlessly handed him the evening paper. He looked, gave a groan and sank his head in his hands.

His secretary went off to make him a cup of strong tea.

The lines between Eyot and London were humming.

'Too hot to print?' The tabloids had picked up the story and were straight on to their northern counterparts. They were ecstatic. 'Wire the photos to us, we'll publish.'

'I think not,' said Fran Coxcombe, reporter, to her colleagues, gleefully contemplating the boost to both career and pocket.

Her editor sauntered in. 'Was Henthorpe really going to put that up to the council?'

'I never said that. Read it carefully, it doesn't actually *say* that this is the fountain chosen by old Henthorpe.'

'That's the impression it gives. You meant it to, I suppose. You'd better hop over there and do a follow-up, Fran, if this Mountjoy woman will speak to you.'

'She won't.'

He grinned. 'Is she a relative of Lord Mountjoy? Must be, I suppose. I expect the mob up at the castle will be pretty peeved, seeing their grand name splashed all over the papers like this.'

'They're used to it,' said a photographer who was passing through. 'Scandal after scandal, that lot. Not a bad pic, Fran, but get an expert to go with you next time.'

The telephone never stopped ringing. One look at the paper, and Henrietta, an old campaigner in these kind of affairs, had taken charge. 'Don't answer the phone. I'll screen all calls.'

'What calls?' said Edmund.

'Journalists of all shapes and sizes, inquisitive friends and relations, ill-wishers, nosy-parkers, you name it. Since the paper was thoughtful enough to print your number, they'll all be trying to get through. I expect it'll make the next editions of the London papers, there's no big story running at the moment, this will be pure gold to them.'

'Oh, nonsense,' said Edmund, audibly grinding his teeth.

'Don't do that,' said Mimi. 'Dentists cost money.' She turned back to Henrietta. 'Surely it's just a storm in a tea cup?'

'Like most news,' said Henrietta. 'No, this is a gift. Cathedral city, Mrs Elgin of the Morality Committee jumping up and down, you related to the nobility.'

'I am not,' said Mimi furiously.

'By marriage, you are. That's good enough for them. Next they'll find out you've got a famous mother, oh, there'll be no stopping them. Now, the one good thing is that, amongst all the tiresome and nuisance calls, there will be one or two worthwhile trade enquiries. It's terrific publicity for you.'

'I could do without it,' said Mimi gloomily. She had dressed that morning in scarlet and pink. Far too lively; she would go upstairs and don a navy outfit for the rest of the day.

'Don't answer the door, either,' said Henrietta. 'Not without checking to see who it is. They'll have your address in no time, and be camped out on the doorstep.'

'That's too far-fetched; good heavens, it's only a story about a fountain.'

'It isn't just any old fountain.'

'What I want to know is,' said Edmund, 'how did they get the picture? And where did the reporter get all that poisonous rubbish from?'

'Gerry,' said Mimi flatly.

That was what really hurt about the whole stupid business. She could have sworn she could trust him. Yes, he'd been a notorious practical joker in his student days, but this? It showed how you could know someone for years and work closely with them, and still have no idea what they might be up to.

'I'm not so sure,' said Henrietta. 'Has he got another copy? It was only a boozy sketch, that first drawing, so he told me. And it's that original one they've printed, not the more detailed and different drawings he did for Elvira. If it's the original, then it's here in the portfolio. Gerry's hardly been in the house since I came. And never by himself.'

'I could ring the paper and demand to know where they got all the information from. And the photo.'

'You could,' said Edmund, 'but I bet they wouldn't tell you.'

'If not Gerry, then who? And when?'

'It's a mystery,' said Henrietta. 'You can accuse me, if you like, I'm the obvious suspect, far more opportunity than Gerry. But it wasn't me.'

Mimi hadn't for a moment thought it was. It was a vulgar and spiteful thing to have done, and you could see that although Henrietta was one to fight her corner, vulgarity was alien to her.

Besides, why should she?

'Ring a friend and give them a shopping list,' advised Henrietta. 'You're going to be barricaded in here for a day or so, whatever you think.'

Mimi and Edmund were too polite to express their disbelief in stronger terms, but they each thought Henrietta was wrong.

Not for long.

The telephone rang yet again.

Then there was a loud peal on the front-door bell. Edmund flew to the downstairs loo and peered out of the window. 'Sylvester,' he said with relief.

He opened the door to find Sylvester there, and several others, total strangers, jostling behind him, with more piling through the gate.

'Quick,' said Sylvester, pushing past Edmund without ceremony and slamming the door shut. 'Several undesirable types coming to pay a visit.'

'Reporters?'

'No question about it, they're all wearing hats with PRESS tucked in the bands.'

'Sylvester!'

'I exaggerate, but you get the picture. And there's a man with a placard proclaiming against works of the devil, and someone who looks as though he's in the double-glazing line. No more answering the door, bolts and bars time.'

'Vincent and Ferdie are out,' said Mimi.

'Good,' said Edmund, shooting the bolt home. 'Then out they can stay.'

'Edmund, the back,' cried Mimi.

'Oh, hell,' he said.

Sylvester pooh-poohed their suspicions of Gerry. They had gone into the sitting-room for a council of war. Sylvester tossed all the cushions out to make room and sat down in his favourite large and comfortable armchair. He was full of energy and purpose.

'No, no. Not Gerry. You take my word for it. And Henrietta? Impossible.'

Mimi had an unholy idea that he was enjoying every moment. There was nothing Sylvester liked so much as an intrigue, ruffled feathers, people doing absurd things and striking ridiculous attitudes.

'No, I think you've got to look closer to home for this one, Mimi. Where's Vincent today?'

Vincent.

Edmund and Mimi looked at each other.

'Has he ever seen the drawing, though?' she said at last. 'I never showed it to him, and I'm sure Gerry wouldn't.'

'He snooped,' said Edmund.

She opened her mouth to object and then shut it again, remembering dozens of Vincent's snoops from his forays into her teenage diaries, his steaming open of letters not addressed to him, his uncanny skill at eavesdropping, his unscrupulous if languid prying into anything and everything to do with family, friends, acquaintances and even complete strangers.

'Vincent,' she said in cold fury.

'Vincent!' said Edmund, enraged.

'Vincent,' said Henrietta in suitably surprised tones, as though she hadn't guessed straight away that Vincent was at the bottom of all this. 'Of course. Vincent. He can't have realized, he must have been indiscreet, I expect the reporter wheedled all kinds of misinformation out of him without his realizing it.'

'Wheedle?'

'Vincent not realize what he was doing?'

'The skunk.' Mimi had no doubts at all, now the unspoken suspicion was out. 'He's done it quite deliberately, to pay us back for refusing to go out and buy them food. And he's in a temper because I wouldn't accept delivery of his furniture from the auctions he's been to. He's having to pay for storage, and he can't bear it.'

'You never told me you'd done that,' said Edmund, surprised.

'Well, I did. The nerve of it, half a lorry-load of chairs and a table, and some bronzes and a hefty sideboard affair. And he never said a word about it, just told the delivery firm to bring it all here. He was furious when he found out I'd sent it away. He said I was being unreasonable, and that it could all go into the rooms we aren't using on the second floor.'

'Ha,' said Edmund. 'We might have guessed he'd have his eye on those to use as storerooms. Very predictable, Vincent.'

Mimi was remembering something else. 'I should have known. I bet it was the reporter who telephoned yesterday morning, just as I was going out. Vincent answered it, told me it was a wrong number.'

'You have to hand it to him,' said Edmund. 'You said he'd get his own back, Mimi. And he has.'

And she knew that he had, and that there was nothing she could do to him which would make the slightest dent on his supreme self-esteem. Brother or not, at this moment she hated him.

'No point spitting and swearing about Vincent,' said Sylvester briskly. 'All water off a duck's back if you ask me. Although I shall make very sure that Elvira knows what a nasty, low trick he's pulled.'

'She'll probably admire him for it,' said Mimi crossly.

'Not Elvira.' Sylvester was definite. 'She has a very strict code, has Elvira, and she won't tolerate a piece of nasty brotherly treachery like this.'

Henrietta got to her feet. 'The phone's making strange noises, I left it off the hook. I'd better get back on duty.'

She vanished back to the office, whereupon the telephone bell sounded shrilly through the house. It was answered immediately, and she reappeared at the sitting-room door. 'Gerry,' she said. 'Do you want to talk to him, Mimi?'

'I'd better.' She hauled herself up from a cushion on the floor and made for the hall.

'Gerry? No, it isn't funny at all. It's a disgrace, and of course, Vincent's at the bottom of it.'

'Well?' said Sylvester, five minutes later, as Mimi came back to join them in the sitting-room.

'He's not particularly bothered. He says it'll all blow over, and he's going to tell Elvira what Vincent's been up to, doesn't think it'll affect the commission from her at all. Which isn't what's worrying me. It's the council job that's the problem.'

Sylvester and Edmund had been talking tactics. They outlined their plans to Mimi.

'One, send the *Post* a picture of the boar and ask them to print a correction to the story.'

'Which, if they do, will be on the bottom of page ten,' said Edmund cynically.

'Sssh,' said Sylvester. 'Two, wait and see if the nationals pick it up. I'm sure they will, but they might take a different line. Three, issue a press release saying that the photo of the sketch was taken without permission, that it was a preliminary drawing for a work in progress for a distinguished client who wants the fountain for his remote private grounds.'

'They'll be hell-bent on finding out who that is.'

'You can make it sound as though it's for a foreign customer. Male and kinky. That'll put them off the scent.'

The phone had gone on ringing intermittently. Henrietta put her head round the door to tell them that *Gay Gazette* had just called to ask permission to do a big photo-feature on the proposed fountain, together with a profile of Gerry.

Sylvester and Edmund thought that was very funny. Mimi, who felt as though she had no shred of humour left, didn't.

It wasn't a good night, and Mimi woke early with a dull feeling in the pit of her stomach. She remembered why, and rolled over, burying her head in the pillow. Beside her, Edmund slept soundly and peacefully. She toyed with the notion of waking him up, why shouldn't he suffer too, but her better nature prevailed, and she struggled out of bed.

She pulled back a few inches of curtain. Fortunately, their bedroom windows looked out to the side and not out on to the street where the odd hopeful photographer had been camped until far into the night. Rain lashed against the window, and the huge beech in next door's garden was swaying in the wind.

Good.

That would keep the pests away.

At that very moment there was a ring at the door. At this hour? She stumbled into her slippers and went downstairs, slowly, to have the by now customary look from the downstairs loo.

The rainswept street was mercifully deserted, and Gerry was

standing at the door. She pulled back the bolts and let him in.

'It's blowing a gale this morning,' he said, unwrapping himself from a gigantic mac and giving it a good shake, showering her with damp droplets. 'I thought you might like to see the London papers.'

'Oh, no.'

'Oh, yes. Get an eyeful of the tabloids, the coverage has to be seen to be believed.'

Sophisticated London's joyful certainty of printing the full photo had had to be dropped. Not even the most daredevil of the rags dared show the complete glories of Gerry's drawing. The editor of the *Mercury* had sighed and vetoed it at a glance. He'd told his reporter to print, but to blot out the offending parts.

'Posing pouches,' said Mimi, awed.

'Is that what they are?' He peered at the black blobs. 'I thought perhaps codpieces.'

'It's far worse than if they'd left the figures uncovered.'

'Yes. That was risqué, bawdy and rather amusing. Now, it's merely obscene.'

# 27

The more pretentious papers droned on about dangerous rifts in local government exemplified by the internecine warfare which had broken out in Eyot.

They scorned the prurient approach of their lesser brethren, but nonetheless printed as much of the fountain and its shapely male figures as they dared, affirming in strong prose exactly why they couldn't print the whole thing, with much mention of the archaic laws relating to male nudity and erect members as compared with female full-frontals which were two-a-penny and bothered no one except the Mrs Elgins of the world.

'They'll be hawking postcards of it in grubby bookshops next,' said Mimi with distaste. 'And it's such a lovely piece of work, Gerry. If rather rude.'

Much to her surprise, Gerry gave her a hug. 'Thank you for saying that, love. Well, I'm here for the day. I only just made it, there are reporters pounding up the street even now. One knew who I was and offered me a thousand quid for an exclusive.'

'No!'

'Yes, but I turned it down.'

'Perhaps you shouldn't have.' She knew how hard up he always was.

'Elvira wouldn't like it,' said Gerry austerely. 'I shall settle down to some serious work here; Elvira knows I'm not going out to Hustle today. And with my mind on my own well-being – I haven't spent all that time with Vincent for nothing – I shall start by making coffee. How is Henrietta going to get in?'

'Through the neighbour's house.' Mimi lowered her voice

as if fearful of being heard by loitering pressmen. 'There's an interconnecting door on the top floor, in case of fire. Nobody knows about it except us and next door. He won't let on, he hates journalists.'

'Isn't Benedict up there?'

'Yes, but he's in the middle of three days' meditation, only surfacing to do an hour or so's work and to nip downstairs for a frugal meal. He wouldn't notice if Cromwell's New Model Army trooped through with muskets. It's quite restful here just at present, because Vincent and Ferdie were out when the story broke, and haven't come back.'

'I know where Vincent is,' said Gerry. 'He's hopped over to Holland.'

'Holland!'

'To buy some special item of furniture for Elvira.'

'Heavens, over to Holland, just like that.'

He laughed at her. 'It isn't far, especially not when you're near the North Sea. You catch a boat from Hull, you know; out one night, back the next.'

'It seems far when you aren't in the habit of going anywhere much abroad. In fact I'm starting to feel that a trip to London is an expedition.'

'Eyot has that effect on people after a while. It wouldn't bother Vincent, though, anywhere to achieve an aim.'

'And never a word to us.'

'Do you wonder, when you see what he's let loose?'

'Do you suppose that Ferdie's gone with him?' A note of hope crept into Mimi's voice.

'Is that likely?'

'Couldn't be more unlikely. Or perhaps he's gone back to London, oh, the relief if he has.' Mimi mused for a moment on this delightful prospect.

Gerry pushed a cup over to her. 'Drink up,' he said. 'And I'll make you some breakfast, if you've any food in the house.'

'Plenty, for the moment, with the two chief locusts away. Titus has promised to bring us a food parcel later today. Oh, how ridiculous it all is.'

'Tiresome.' He was having a skirmish with the toaster and yelped as he burned his fingers. 'Ouch, that hurt.'

'Vincent did something to that, and it hasn't worked properly since.'

'He simply looked at it, I dare say.'

Henrietta arrived on the dot, and passed unnoticed through Benedict's eyrie while the meditating painter sat motionless and cross-legged on a fat cushion.

Titus and Phoebe followed an hour later, similarly unremarked. Titus looked tired and strained; Phoebe's eyes were bright with the excitement of it all. She hurled herself at Mimi, giving her a rib-crunching squeeze, and then glared at Edmund.

Even Edmund must notice how Titus is looking, thought Mimi, winking furiously at him. He stared at her; bother him, how slow on the uptake he could be. Then he turned to Phoebe and apologized profusely and graciously.

'That's all right,' she said magnanimously. 'Can I come back? I'm a terrific nuisance to Titus, and Q is beginning to say she'll have to come out of hospital, which makes all the nurses click and tut. It would be better for me to be here with you. If you don't mind. If I'm not too much trouble.'

'Not at all,' said Edmund. 'You can keep watch on the street and front door for us.'

'A spy.' She was delighted at the thought.

'It would be a tremendous help,' said Titus gratefully. 'I'm due to take some time off about when the baby's due, but that means it's very difficult just now for me to get out of being in the department.'

'I don't mind,' said Phoebe buoyantly. 'It's fun here with all this going on. Have there been any more bumps in the night?' This with a sidelong look at Edmund.

'No, thank goodness,' said Mimi. She'd pushed the ructions in the study to the back of her mind these last few days; she had too much on her mind to worry about that as well. The whole business seemed to have died down, after all. And Will hadn't had any suggestions to offer. He'd rung them, saying he was sure that the whole affair was outside the normal scope of ghost-hunting, but he was following up a similar case in America. It would take some time, but he would get to the bottom of it eventually. These cases took time and patience.

And was Edmund sure that he wouldn't like the witch to try again?

Edmund was quite sure. So was Mimi. Feeble, all talk and no do, these musicians, she thought, unfairly and uncharitably.

'Edmund must not be annoying him any more,' said Phoebe. 'Unless he's off stirring things up somewhere else.'

'There's bound to be a perfectly natural explanation for it all,' said Mimi. 'Someone sleep-walking, or a freak wind down the chimney. Or a case of multiple personality, someone not knowing what one of their other selves is up to. Anyway, it's over now, and I'm not going to fret about it.'

'There have been rumours of trouble in the history department,' murmured Titus.

'He can do what he likes there,' said Edmund complacently. 'Will can take the witch for a visit if he likes, that'd stir them up a bit. It's of no consequence to me, for I'm not going back to the department, now or in the future.'

This was news to Mimi; how like Edmund to announce a major change in his life in front of a heap of people, in the middle of a crisis. Secretly, though, she was pleased. Away from the university, his work might go better. And joy of joys: no university, no Inez.

'Where are you going to put Phoebe?' asked Edmund.

'In her old room,' said Mimi. 'I'll move Vincent's things back into Ferdie's room, they can sort that out for themselves, what a mercy neither of them is here.'

'Hm,' said Titus. 'I have heard a rumour, and it may be only a rumour, that the *Post* has got some more photos which they're planning to print. Of some works by Ferdie. Quite hot stuff as well, one gathers.'

Silence, broken by Edmund cursing.

'The torsos,' said Gerry. 'It's those torsos of his.'

'Lively items, are they?' enquired Titus.

'You could say that.'

'One hears it's all hotting up at the Mountjoy residence.' Dr Cara Sicilienne took a bite out of a sticky bun and washed it down hastily with some bitter coffee.

'Edmund's house, I suppose, not the castle.' Daphne removed

the grubby ashtray from their table and slid it over to an empty one nearby. She had no interest in the castle.

'Of course. That child Phoebe's back, and they're in a state of siege.'

'Is Ranulf – wasn't that the name that was mentioned – helping out?'

'No, he's been wreaking havoc in the History department here instead; he had a go at Inez's room yesterday.'

'Really? I wouldn't have thought there was much there to take offence at.'

'It's the principle of the thing. He seems to have it in for historians in general now, at least any associated with Edmund. Quite out of control.'

'Aren't you concerned? These historians are your brood, after all.'

'Not in the least. Plenty more people full of threadbare ideas where this lot came from. The one or two who have any notion of what they're doing will cope with it as a minor hiccup. Maybe the others will take fright and rush off to find proper jobs.'

'Lucky you, if so.'

Titus went back through the attic and the neighbour's house. Mimi and Gerry tried to get on with some work; Edmund shut himself in his study and brooded. Phoebe liaised with Henrietta, delighted to keep watch on the unruly throng still hanging about outside.

'Oh, look,' she cried out. 'It's Ferdie. And Vincent. Vincent's coming through, but Ferdie's stopped to talk to someone, goodness, what an ugly man. Now Vincent's gone back to get him, they're arguing, Vincent's dragging Ferdie away. I wonder why.'

'I don't,' said Mimi, who had joined Phoebe at the window. 'I suppose we'll have to let them in.'

'No,' said Edmund.

'They'll get up to more mischief if you don't,' said Henrietta.

'Oh, very well. God, how I loathe the pair of them.' He went grumbling to open the front door, shouting and yelling imprecations at the assembled press while Vincent and Ferdie slid in.

'Hello,' said Vincent. 'Nice to be back. What's for lunch, Mimi?

I'm starving. I'll just pop up to my room for a quick shave, shall we say in twenty minutes or so.'

Edmund's hackles rose. Anyone would think it was Vincent's house, look at the way he walked in as if he owned the place, issuing orders in his cool, arrogant way, expecting everything to revolve around him. He bounded up the stairs after him, and leapt in front to bar the way into the big spare room. 'Sorry, not in here. Phoebe's back, so you're in there with Ferdie.'

Vincent went white with anger.

Ferdie snored, there was hardly room in there for one human being, let alone two men, Phoebe would have to go. Or she could sleep on the landing.

'Phoebe stays where she is. Of course, you could always join Benedict in the attic.'

Vincent was always inclined to continue an argument to the bitter end, but there was something in Edmund's face which made him, for once, a little wary. He shrugged. 'Oh, very well, but I'll make you sorry for it.'

'Don't threaten me,' said Edmund furiously.

'Not you, dear brother-in-law. I shall have my revenge on Mimi.' And before Edmund could broach the little matter of the article in the *Post*, Vincent had slammed the bathroom door and ran the bolt home. Edmund was left seething on the landing.

The atmosphere in the house was heavy with division and dark undercurrents of conflict. Only Benedict, lost in distant realms, wasn't affected by it. By bedtime, Edmund felt as though he'd been hauled up and down on a cheese-grater.

'How could any of you bear Vincent? How did he survive school? Why didn't your mother curb him before he became what he is?' He was snarling and frothing through his toothpaste, and his pepperminty words were indistinct, but Mimi knew full well what was the matter.

She soothed him as best she could, but it was hours before he dropped into an uneasy sleep, only to be roused very little later by familiar sounds from downstairs. God, the presence was back. He would rush downstairs, accost whatever it was, tell it to bugger off.

What was the point? He knew there would be no one there.

He reached out for his bottle of pills and swallowed two. Then he lay there in the dark, hating Vincent, worrying about his work, fretting about Mimi's anxious face, her efforts to calm him down, to placate Vincent, to keep Ferdie under control, to feed a large household and to keep her threatened business going.

Then he sat up.

He'd had enough.

He'd come to a decision. He was going to go to France. A friend had offered him the use of a house there if he ever needed it. Right, he did.

His friend was abroad for a year, where had he gone? America, that was it. Well, he wouldn't be in France in that case. Unless he'd lent it to anyone else, there should be no problem. It was the right area for his work, it would be wonderful to be back in France, he would take his notes, his books, his manuscript and finish the bloody book.

And Mimi's brothers?

Ha, they could stay and fend for themselves. It wouldn't be for long, they'd soon tire of having to buy food, and pay for it, and cook it. Not to mention washing-up. And no one would wash their shirts or underpants, make their beds or do anything for them. He would pay Mrs Sconce to have a holiday.

He was so delighted by his scheme that he woke Mimi up to tell her, only to be greeted by a sleepy, cross wife who told him he was mad and turned over to go back to sleep again.

'I had such a strange dream last night,' said Mimi the next morning. 'I dreamt you woke me up and said we were going to France.' She smiled at Edmund, wondering why he was up and dressed so early, it was most unlike him these days.

'It wasn't a dream,' he said briskly. 'Start packing, we *are* going to France. I've just spoken to Bill, we can have his house in France for as long as we want. It's near Quimper. It sounds charming, from what he said, a converted mill. I've rung the ferry and booked tickets, we want to be off by twelve at the latest.'

'Are you mad? I can't go to France with all this on.'

'It's exactly when you need to go to France. I've had a quick word with Gerry and Henrietta, and they both agree it's a brilliant idea. Henrietta has agreed to stay on for as long as we're away.'

'We can't possibly go away. What about my brothers?'

'Ha, your brothers! They'll have to cope on their own, and I'll be much surprised if they aren't heading back to London before the week's out.'

'We can't leave them with the run of the house.'

'Yes, we can, and moreover I shall have the gas turned off. Henrietta won't need it, and it'll make it difficult for them to cook.'

'They'll starve.'

'Good.'

'Then there's Phoebe.'

'I rang Titus, he's spoken to Quinta, she's agreed that Phoebe can come with us. It'll do her the world of good, sun, warmth, a chance to breathe some sea air. And she'll be company for you; I shall be working day and night. Titus will be coming round any minute with her passport.'

France! No office, no reporters. Blissful sunshine, delicious food. Edmund all to herself. No lurkers in the study. It was, she decided, her duty to go, he needed her.

No he doesn't, her darker self muttered. What he needs is to write his book.

But he would have to be free of the distractions of daily life if he was to concentrate, he couldn't be troubled with domestic matters as he would be if he was on his own.

Why? He wasn't a child. He could eat out, learn to use the washing machine. French equipment couldn't be very different, and he spoke French. He should go alone and she should stay put, get on top of things here. That was the most reasonable plan.

To hell with it, her darker and less rational self said. I'm going, and that's that.

Now, practicalities. She'd pack all the summer clothes she'd hardly worn this year. 'Edmund,' she called out over the banisters. 'Did you ever take those blue trousers to the cleaners?'

Vincent's jaw dropped when Edmund told him what was planned.

'Oh, no you don't,' he said when he'd recovered his wits. 'You go, leave Mimi here, a house like this needs looking after.'

'Sylvester will keep an eye on things and Henrietta will be here every day as well.'

'You think your going away will get rid of us.'

'I live in hope.'

Vincent's eyes narrowed as Edmund went upstairs, calling to Mimi to get a move on.

'Quimper,' Vincent said to himself, tapping his white teeth with a pen picked up from the hall table. 'I wonder.'

Ferdie reacted sullenly to the news. 'It's too bad. First mother, now Mimi. They've got no family feeling.'

'Revenge,' said Vincent, 'will be sweet. Do you remember Darius?'

Ferdie frowned. 'Vaguely. Not my cup of tea, heavily into women, wasn't he?'

'Was, and is,' said Vincent with satisfaction. 'A rake, full of charm and skills to delight a woman. I think I'll drop him a line.'

Ferdie looked at Vincent and shook his head. 'You wouldn't do that.'

'I would.'

Mimi mistrusted Vincent's amiable farewells. He was plotting something, she was sure, but she was too flustered and pressed for time to investigate further. Probably some scheme involving Elvira; she was prepared to bet that Vincent would shortly be installed in great comfort in Hustle Manor.

'Not if I have anything to do with it, he won't,' said Gerry firmly.

Mimi didn't rate his chances against Vincent's snakelike skills for one moment.

'What did he say about your going?' said Gerry curiously.

'Rage and fury, of course, but he knows when he's beaten. He's even said that he'll get in touch with a friend who lives near where we're staying. He knows Ma, apparently. Vincent's going to tell him to look us up.'

That sounded harmless enough.

Mimi stuffed her and Edmund's passports into her bag. They had nearly forgotten them, a sign of how distracted she was. She had another fit of the frights. What was she doing? You couldn't just take off for France like this.

'Why ever not?' Sylvester had elbowed the two remaining reporters out of his way and was leaning in through the car window. 'It's only France, for heaven's sake, you're not off to the Amazon jungle. Are you so attached to Eyot?'

'No, but . . .'

Edmund started the car, the luggage piled haphazardly into the rear shifted about with several alarming bumps and bangs, and they were off.

'Lovely,' said Phoebe, stretching herself out on the back seat. 'Adventure.'

# 28

Phoebe sat sprawled on the terrace, dozing in the warm air.

Mimi noticed idly that Phoebe's clothes, although loose on her currently skinny frame, were not the right size for her. She had clearly grown since the previous summer, and her shorts were very short and her T-shirt barely reached the top of her belt.

She'd take her into Quimper and buy her a few summer things. Phoebe would love having some French clothes to show off to her friends when she was back in England, and she'd have all summer to wear them. Always supposing real summer reached Eyotshire before it was time for the gales and fogs of autumn.

A cat made its neat way across the grass and flopped down in the shade of a cypress tree.

French conversation drifted in from the lane where two neighbours were discussing Edmund in loud, interested voices.

A few gulls circled and mewed above them in the deep blue sky, which was streaked only with the slightest wisps of cloud. Mimi thought of the great mountains of black cumulo-nimbus doubtless hovering above Eyot, and shut her eyes, her senses drowsy with the heat and the bright, clear light and the peace.

Bill's house was in a village outside Quimper, in a dusty lane. Its garden was backed by fields, the other houses were set in their own gardens, secluded and private. This house had once been the village mill, and was mellow with ancient stone and charming windows with gently pointed arches; accolades, Edmund said they were called.

Inside, the conversion had been done with style and drama, and the huge, circular grinding stone had been left in place to form the centrepiece of the big downstairs room. After living in a terraced house in the centre of a busy city, the tranquillity, space and sunlight were very soothing to the spirit.

She would walk to the centre of the village by and by, a ten-minute stroll to get fresh baguettes for the evening. From the moment of arriving in France, Phoebe's appetite had taken a turn for the better, and she could consume vast quantities of the local bakery's bread, croissants and patisserie. Mimi had watched with awe as she put away three strawberry tarts in quick succession.

From inside the house came, from time to time, the tap-tap of Edmund at work.

'What a good idea it was to come here,' said Mimi. 'Clever Edmund to think of it, away from that university, away from all the nuisances of my fountains, away from my brothers, away from the fiend in the study.'

Phoebe adjusted her sunhat and pushed her sunglasses up on her head. She gave Mimi a very direct look of her intense green eyes. 'Not exactly,' she said. 'He's not a fiend, anyhow, if you're talking about Ranulf. And he's here.'

'What?' Mimi gave up relaxing and turned her attention full on Phoebe. 'Who?'

'Ranulf. That's the name of the man who was in the study at night. And up at the university. Didn't Edmund tell you he knew his name?'

What an extraordinary child she was, the things she came out with, and spoken with all the conviction of truth.

'Cross my heart,' said Phoebe. 'He was in the car beside me. That's why I had to put my legs down after we stopped at Welton. I mean, he isn't really there, so I could have left my legs where they were, but it seems a bit rude, feet through his tummy.'

'Welton?'

'Yes, where we stopped for petrol. That's where he got in, he was marching up and down on the forecourt, waiting for us.'

Mimi had to laugh, it was so absurd. 'I hope he had a good crossing.'

'Oh, yes. He had lots to say. It used to be dangerous crossing the Channel in his day. You had to wait for the right winds, and it took hours and hours. Days, actually, and they used to sink all the time.'

'I don't expect many people did cross the Channel then,' said Mimi, sinking back into a doze. It was too warm and pleasant to worry about Phoebe's bizarre fantasies. She didn't remember being so fanciful herself as a child, but she was very different from Phoebe.

'Ranulf had to, a lot. Backwards and forwards, off on a crusade, then back again, then off to France and back again, and then Rome. He went all over the place.'

'Very enterprising.'

'He didn't have any choice. Where Sir Hugo went, he went too.'

'Who was Sir Hugo?'

'Sir Hugo Mountjoy. He was a Templar, a proper one, a knight. You know, with a funny red cross on his front. He's the one in the Mountjoy chapel. Ranulf was his bastard half-brother, and his lifelong servant. Sir Hugo became a Templar, so Ranulf had to as well. Not much freedom of choice in those days,' she added with disapproval.

'Mmm,' said Mimi, drifting into sleep, only to be shaken awake by Phoebe.

'There are eyes in the hedge.'

'Now, Phoebe, this nonsense has got to stop.'

'Look.'

'All right, yes, there are eyes. It must be the cat that was here.'

Phoebe pointed silently to the shade of the cypress tree, where the cat was lying, its tail twitching lazily, its own tawny and unblinking eyes focused on the other eyes in the hedge.

'Ullo, English,' said a voice, and the hedge rustled and disgorged a girl, slighter and smaller than Phoebe, with dark hair, merry eyes and a pair of crutches in her hand.

Mimi's French was reasonable and rusty, Phoebe's rudimentary, but it was Phoebe who quickly discovered more about their unexpected visitor. 'She's had an operation on her leg, because a bone she broke didn't heal properly. So she's off school, just like me. Can I go next door? She's got a parrot she wants to show me.'

Mimi hesitated, not sure. It was such a responsibility, looking after someone else's child. She hardly supposed that next door housed a gang of child molesters or kidnappers, but then she had no idea who did live there.

She didn't want to interrupt Edmund. On the other hand, the intermittent typing had petered out altogether now, perhaps it would be a good moment.

'Next door?' he said, looking particularly vague. 'Oh, Bill mentioned them, they're old friends of his, nice people, from what he said. Phoebe won't come to any harm there, it'll be company for her if they've got a girl about her age.'

Phoebe danced through the door. 'Thank you,' she said. And then, remembering her manners, she asked Edmund how his work was going.

'It isn't,' he said shortly.

'Oh, Edmund,' said Mimi, all the brilliance and peace going out of the day for her. 'Truly not?'

'Hopeless,' he said in a despairing voice. 'Wading in mud. Never mind, I'll plug on. Off you go, Phoebe, mind your Ps and Qs, the French are very hot on that.'

Phoebe made a dash for the hedge, then slithered to a halt, turned round and came running back. 'I know you don't believe a word I say, but Ranulf's out there in the garden, he is really, and he could help you an awful lot. I mean, he was there then and so on. You just have to ask him, that's all.'

This time she went, struggling through the hedge with her new friend. Mimi could hear their piping voices fade as they went towards the French girl's house.

Edmund bent ostentatiously over his work and Mimi, knowing that he wanted to be alone with his misery, went back to the terrace.

Edmund scrunched up another sheet and tossed it on to the floor, which was littered with similar paper snowballs. At this rate he'd have to go into Quimper and buy more paper.

How long had he been at it today? Four, five hours? And what had he achieved? Nothing. Not one paragraph, or even a sentence that was any use. And it had been the same yesterday, and the day before.

All writers hit rough patches.

He hadn't written one paragraph or word that would do for

weeks. It wasn't a patch so much as a permanent state of futility. He leant back in his chair, stretching his arms out above his head and yawning.

Phoebe and her friend must be out in the garden again, he could hear their lively chatter. They probably only had a hundred words of each other's language, but they talked non-stop. Phoebe was telling her friend about Ranulf. He gave a wry smile. If only his invention and imagination was as fertile as a twelve-year-old's.

Then he pulled himself together. Imagination? Invention? What was he thinking about? Those weren't what you needed for the kind of book he was writing.

He started another blank page, then stared, surprised at the single word now on it. It wasn't at all what he'd intended to write.

Ranulf.

Who exactly was Ranulf? Damn it, he remembered the name, but he knew virtually nothing about him. He tapped his pen on the desk. Ranulf.


Mimi woke to a room flooded with sunlight, and an empty place beside her.

Edmund must have gone to the loo. It was only five o'clock, far too early to wake up, even on such a wonderful-looking day. She yawned, turned over, half-drowsing, waiting for the familiar sensation of Edmund stretching out beside her and giving his pillow a hearty thump before he sank back into sleep.

She stirred again, glanced at the clock.

Twenty past five.

Yawning, she got up, went over to the window. The stillness of the very early morning hung over the grass and the line of trees, only broken by three rabbits scampering after each other in crazy circles, pausing for a quick ear-twitch and then diving into the undergrowth.

Where was he? She walked softly along the passage, not wanting to disturb Phoebe. Through the open door of her room she could see her spread out on her bed, face down, looking like an abandoned star fish. Utterly asleep. She pulled the door to, and went downstairs.

In the kitchen there was a cooling pot of coffee, the meagre remains of yesterday's baguette and an apple core. Clear evidence that Edmund had been here. He never threw his apple cores away; their house at home was dotted with them, often undiscovered until they emerged weeks later as withered mummies from behind radiators or under cushions.

Disgusting, but where was he?

Tap, tap, tap.

Could he be working? At this time of the morning? Edmund, whose wits only came to at about ten o'clock?

She went to his room and listened outside the door. She turned the handle, but the door didn't open. 'Edmund!'

'Go away.'

Go away? 'Are you all right?'

'Of course I'm all right, but I'm working and I want to be left alone. Go back to bed.'

'I thought I heard voices in there. Are you alone?'

'Who would I be with? Houris from the village? I'm working, I said. Go *away*!'

## 29

'He's possessed by his muse,' said Phoebe solemnly, her eyes bright with enthusiasm.

They were having breakfast on the terrace. That is, Mimi and Phoebe were; of Edmund there was no sign.

Phoebe helped herself to another roll from the basket on the table and dug her buttery knife deep into the pot of apricot jam before spreading it liberally on the bread. Mimi opened her mouth to protest, looked at Phoebe's happy face, and said nothing. She remembered buttery knives and jam when she was that age, and, after all, it wasn't her business to rebuke the child. Live and let live, she told herself.

Phoebe licked her fingers, looked with satisfaction at the roll, and crammed a large portion of it into her mouth.

'Phoebe, it's been six days.'

'I don't expect muses take any account of days and time and that sort of thing.'

Maybe not, but Mimi did. Every day, Edmund had risen at the crack of dawn, made a hasty breakfast and then locked himself in his room, emerging after several summonses at lunchtime only to seize a plate of food and carry it back into his room.

In the evenings, he reluctantly abandoned his writing for half an hour. He came out uncommunicative and abstracted, to bolt down whatever delicious food Mimi had bought or prepared. Then he hurtled back into his room for another session which lasted until long after she finally fell into a lonely sleep.

'I haven't exchanged more than a dozen words with him.'

Phoebe wasn't having that. 'I don't know about exchange,

but you said more than a dozen words to him through the door yesterday.'

'He's very annoying, and it's extremely bad for him, cooped up in there all day. No company, no exercise.'

Phoebe shot a quick glance at Mimi and went on eating. No point in telling her that at night, after she had gone to bed, Edmund left the house, going off on a long walk, talking furiously and loudly to himself, as the neighbours thought, delighted to find such a madman in their midst.

Phoebe knew differently, but then she could see Ranulf. And she wasn't going to talk about it any more, because no one believed her. Adults never did. Her friend from next door, Héloïse, did, but then she was her own age, and Celtic, and fey, and took Ranulf in her stride.

Phoebe polished off her roll, and announced that she was going out with Héloïse and her mother for the day. They were going to the sea for a picnic.

'Lovely,' said Mimi, wondering if she could ask to join them. Then she pulled herself together. It was all very well not nagging at Phoebe about butter and knives, but some things still mattered, and she owed it to Quinta to take care of her daughter. 'Have you cleaned your teeth? And remember to put on lots of sun cream.'

'Héloïse's mother makes me, she smothers us in it, very embarrassing, on the beach. And yes, I'll wear my sunhat, every minute. Bye.'

Another day stretched out in front of Mimi. No, today wasn't going to be like yesterday and the day before, hanging round in case Edmund suddenly wanted her, darting out to buy food, spending hours over special meals, constantly on the alert in case the tap-tapping stopped.

Of course, it did, from time to time, but only to resume within a few minutes. Bill's study, where Edmund was ensconced, doubled as a guest bedroom and had its own shower and loo. So she didn't even see him when he needed a pee, damn him.

Today would be different. Today she would go to Quimper, wander about, buy herself lunch. A fishy lunch; Edmund loathed fish. Then maybe she'd drive to the coast, have a swim. She opened the fridge. Paté, cold meats, some tubs of salad. Orange juice, wine. Yoghurts, but he would have to be starving before he touched a pot of yoghurt. There was fruit in the bowl on the table. She pulled a sheet off the shopping pad and wrote a message in large, firm letters. 'GONE OUT. BACK THIS EVENING. FOOD IN FRIDGE. FRUIT ON TABLE.'

She attached it to the fridge door with a magnet in the shape of a champagne bottle. Then she hesitated, wondering if she shouldn't go to the boulangerie to buy him some bread; Phoebe had left nothing but crumbs.

No.

Edmund had a perfectly good pair of legs. If he wanted bread, he could go and get it for himself.

Fired with new determination, she swept out of the front door, resolutely not looking sideways at the closed door in the little passage. She scrunched across the pebbles outside and opened the car door.

This was much better than sitting about the house fretting over Edmund. She swerved round the wheelie bin which was parked in her gateway, and turned into the lane. She told herself she should be pleased with all this frenzied activity on Edmund's part. It had to be more promising than the previous weeks and months of painful effort which had produced nothing of any use.

Although this demonic possession did seem strange for a work of scholarship. Dumas rather than Braudel, one would have said, but never mind. If it got the book finished, and Edmund's spirits raised, and money in the bank, then she should stop resenting it. Even if it had turned her husband into a snarling recluse.

It showed how little she really knew him. Maybe that was what marriage was all about, years and years of finding out what another person was really like. Maybe that was why so many marriages fell apart. When you discovered the real person, and decided you didn't like it all that much.

Or when you'd unpeeled the layers of their personality and discovered that there was nothing at the centre.

No danger of that with Edmund, he was clearly full of centre, even if his true nature was turning out to be other than she had expected or known.

At the corner of the lane, she nearly collided with an elegant

Mercedes turning off at speed from the main road. Road lout, she thought furiously, peering forward to see if the road was clear. Then to her surprise, the Mercedes, which had screeched to a dramatic and dusty halt a little way along the lane, reversed and drew alongside her.

She frowned, and braced herself for some insult about her driving. The driver was an attractive-looking man; pity about his manners.

He looked amused at her severe expression, and asked in a pleasing baritone voice, 'Are you by any chance Mimi Mountjoy? I'm Darius Flint, I heard you were staying here and was on my way to look you up.'

Mimi liked Quimper anyway, but it was twice as much fun with Darius. He was full of vigour and energy, whisking her into a hair salon when she looked in a shop window and decided her hair was a fright, insisting on taking her to lunch at a delightful restaurant tucked away in a back street which she knew she would never have found by herself, taking her round the market and making her buy all kinds of unusual food which hardly seemed suitable for her modest household.

She protested at his devoting the day to her, and to his extravagance, but he laughed at her, quizzing her with his hazel-grey eyes and mimicking her with lively gestures of his hands.

'After all, I know your mother well, why shouldn't I get to know you?'

'You know my mother? How?'

'Oh, we met in London, as one does, parties, concerts, theatres. I know your brothers, too.'

'Oh?' she said, less enthusiastic about that. 'Of course, we have no idea where my mother is. She went off on a boat.'

'I know, such an outré thing to do, a banana boat, too. But she's back in civilization now.'

'Is she? Really?' Her heart leapt. If her mother was back, in London, then surely her brothers would troop back for their home comforts.

'She's in Paris, not in London. And you mustn't tell the boys, not on any account. She wants them to set themselves up with places to live before she lets on where she is.'

That disturbed Mimi. Darius was excellent company, but he was still a stranger, and here he was, telling her about her mother, and where she was, and her plans. Which, if her mother wanted it kept secret, he shouldn't have done. Although why he should know, and not her . . .

'Forget it,' he said. 'We don't want to talk or think about anything which brings clouds across your lovely face. I want you to smile and enjoy everything. No, not like that, a glassy grin is not what I had in mind. That's better, I shall have to make you laugh, I can tell. Which is fine, because I'm very good at making people laugh and smile.'

She could quite see that. It was impossible to be gloomy or thoughtful for very long in his company. He was too lively and full of wit and fun. And a powerfully attractive man with it, there was no question about that.

It was such a long time since she'd had a flirt.

# 30 ♪

Phoebe was rigid with disapproval.

'It's not that I precisely mind being left by myself this evening, although it is the fourth night in a row, you do realize that.'

'You aren't really on your own, Edmund's here.'

'And he's about as much company as the wheelie bin out in the lane. No, don't fuss about me, I'll simply go next door and watch TV with Héloïse. It's a bit miserable going to bed by yourself, but I don't object that much, one has to grow up, I know. And in any case, la mère d'Héloïse has asked me to stay over tonight, so I shall.'

'Very well, then.'

'Just the same, does Edmund know you're out gallivanting every night with a mysterious Lothario who plays the flute?'

'What's the flute got to do with it? Darius is a successful professional musician, with his own recording company, not some busker I've picked up in the street.'

'It doesn't matter who he is, you shouldn't be out with him every night. Not when you've got a perfectly good husband of your own.'

'That's enough. Edmund is occupied with his own affairs, and I choose to spend time with an old family friend. And I don't want any more impertinent remarks from you.'

Phoebe was not at all abashed, but merely gave Mimi one of her penetrating looks. 'Does Edmund happen to actually know this old family friend?'

'He's a friend of my mother's. And since Edmund doesn't care whether I'm in the house or not, it can't matter to him where I am or who I'm with. And frankly, Phoebe, it's none of your business.'

'That's what adults always say when they get up to something they shouldn't,' said Phoebe, escaping before the storm broke over her head.

Mimi was nettled by Phoebe's remarks, and she did feel guilty about scudding off and leaving her to her own devices. But Phoebe would much rather be next door with someone her own age, so she was really making a fuss about nothing. And she couldn't endure any more evenings with Edmund barely present in flesh and not at all in spirit.

She had never imagined she could feel so out of sympathy with Edmund. Almost, it was as though she didn't exist. Some holiday this had turned out to be. She thought back to the idle joys of their honeymoon, when they were so much in love, so full of ebullient lust, so carefree.

Well, too bad. She checked that she had plenty of spare film in her bag, picked up her camera and went off, not even thinking of looking back at his room. And no notes left for him, no fridge full of carefully chosen food. Let him cope by himself. He was almost as bad as her brothers, expecting everything on tap. He was one to complain about parasitic Vincent; how much did he help?

A lot, her reason told her. Edmund was a keen and valiant supermarket-goer, and perfectly ready to lend a hand in the kitchen. And when she was concentrating on her work he would bring her drinks and snacks, and read her catalogues and make funny remarks about the fountains and garden pots.

And had she forgotten that he had looked after himself for years perfectly well, in Eyot and abroad? He hadn't got scurvy or rickets or expired from food poisoning, not as far as she'd heard.

She started the car. Had she married a man because he was domestic? What a depressing thought. No, she'd married Edmund because it made her spine tingle just to look at him, because of the back of his neck and his hands and the inside of his wrists and his voice, and his quick understanding and humour and his ease in the world and his shrewd observations of his fellow men. And because, unlike her mother, he was full of encouragement about her work.

She blinked, and made herself concentrate on her driving.

They were two individuals, for God's sake. He chose to shut him-self away with his book, fine. Meanwhile, she had chosen to find herself some beguiling male company and go out photographing fountains by moonlight.

The evening began promisingly. She and Darius ate and chatted their way through a delicious and leisurely dinner. He was at his most amusing and full of extravagant compliments, and she sparkled from the good food and wine and his flattery.

They finished their meal, and went out into the warm evening air, Mimi feeling relaxed and happy.

Then, what a shock. A large shape came suddenly out of the shadows and nearly sent them flying. A well-known voice boomed an apology.

'Good gracious,' cried Mimi. 'Sylvester!'

'Mimi? Why, how delightful. My God, is that Darius?'

David and Goliath, thought Mimi. Only one always supposed Goliath to be dim-witted like others of his gigantic kind, and no one would call Sylvester's wits anything other than razor sharp. His eyes, too, were keen, and took in far more with a single glance than she would have wished.

He was courtesy itself. 'Well, well, this is very nice. Come and join me in a drink. Hilaire's bar over there is just the place.'

'We're going out to a village near here to photograph a fountain,' said Mimi quickly. 'By moonlight.'

'Ah, a working evening,' said Sylvester drily. 'I think the moon will be with us for a few hours yet, and you must allow me to enjoy a little of your and Darius's company. I haven't seen you for years, have I, Darius? You haven't changed a bit, I must say. Trim as ever, but of course you small chaps have to stay neat.' He turned to Mimi. 'Edmund not with you?'

'He's working.'

'Ah, just as well I didn't drop in on him, then. Mustn't disturb the writing. I hope it's going well.'

'All-absorbing.'

'Excellent.'

He guided them into the bar across the square, which immedi-ately seemed full; a usual Sylvester effect. Mimi couldn't help regarding him with affection, although for reasons she didn't care to examine, she would rather not have bumped into him just now. She was longing to ask how he'd left everything in Eyot, was Henrietta coping, what about Gerry. And, most of all, what were her brothers up to?

Only it didn't seem the time or the place; she found she didn't care to talk to him about personal and family matters in front of Darius. What on earth was he doing in France? He hadn't said anything about a trip over.

Darius didn't seem exactly overjoyed to see Sylvester. He asked for a black coffee and was disinclined to answer his jovial questions about his music, his recording company, and someone called Giselle.

Mimi didn't like the sound of Giselle. Who was this Giselle?'

Darius stirred himself and launched into anecdotes about a recording of Debussy's complete flute music – not precisely to Sylvester's taste, judging by the look that crossed his face – the forthcoming festival of French music here in Brittany which he was heavily involved with and a scandalous story about a clarinettist and a horn-player rejoicing in the name of Angelica Simpkins.

Mimi sipped her wine and listened.

'We shouldn't talk shop.' Darius gave her one of his charming smiles. 'Very boring for non-musicians.'

'Ah, but Mimi is a musician. Didn't she tell you?'

'You play an instrument? Of course, I remember now, Vincent once told me that his sister played the piano a little. Tinkled the keys as he called it.'

Sylvester's eyebrows rose. Mimi twisted her glass round on its stem. 'I used to play. I don't much nowadays.'

'You must have been at college with Angelica,' Sylvester said to Mimi.

'Yes, I was.'

'That kind of a musician, then,' said Darius, sounding slightly huffy. 'Trained.'

'Yes.'

'Angelica was bewitching even then, wasn't she?' Sylvester went on. 'I can't think how many happy partnerships and marriages she broke up. A born seductress of course, and the nasty thing is, I believe she used to do it just for the hell of it.'

'Did she?' Mimi didn't want to think about Angelica.

'There are men and women like that. Often faithful in their way to one person, but out tom-catting, meanwhile, seeking whom they may devour.' Sylvester drained his beer. 'Unsavoury, really.' He rose. 'You'll want to be off to take snapshots of this fountain, what a charming notion. Mimi, have you a spare bed for a few days? Tell Edmund I shan't bother him, and I won't bother you, either, I shall be out working for long hours.'

'Oh?' said Darius. 'Working? Performing?'

'No. There are some manuscripts in a private collection here which I want to look at. A hitherto unknown cello concerto by C. P. E. Bach, so the owner thinks. I've been meaning to get over and look at it for some time. A week's recording was cancelled at the last moment, so I came.'

Mimi pulled herself together. However strained things were between her and Edmund, she wasn't going to turn an old friend from their door. 'We do have a room, and it would be lovely to have you there. Phoebe will be thrilled.'

'Only one spare room?'

'Edmund works in the other.'

'Then I shall be doing you a service, because Inez is on her way to France.'

And before she could recover her wits, he had bid them good night, told her he would turn up tomorrow and surged out into the square.

'Who's Inez?' asked Darius.

'She's a learned type from Eyot University. A friend of my husband's.'

'A good friend, I hope, to distract his attention,' he said, taking her arm and guiding her towards his car.

'I think I'll leave the photos for tonight,' she said suddenly. 'I'm tired.'

'But no! It's because Sylvester came crashing in like that. He's upset you.'

'Upset me? Oh, no, not really.'

'So sensuous, marble and water by moonlight.'

'Clearer by daylight, perhaps.'

And then, as she got into her car. 'Who's Giselle?'

'Giselle?'

'Sylvester mentioned Giselle.'

A long pause.

'Giselle's a friend. Sylvester met her once. Good night, my sweet, and drive carefully.' He leant down and brushed her lips with his. 'We meet tomorrow, for lunch. I have a friend who has a delightful house, close to a beach, we can have lunch there, he is away, we can be just the two of us, and then we can swim. Be by the bridge here at eleven, okay?'

'At eleven.'

# 31 𝄢

Sylvester rolled up at their house in time for breakfast, to be greeted coolly by Mimi and with cries of joy by Phoebe.

'Sylvester! Why are you here? Are you staying with us? Mimi never said.' An accusing glance in her direction.

'Good morning, Sylvester. Phoebe was asleep when I got back last night, so I didn't tell her I'd seen you. Have a chair. Have some coffee.'

'I've got a new friend, she lives next door.'

'I hardly expected you this early.'

'She's French, and she's got a funny leg.'

'I'll have to see about your room, I was going to make it up later.'

'She's called Héloïse, and she's got a parrot.'

'I'm afraid Edmund shuts himself away with his book; we aren't likely to see him before this evening.'

Sylvester clapped his hands over his ears and begged for pity. Mimi poured him some coffee and Phoebe went flying next door to summon Héloïse to meet him. She popped her head back through the hedge, looking, with the leaves surrounding her copper curls and pale face, like some tree nymph from a more pastoral and classical age. 'Did you bring your cello?'

'Naturally. Do I ever go anywhere without my cello?'

'Oh, good, because Héloïse doesn't know much about cellos, and you can play to her.' She vanished.

'Can I just?' Sylvester helped himself to a buttery croissant.

'Haven't you had breakfast? I'll fetch another plate.'

'In point of fact I have, but these look so delicious, I thought I might tuck one in.'

'Lily will know.'

'Nonsense. All this heat, and I propose to do some swimming, I shall return to Eyot a svelte man.'

'I do hope not, I can't imagine you svelte. Besides, think of the shock to Gabriel.'

'Gabriel's getting rather naggy about my waistline. Not from an aesthetic point of view, but he's worried about my cholesterol levels and so on. You know how people who've spent any time in the States are. I've told him that all these funny spreads and processed oils are poison to the system, much better stick to butter and olive oil, but it's like telling the Pope that the Presbyterians have got it right. A drop more coffee, please, if there is some.'

'I'll make some more. Then I'll have to leave you to your own devices; I'm due in Quimper at eleven.'

'Meeting Darius, eh?'

Mimi gave him a look.

'Don't do it, that's my advice, although I don't suppose you'll take it. He's a menace, he always has been. He's a womanizer of the most destructive kind. No, don't look at me like that, I know what you're thinking, what do I know about heterosexual relationships? Plenty, when it comes to types like Darius. He's a scalp-hunter. He cozens women with his lively and appealing ways, sleeps with them, then laughs at them and tells everyone about them.'

'Pure spite, remarks like that,' said Mimi defiantly. She was developing a horrid cold feeling at the pit of her stomach.

'Meanwhile, he spends his real life comfortably at home with Giselle, who's so besotted and dim that she puts up with his exploits. He had to come and live in France because he got such a bad name in England. No one will employ him as a musician there any more, he's made so many enemies.'

'He's a friend of my mother's. He looked me up. Edmund's hors de combat, Darius is showing me around. No harm, no menace, no sinister undertones.' The chilliness had spread to the base of her spine.

'And then one day, there'll be a friend's flat, just the two of you, a light and piquant lunch, too much champagne, and woof, flat on your back, and he's laughing at you all the way back to Plotin.'

'Plotin?'

'That's where he and Giselle live.'

There was something in the name Plotin which gave her pause for thought. It was so ordinary a name. It sounded like the place where a man would lead a civilized domestic life. And had he ever mentioned Plotin, or suggested she visit him there? He had not.

'Are you sure about Plotin?'

'I am indeed. I've stayed there. They have a very pleasant house, very French bourgeois, which is what Giselle is. Darius has had a studio built on at the back, although his main work is done in Quimper. They have drinks with the neighbours, go out to Sunday lunch at the local hotel, go away for August. Then he gets restless, wants to prove himself, so he jumps into his vulgar car and zooms off to find a prey.'

'Darius has a very elegant car. A Mercedes sports car.'

'As I said, vulgar. Red, is it? Sure to be.' He nodded and took another croissant. 'Never a pick-up, it's always someone he's been introduced to, or a friend of a friend, he has his standards. Besides, where's the fun if no one knows who his latest conquest is? No gossip, no crowing, no point. Best of all are married women, because he takes care that the husbands know about it, and then he has the pleasure of seeing their marriages shake and even founder.'

'This is all nonsense. I don't believe a word of it.'

'Some men don't mind their wives banging around with the Dariuses of this world; most do, just as the wives would object if their husbands whizzed off into the blue with an Angelica.'

'Oh, bugger Angelica.'

'I expect they do.'

'I heard that,' said Phoebe, appearing behind him. 'That was very, very rude, Sylvester.'

Sylvester reddened and looked very apologetic. 'Forget I said that, young Phoebe.'

'Huh,' said Phoebe, sensing that for once she had the upper hand. 'Héloïse isn't back yet, she's had to go to le clinique for physio. She'll be back soon, then you can meet her.'

'Thank you. Meanwhile, since Mimi is in a brown study, you can show me where the coffee is kept.'

'Merde, alors,' said Phoebe, looking at Mimi's worried face.

Mimi came to her senses. 'Phoebe, you are not to say merde.'

'My French is getting awfully good,' said Phoebe, taking Sylvester by the hand and pulling him out of his chair. 'I know dozens of really bad words now, Héloïse taught me, much worse than merde. Only I mustn't say them, or I'll shock Mimi. I'm saving them up for school, I want to see if Madame Mouchoir knows them, I bet she doesn't.'

At eleven o'clock, Mimi was at the local supermarket with Sylvester and the two girls.

At half past eleven, Darius was still waiting by the bridge at Quimper, furious and alone.

'How did you come to meet him?' Sylvester asked casually as he cruised up and down the aisle investigating mustards.

'He knows my family. I told you, he looked me up.'

'Does your mother have your address in France? That's very surprising.'

That hadn't occurred to her. How had he known where she was? 'Vincent. Vincent said he had a friend here.'

'Listen, ducky, he and Vincent are lifelong cronies.'

'Oh, no!' What a fool she'd been, how naïve to trust Vincent for a second. She'd known he was up to something.

'Yes. Vincent will have given him your address, probably told him to look you up, may even have said you were ripe for the plucking.'

Which I wouldn't have been for a moment if Edmund hadn't lost himself in that bloody book, she thought, going pale with rage at Vincent's skulduggery. But he had been, and she had become resentful and bored and lonely, and fallen right into Vincent's trap. 'Vincent is unspeakable,' she said. 'How could he?'

'He did it for revenge,' said Sylvester. 'Revenge on both you and Edmund. Very neat.'

Mimi hurled a pot of tarragon mustard into her basket. 'Vincent is vicious.'

'Very.'

'I don't know why you're getting all these things,' said Phoebe inspecting the contents of the trolley as she and Héloïse plonked them down on the checkout counter. 'Pink shoe polish, quelle horreur, who has pink shoes? And why cat food, is it for our supper? Are times hard?'

'Oh, hell,' said Mimi, looking with dismay at the strange collection of items laid out in front of her. 'Oh, shit, she's starting to ring them up, stop, arrêtez, arrêtez s'il vous plait.'

'If I can't say merde, then you shouldn't say shit,' said Phoebe primly. 'Zut, I think the checkout girl is going to have a fit, and she's calling the manager. Héloïse had better explain.'

'Exactly what did Héloïse say to that man?' asked Mimi a little later, when they went out to the car with a more suitable load in their trolley.

'That you had a problem with names of things, because you fell on your head off a horse, cheval, you know.'

'Really, Phoebe.'

Sylvester was vastly amused. 'You were lucky. Young Héloïse was intending to explain it was all to do with hormones, but I said you were either too old or too young for that.'

'Oh, thanks.'

'Blame Vincent.'

'I do.'

Vincent's ears weren't burning, because he was cold with rage.

The house was a pit.

Piles of washing-up overflowed out of the sink; none of them knew how to operate the dishwasher, and Benedict had fused it.

There was no hot water because the gas had been switched off, and none of them had the necessary domestic knowledge to track the pipes to the meter, which lurked in the basement, and turn it on again. Moreover, the evenings and nights were chilly, and there was no heating. Vincent had dug out an old and erratic fan heater, which he guarded jealously. Since it growled and emitted sinister sparks, his younger brothers felt that, on the whole, he was welcome to it.

The beds needed changing, and the pile of clean linen had been exhausted. Vincent felt sure that there was lots more somewhere, but he couldn't find it. Perhaps it was in Mimi and Edmund's room, which had been locked. He had called for

Ferdie to apply his expertise, but his skill was with credit cards and modern locks, not this solid Victorian affair.

There was a nasty smell of decay in the fridge, and the cupboards had an assortment of things no one wanted to eat, such as cornflour and cocoa powder. They had tried the cocoa, but found the instructions too complicated.

'We'll starve if Mimi doesn't come back soon,' said Ferdie plaintively.

'At least your ugly friends take you out to dinner from time to time.'

'Only the ones I don't care for. The others expect me to pay for them, and how can I? I'm penniless again. Do you suppose Benedict has any money?'

'If he has, he won't lend it to you,' said Vincent. Benedict was notoriously close with his earnings, and he had learned over the years what bad borrowers his brothers were.

'You can always go out to Hustle Manor, batten on Elvira whatsit, that's what you usually do,' said Ferdie. He was slightly envious of his brother's way with older women. It seemed to him to be a cushy arrangement, with none of the scenes and traumas and occasional violence of his own way of life.

'No, I can't,' said Vincent shortly. 'I asked, but she laughed and said she wasn't having visitors at present.'

'That isn't true,' said Ferdie, watching his brother to see how he would take the news he was about to impart. 'I happen to know that Gerry's spent several nights out there recently.'

Bang.

'Was that Vincent going out?' asked Benedict, still in his pyjamas, although the day was far on. 'Is there anything to eat?'

'Yes, it was, and no, there isn't.'

'I do wish Mummy would come back to London.'


'I hear that Inez is going to France to find Edmund,' said Dr Cara Sicilienne, perching herself on a high stool at the bar beside her colleague from the English department. 'Double whisky please, with ice.'

'She thinks he needs her help.'

They laughed, making the student behind the bar hurry up with his dispensing of drinks, what a sinister pair they were, no wonder half the University was terrified of them. Daphne gave him a smile, and he shot down to the other end of the bar, quivering and dropping a glass or two as he went.

'She won't be welcome.'

'No, Mimi will have to cope with her, won't she love that.'

'I wonder how the book is going.'

'It should be nearly finished, by my reckoning. Then we'll see.' Cara raised her glass in salutation. 'Here's to it. Won't Junius Paxley be stunned?'

More laughter. The bar-tending student cringed and abandoned his post to flee for refuge in the gents.

In Plotin, an angry Darius braked sharply outside his house, and slammed the car door behind him. Bloody woman, standing him up like that. And then he'd got Sylvester on the phone when he'd rung her house; no, Mimi hadn't been in Quimper, she was out all the rest of the day, something to do with her work, was there a message?

Darius hadn't dared to be rude, not to Sylvester. He, Darius, might be doing very nicely in his way, but Sylvester was altogether in a different league; he had the friendship and the ear of too many important people in the music world and was altogether far too big a shark for Darius to take on.

Reason reasserted itself, and he shrugged as he let himself into the house. 'Giselle?'

Win some, lose some, he thought, as Giselle enveloped him with delight at his being home when not expected. No lover hidden in her bed, he knew that for sure; really, a faithful wife was worth having. And he didn't lose many of the other sort. He was going to have a word or two to say to Vincent about his sister when he saw him again.

Sylvester showed no surprise or alarm when a distracted Edmund came grudgingly out of his room for dinner.

'Hello, Sylvester. You here?'

'Not only here, but acting chef.'

'Good, good,' said Edmund, although it was clear he could be eating sawdust with mayonnaise for all the notice he took of what was on his plate. Well before the others had finished, he had risen and hurried back to his room.

'I am so sorry,' began Mimi.

Sylvester turned on her. 'Don't you ever apologize to me for what Edmund does. It won't do, he's a grown man, if he wants to be ill-mannered, that's up to him, and it's for him to apologize, which, of course, he won't.'

Mimi's blood was up. 'It's all very well, Sylvester, you can be grand about it, this is your first evening of him. He's been like this for days and days; for anything I know he'll go on like this for ever.'

'Pooh, of course not. He's in a kind of trance, can't you see? It's called inspiration, and he's a lucky man; that kind of manic creativity is more often sought than found. I'm not offended, and you shouldn't be either. For all you know, he could be composing the Messiah in there. Don't be so self-centred. Now, did I see a bottle of Calvados lurking on the side? A little glass would go down very well before we tackle that promising tarte aux abricots.'

# 32 ∫

'I insist. I have to see Edmund.'

'No.'

Inez had arrived at lunchtime, glowing with health and full of serious and scholarly purpose. She did have a sensational figure, Mimi had to admit. And her lustrous brown hair and smudgy bedroom eyes were outrageous. True, she had a thin nose, which was a serious drawback from a perfectionist point of view, but what man would waste time looking at her nose?

Her voice was flat and prosaic, carrying no message of the harem. 'This is urgent departmental business. University matters.'

'Too bad.'

'Edmund will want to see me.'

'No, he won't.'

The door of Edmund's room flew open. '*Will* you be quiet out here? Why are you standing about in the hall talking at the tops of your voices, is this really necessary? How the hell am I supposed to think with all this row . . . ? Ah, Inez. Just the person I need. Come in.'

The door shut behind them, leaving Mimi speechless, and Sylvester, an interested observer of the scene, much amused. 'Rolled you up, foot and cannon, I'd say.'

'How dare she? How dare he?' Mimi was uncertain which of them she was more furious with. 'Shaking her bosom at me.'

'Don't fret, it's something in her mind Edmund wants, not a more voluptuous offering.'

'How do you know?'

'Because I do, and so do you. You've built up this fantasy about

Inez and Edmund. Yes, he went to bed with her, a good time back, long before he met you. So what? I expect you went to bed with lots of well-endowed men before you met Edmund.'

'Sylvester!'

'Don't be prissy. Inez is domestic, unoriginal, and essentially dull. Edmund grew very bored by her limited imagination and total lack of humour.'

'How do you know?'

'He told me so. Inez will one day meet some man who also has no sense of humour, and they will get on splendidly and raise a horde of humourless children.'

He fell silent; Mimi grew suspicious. 'Out with it.'

'With what?'

'With whatever wicked thought has just crossed your mind.'

'That's entirely my affair. Now, I shall head for the Château de Keroüalle, where I intend to spend many happy hours wrestling with the more serene joys of Carl Philipp Emanuel's blissful music.'

'What are Bach papers doing here in France?' she asked, interested despite herself.

'The present owner's grandfather married the daughter of a noted German musicologist and collector. He left his collection to his daughter, much, one gathers, to the rage of his German colleagues. After I have done my stint there, I will return and take you out to dinner. Phoebe, too, if she wants to come.'

'What of Edmund?'

He looked surprised. 'What of him? Food holds no delight for him just now, one can see that at once. Leave him a plate of the French equivalent of hominy grits, that'll keep him going. And a pear or two, very beneficial for the digestion; it must be extremely constipating, all this writing. You'll have to send him to a health farm once he's finished.'

'Inez isn't staying here,' she said, her mind reverting to darker matters.

'No, since I'm here, and she can't have Edmund's room, she most certainly isn't. Besides, I do believe you'd creep into her room and do her in if she stayed. I noticed a pleasant-looking hotel in the village as I came through, perhaps they have a room. Or Quimper? Of course, she may not be planning to stay.'

'People do not travel all this way from Eyot and go straight back again. I expect she's brought her bikini.'

'Stop grinding your teeth, and look up the number of the hotel.'

Inez clearly felt that hospitality was lacking in the Mountjoy establishment, but she was so pleased to have got the better of Mimi over access to Edmund that she merely gave her a hurt look.

'They have a little restaurant attached, very convenient.'

'I would like to be able to talk to Edmund over dinner.'

'Don't push your luck. He doesn't dine these days, in any case.'

'He's working so hard,' said Inez in reverential tones. 'I could see ever such a big pile of finished typescript. He wouldn't let me see a single page of it, though, which is a shame. I'm sure I could be very helpful at this stage.'

'So why did he want to see you?' said Mimi, who'd been longing to ask, but had too much pride.

'To ask me some very strange questions,' said Inez with a sniff. 'I did a paper once on sexual relationships within the Templar order, and that was what he wanted to know about. Just checking, he said. I can't think where he got his information, I must say. Most of it seemed very inaccurate, not at all in line with the main authorities.'

If it's got sex in it, then it can't be all about finance, thought Mimi at once. What was he up to?

'Is Plotin near here?' asked Inez unexpectedly.

'*Plotin?*'

'It's a village, I believe. Or perhaps a small town.'

Mimi stared at her. 'Why do you want to know?'

'My cousin lives there. I'm sure he'll put me up for a few days, then I can come over whenever Edmund needs me. I'll leave my number.'

I shall burn it and hide the phone, Mimi decided. 'Cousin? A French cousin?' she asked.

'No, he's English. His wife's French, though, from Plotin.'

'I know someone who lives in Plotin. A friend of my brother's. Called Darius.'

'My cousin is called Darius so I expect it's him. It isn't far, is it?'

'I'm not sure, why don't you look at the map?'

'Isn't that typical? You think you've heard and seen the last of someone, and then you haven't.'

'No reason why you should meet up with Darius again,' said Sylvester reasonably. 'He won't be in a hurry to see you again, you made a fool of him.'

'No,' said Mimi. 'He made a fool of me, and I'd rather Edmund didn't get to hear about it.'

'He will. Some kind soul is bound to tell him, with embellishments. Better tell him yourself, that you met up with Darius and had dinner with him and so on. He'll have to take the rest on trust.'

'Will he?'

'Probably. Nice man, Edmund.'

'It's all for the future, anyhow,' she said. 'I could tell him I was dating Lucifer just now, and he wouldn't pay any attention.'

Mimi was getting used to her solitary lifestyle. Some nights, Edmund didn't join her in bed at all. Not that it made any difference, for when he did, he fell straight into an utterly deep sleep, no sleeping pills necessary these days, she had noticed, and he was always gone in the morning long before she was stirring. She supposed he slept in the room downstairs, damn him for his indifference.

What time was it now? Seven o'clock. She banged the bolster into a more peaceful shape, she didn't have to get up yet.

There was a patter of bare feet, and a tousled Phoebe appeared at the door of her room.

'What is it?'

'There's someone arrived, they're knocking at the door.'

'Who?'

'They came in a taxi.'

Mimi, with a suspicion that it must be Inez come back to plague her, pulled on her robe and went downstairs to do battle. She unbolted the door and glared.

'Hello, Mimi. Why are you looking so cross?'

'Benedict!'

This time Mimi was absolute. 'No, no, and no. There isn't a room, there isn't a bed and you aren't sleeping on the floor or camping out in the garden. I don't know why you're here, but you can go away.'

'How can you be so hard? I had to come, I need to paint here, for this commission, it's the light, you see. Not quite right in Eyot, especially not when it rains all the time. I won't take up much room, I promise, and I'll be ever so quiet. You'll hardly know I'm here.'

'I will, and you won't be.'

'Is Edmund cross with me?'

She looked at her brother with exasperation. 'He's working. He's working incredibly hard, and he can't be disturbed. No, Benedict, I mean it this time. You are *not* staying here.'

Sylvester thudded down the stairs. 'I thought I heard voices.' He smiled, his mischief-loving soul rather pleased at this turn of events. 'Why, it's Benedict.'

'Do you have the number of that hotel in the village?' she asked.

He shook his head. 'No good, they're full up, I heard them talking about it in the boulangerie yesterday evening when I popped in to buy Phoebe a tart. A German family; from what I heard, they're staying here for the rest of the week.'

'There you are, Mimi, you'll have to take me in.'

'No.'

Phoebe was watching and listening intently. She tugged at Mimi's sleeve. 'Why don't you ask Héloïse's Maman if she knows of a place in the village? She knows everyone.'

'Benedict, you stay here. Sylvester, don't let him open his pack, don't let him move, or take a step in any direction.'

'Mimi!'

'You aren't going next door like that?' said Phoebe, full of disapproval.

'This is an emergency.'

Madame Lafargue poured coffee and looked at Mimi with sympathy. She spoke excellent English, was already up and dressed, looking sleek and chic and small and neat and elegant and beautifully made-up in that subtle French way.

Hate, hate, thought Mimi, feeling dishevelled and unshowered.

'There is nowhere, literally nowhere. It is already the season, for foreigners if not for us, and so everything is taken. All the houses and so on, they are booked up year after year. It is a popular area.'

'I know,' said Mimi dismally.

'Is your brother here to see you, or on holiday? He could try nearer the coast, there are more places there.'

'He isn't on holiday. He's a painter, here to work.'

'A painter, how interesting.'

'Maman, Maman,' said Héloïse, who had been getting the lowdown on Mimi's familial affairs from Phoebe and thought it all very interesting. 'Maman, la poterie.'

'Of course.' Madame Lafargue flung her hands up in a very French way. 'I will ring Pim right away, and ask.'

'Pim?'

'Pim and her cousin, lover, friend, who knows, run the pottery. You will have seen it, they have an open-air display as you leave the village.'

'Lovely things.'

'Yes, the local faience, of course, so popular with tourists, but also much better pieces. The firm is well-regarded and sells in Paris. Pim has brains, she runs the business. Marcel is the potter and artist, and there are also assistants. They have studios which they let to painters and artists, in a spirit of community you understand. For an ordinary tourist or visitor, they would not be interested, but if your brother is a painter . . . A professional, did you say?'

'Oh, yes.'

'Excellent. Then we see what we can do.'

Benedict was doubtful. 'I don't like to be with strangers. The atmosphere may not be right for my work.'

'Let me tell you, Benedict, that the atmosphere in this house would be unspeakable if you were here.'

'There's no need to be unkind.'

'And how is life in Eyot?' asked Sylvester, as he swept a reluctant Benedict towards his car.

'Terrible,' said Benedict. 'Do you know . . .'

Mimi sank into the sofa. 'Thank goodness, oh, thank goodness this Pim person could have him. Phoebe, you don't know how lucky you are, no brothers.'

'Any day now,' said Phoebe cheerfully. 'Only I shall be years older than him or her, and I'll show it who's boss. How long do you think it will be before the next one of yours turns up?'

'Don't.' Mimi closed her eyes and put her hand to her head. 'I couldn't bear it.'

'Oh, if Benedict's got your address, the other two'll know where you are. I expect Vincent told him to come, you know what he's like.'

'I'm leaving.'

'You can't. Not while Edmund's in this state. It'd be like waking up someone who's sleepwalking, it could do untold damage to him.'

'Serve him right.'

'Now, Mimi, you don't mean that. Quinta's always saying things like that about Titus, but she really loves him deeply.'

'I'm going to have a shower. If any more brothers appear, I've gone to Mars, on a one-way trip.'

It was three days before Ferdie arrived. Sylvester opened the door to him. 'Only to be expected, your turning up,' he said.

Ferdie gave him an angry look and demanded to know where his sister was.

'Out,' said Sylvester. 'Out all day, gone to Rennes to talk to a buyer, Mimi's drumming up some good business over here.'

'Business! How sordid. It's shameful having a sister with a mind on nothing but material matters. Mind you, she needs to look to her so-called business, that Henrietta's a menace. No sympathy, and an unpleasantly cold and officious nature. She must drive customers away in droves.'

'She's refused to cook and clean up after you, has she? I could have told you not to waste time on that one.'

'All she does is sit about typing pointless letters and answering the phone. She's out a lot, too, Mimi should know that, hardly earning her wages. She's got bags of free time, she could easily do something about the house, it's a complete mess. And I don't know why that woman isn't coming in at all now, the one who used to clean.'

'Edmund cancelled her. You could do a spot of cleaning and tidying yourselves, you know.'

That earned him a very contemptuous look. 'I'm an artist, not a char.' He looked about him with sulky-mouthed approval. 'Not a bad billet, this. Where's Benedict's room? Where shall I leave my kit? And can we rustle up something to eat while I'm unpacking? I'm starving.'

'I don't quite know how to break the news gently, Ferdie, but you aren't staying.'

Ferdie stared at him. 'Don't be stupid. Of course I'm staying. Where else would I go?'

'Benedict isn't here, he's had to stay in the village.'

'Benedict's weak, he lets Mimi walk all over him. Not me. J'y suis, j'y reste.' And as if to make his point, he kicked his bags out of his way and lounged to the sofa, putting his feet up and making himself comfortable.

'No, Ferdie,' said Sylvester, quite mildly. 'No point in settling down; you aren't staying. You'd better come with me and talk to Benedict.'

'How did you manage to get rid of him?' said Mimi, full of admiration. She knew that Ferdie was a much tougher customer than Benedict.

'You didn't meet Marcel, did you?'

'Pim's live-in whatever he is? No.'

'He's very ugly. Thickset body, full of knobbly muscles, and a face like an impish gargoyle.'

'No!'

'Once Ferdie had clapped eyes on him, there was no question, nothing would have got him away. Straight back here to collect his things; we shan't see much of him, except when he wants some money. I told Pim you'd see to his room and keep, by the way.'

Mimi made a face, but it was a small price to pay for not having to deal with Ferdie. Besides, there were some promising lines of business opening up. She'd found some pretty garden fountains and pots and containers which she knew her customers would take to, and interest had been expressed in some of her own stock items.

'Le style anglais, for the garden, is very much in fashion just now,' more than one dealer had told her. Henrietta had sent a portfolio over by express, and even some of her big fountains had aroused keen interest. Gerry's fountain, the cause of so much trouble, had amused rather than shocked. 'Very witty, very charming, but not for the French garden, French families are very conventional in their gardens.'

'It's a one-off,' she had assured them, 'and spoken for.' They raised their eyebrows, and settled down to a peaceful and expert scrutiny of safer shells, dolphins and lions' heads.

# 33

Henrietta sloshed her way from the gate to the front door.

Despite her large red and blue checked umbrella, her red wellington boots and her Burberry, there was still a great feeling of dampness about her. She unlocked the front door, pushing it hard against the pile of post which had fallen through its wire basket and jammed the door. An extra hard shove caused a resilient package to give way, and she fell thankfully into the dark hall.

She stood for a moment, listening, suddenly quite sure that there was no one in the house. She was used to arriving to find at least two of the Ostiman brothers fast asleep, but there was usually some sense of life about the house.

Not this morning.

Benedict had gone to London three days ago, she knew that. Ferdie had gone out early the day before; at least she heard a door bang, and had seen no sign of him since. Vincent had been there last night when she left, tossing a few vicious remarks at her on her departure, as was his wont.

She hung her mac on the stand, and looked into the kitchen. It was just as the brothers usually left it: in an appalling state. She picked her way across the sticky tiles and felt the kettle. Stone cold; no one had been in here this morning. She went back into the hall and hesitated, wondering whether to look upstairs. Henrietta was scrupulous in such matters, and her only legitimate concern was her office. Still, she felt she must have a look.

The phone rang, and she flew down into the hall to answer it. 'Gerry, oh, good.'

'You sound breathless.'

'I ran down from upstairs. Listen, I think they've gone.'

'Vincent and co?'

'Yes.'

Gerry didn't believe it for a moment. 'They'll be back. I expect they're out with boyfriends or girlfriends, as the fancy takes them.'

'I went up to the attic. Benedict hardly has any possessions, you know. Just what can go in a rucksack, and a sleeping roll and his painting things. All gone. Only used-up tubes of paint spilling out of an old bucket he used as a waste bin. So I went and looked in Vincent's room. With some trepidation, I may say; imagine how awful if he'd been in there. He's gone, too. There's just a single large suitcase, all strapped, and a fancy leather label saying Vincent Ostiman on it. His bed is all in a frightful mess, naturally, but there are none of his shaving or washing things in the bathroom.'

Gerry was getting interested. 'How about Ferdie?'

'His room is a pigsty, you can't believe how awful it is.'

'I can,' he said. 'Go on.'

'But on closer inspection, ugh, all I could see that's definitely his is one cardboard box, all taped up with sticky tape, marked, "To be sent on".'

There was a long pause. 'Sent on where?'

'It doesn't say. There's the work in progress as he calls it, out in the stables, but it's got some sacking draped over it, and his tools have all gone.'

'Have he and Benedict taken their stuff from the bathroom as well?'

'Yes, no shaving things, towels all over the floor, of course, and bits of soap and so on, and a toothbrush with about three bristles on the bathmat.'

'They've left no note, no clue, about where they've gone, or if they'll be back?'

'Nothing, but then they wouldn't. They regard me as an unwanted intruder in the house.'

Gerry thought that was extremely funny, but Henrietta's mind was running on practical matters.

'Do you think I could risk ringing Mrs Sconce? Edmund said

to get hold of her if Mimi's brothers went, but would she take fright and give notice, with the house the way it is?'

'No, she'd regard it as a challenge, she's a tough cookie, is Mrs Sconce. Look, I'll have a quick word with Elvira and see if I can persuade her to drive me into Eyot. She said she had some shopping to do. Then I can come to the house and have a recce.'

'Isn't it your day at the Cathedral School?'

'Yes, but I'm not going in any more. I've resigned, with effect from the end of term, and got a friend to cover for me for the rest of this term.'

'Gerry!'

'Yes, well, my circumstances have changed. I'll tell you when I come. If I can't twist Elvira's arm, I'll catch a bus. Mind you disinfect a cup or two, I don't want to catch anything.'

Gerry squeezed his way into the hall an hour later, followed by Elvira.

'I had to come, out of sheer nosiness,' she said. 'Dear God, what a mess. Oh, poor Mimi, it looks as though the vandals have been on a visit.'

'They have,' said Henrietta. 'Come through to the back, I bring in my own coffee-maker and supplies each day.'

'Very wise,' said Elvira, peeping into the kitchen. She opened another door. 'Is this Edmund's room? The haunted one? Gerry told me all about it, quite fascinating. Of course the Mountjoys are perfectly mad, all of them, and they always have been. This room looks quite neat.'

'Yes, even Vincent didn't quite dare to mess it up. Although judging by the dirty glasses and the cigarette ash, he must have been sitting in here in the evenings, I didn't notice that.'

'I didn't know Vincent smoked.'

'He doesn't,' said Gerry, who'd been having a closer look. 'The cigarettes have had other uses.'

They gazed, shocked at the neat burn holes all over the brocaded chair.

'The beast,' said Henrietta.

'He was furious with his mother for giving Mimi that chair,' said Gerry. 'I expect it can be put right.'

'It's the venom,' said Elvira. 'Such charm, and all the time a viper behind the mask.'

Gerry shot her a quick look, but merely said that Vincent didn't care to be thwarted.

'I bet he had a good look round,' said Henrietta, feeling quite indignant at this invasion of Edmund's sanctuary. 'As if Edmund hadn't had enough trouble in here.'

'I suppose it couldn't have been Vincent all the time, wreaking havoc in there?' asked Elvira, following Henrietta down the passage to the office.

'No,' said Gerry. 'It began before he turned up, and besides, it wasn't a practical joke. Definitely a visitation from other realms.'

Henrietta agreed with him. 'I haven't got any time for ghosts or spirits or communications with planes and whatnot, all a lot of nonsense in my opinion, but whatever was bothering Edmund, it wasn't flesh and blood as we know it.'

Elvira gave a pleased sigh. 'How delightful, I'm longing to meet Edmund, when is he back? Is he as delectable as all the other Mountjoy men?'

'I suppose so,' said Henrietta, whose own tastes ran to blond men of the most traditional English country type. 'Fairly powerful personality, and very clever, but not exactly restful.'

'Typical of that family. Now, my dear, make us a cup of coffee, and we'll plan what to do. Mimi might come back any time, she's been away for ages, and it would be a terrible shock if she saw the house like this.'

'I spoke to her a couple of days ago,' said Henrietta. 'Edmund's still engrossed in his book, she's no idea when he'll be finished. I think she's toying with the idea of bringing Phoebe back and leaving him there.'

'Phoebe?'

Gerry explained.

'Mimi had much better stay with her husband,' said Elvira, with the authority of years of husbandly experience. 'If he's been working flat out, then he'll be full of beans when he's finished. She'd better be there, or he'll find solace and relaxation with some local mademoiselle, and she wouldn't like that at all. She's not the type to cope well with unfaithfulness, even of the most

frivolous kind. In which case, of course, she should never have
married a Mountjoy, but having done so, she'll need to keep an
eye on him.'

'I do wonder where the Ostiman brothers have gone,' said
Henrietta, reverting to the topic uppermost in her thoughts. 'I
mean, can we be sure they've really gone for good?'

'No question at all about where they've gone,' said Elvira with
a cynical laugh. 'I've heard all about these brothers from Gerry.
It's as plain as the nose on your face: they've gone to France.'

'Oh, no,' said Henrietta, dismayed. 'Surely not.'

'That's where they've gone, all three of them, to plague the life
out of Mimi over there. She'd better stand up to them this time,
because if she doesn't, her husband will really start to rebel, and
besides, she can't go through life with three brothers following
her about like tin cans on a string. You ring her up, Henrietta,
and see if I'm not right.'

Mimi put down the phone with a sigh.

'You've got your "Shit, it's Vincent" face on,' said Phoebe
perspicaciously.

'Phoebe, how many times do I have to tell you not to say shit
and merde all the time? How am I going to explain your terrible
language to Quinta and Titus when I get back to England?'

'At this rate, we're here for the duration,' said Phoebe unrepentantly, stuffing the last of the croissants into her mouth.
'So I wouldn't fuss, if I were you, at least not about my colourful
vocabulary.'

'Is she right?' asked Sylvester. 'Was that call about Vincent?'
He reached across the table for jam and a final crust. 'Is this all
you've left me, Phoebe? I shall fade away if you go on like this.'

'Not you,' she said, giving him a good squeeze as she went
past.

'Where are you going Phoebe?' Mimi asked.

'To Héloïse. We have a scheme going, I'll be back this afternoon, because Héloïse has an appointment with Monsieur le
Docteur. She says he's horrid, and like a monkey, and there's
a blissfully handsome one, only her mother won't allow her
anywhere near him. Bye, Mimi, don't let Vincent prey on your
mind, perhaps Pim will have him as well.'

'Phoebe's growing up fast,' commented Sylvester. 'Is Vincent on his way?'

'There's no evidence,' said Mimi hopefully. 'Only presumption. That was Henrietta on the phone, she thinks the three of them have left Eyot for good. I told her that Ferdie and Benedict were here, although not, thank God on the premises, but that we hadn't seen or heard from Vincent. She thinks he's on his way.'

'Bound to be,' he said. 'Want me to deal with him if he tips up?'

She pulled a face. 'I must stand up to him at some point, he's getting more and more troublesome, and now that he's peeved he does such ghastly things. Almost, I wish he'd marry Elvira, just to get him off my back, but really, I like her too much.'

Sylvester snorted. 'Elvira has far too much sense to take up with Vincent on any long-term basis. Besides, she's got other fish to fry. Still, you're right, got to do something about Vincent, because though it may be fairly peaceful just now with Edmund incommunicado, that won't go on for ever, and I think he's had enough of your dear siblings.'

Mimi wandered out on to the terrace, feeling the heat from sun-baked stone on her bare feet and the warm breeze on her face. 'It should be perfect here, and yet I worry about Edmund and worry about my brothers, and I can't see how it's all going to turn out.'

'I expect your brothers will find out where your mother is and go back to her.'

She shook her head. 'I didn't tell you, but Mum's in Paris. Determined to keep her exact whereabouts a secret so that the boys shan't come and pile in on her.'

'Do you have her address?'

She shook her head. 'No. I wish I had. Perhaps Junius has it, and he'd give it to me.'

'Don't count on it,' he said, after blowing out his cheeks in a thoughtful way and making a whistling sound. He plucked a twig off one of the cypress trees and rolled the leaves between his fingers, releasing the heady, entrancing scent. 'Your mother wouldn't trust you.'

'Why not? I'm not going to camp out with her; I've got my own home and life, thank you.'

'What's the betting those brothers wouldn't get the address off you? You always give in to them in the end.'

She winced. 'That's not fair.'

'It's how it is. You placate them. Pacifism is always fatal. It does not a jot of good as far as your brothers are concerned, because their demands simply get more outrageous. No, it'd be more than his contract is worth for Junius to tell you where your ma's hanging out.'

'It's all very well for you to say I have to deal with them, but how? You know how impossible they are.'

'It's not an easy one.' Sylvester reached down into a crate on the ground for a bottle of fizzy water. He wrenched at the cap, and it came off with a wild hiss, showering him, Mimi and the table. 'Sorry,' he said, pouring out two glasses of the water and putting the bottle down on the table with a thump. 'If you don't put your foot down pretty soon' – another thump – 'you'll end up having to choose between them and Edmund.' Thump, thump.

Mimi took the bottle away before it exploded again. 'What a thing to say. How could there be any choice? Edmund would always come first.' Her eyes narrowed. 'Always supposing he resumes normal life at some point.'

'He will, and by that time, you'd better have a brother strategy fully worked out. This Pim arrangement is fine for a while, but what then? And it won't do for Vincent.'

Vincent was too cunning and subtle to risk another head-on clash with his sister right away. He arrived in France on the overnight boat, but when he reached Quimper he took the road out of the city that led to Plotin.

He'd stay with Darius for a day or two, find out how things had worked out between him and Mimi. He felt pleased about that, a masterstroke, he thought, and wouldn't he enjoy letting Edmund know what had happened, with as many salacious details as he could wring out of boastful Darius. The thought of Edmund's discomfiture pleased him so much that he arrived at Plotin in an excellent humour.

The front door was open, and he walked in, calling out for Giselle and Darius. Then he frowned. Who was this totally strange woman, clad in a tiny sundress that did full justice to a superabundantly endowed figure? Surely Darius hadn't broken his cardinal rule and brought home one of his conquests to his own house?

'Who are you?' he asked.

'Inez,' she said. 'I'm a cousin of Darius's, I'm staying here. Did you want to see them? They aren't here; they've gone to Paris for a couple of days.'

Mimi had been cast into a state of gloom by Sylvester, and she was glad to see his car roaring off towards the château. Troublemaker, she told herself, wandering disconsolately back on to the terrace. People had to cope with their families, and with the families they had married into, why shouldn't Edmund?

Sylvester was getting her all worked up about nothing.

Besides, it wasn't her problem, it was her mother's. She must find out where her mother was. She had brought the boys up, she had never curbed their idle, parasitic ways; it was too bad of her, then, to scuttle off leaving Mimi to pick up the pieces.

Her mother was a very selfish woman.

The thought popped into her mind unbidden, unwelcome and very surprising.

Selfish?

Never. Her mother was an artist, she had had to work hard for a living after her exasperated husband had vanished into the Mexican sunset with a girl from the circus. Eccentric, yes. Abstracted. Fanatical about her work, professional to her finger-tips. That, too. But never less than a devoted mother.

Devoted to who?

To the boys, that was who to.

She tossed her head as though to shake off an irritating insect, but the disagreeable thoughts still buzzed in her brain.

Would her mother ever have put up with her living at home long after she was grown up?

No. In fact, her mother had insisted on her going into digs as soon as she went off to college, very meagre and uncomfortable digs, too, until she had moved into the house in Fulham with Gerry and his friends.

Sons, yes, she would go to any amount of trouble for them. Daughter, no.

And then, when it had become too much for her, she went off, dumping the whole problem – which was entirely of her making – in Mimi's lap. She must have known the boys would simply move en masse to her house.

And she must have known that it would put a tremendous strain on Mimi's marriage.

And Mimi had a horrid idea that she didn't care a bit. She probably thought the best thing would be for her to stop being married, and settle down to being a lifelong carer and provider for her brothers.

And that was another thing. Her work had never been important to her mother. It isn't Art, she could hear her saying, her voice full of scorn. Art matters, nothing else is of the same value.

Was Vincent's antiques wheeler-dealering art? In her mother's eyes, it probably was. Dealing with beautiful old objects was quite different from grubbing round in ponds with a pump.

Mimi sat down, feeling almost faint. Did her mother love her? She'd never questioned it. There was her mother, there were her brothers, there she was, in the family, one of them.

Only not exactly one of them. Her status was different, and Mimi suddenly saw, quite clearly, that her mother had never loved her as she had loved her sons. And with this revelation came a kind of release and a huge feeling of relief. For if her mother didn't love her, then she never would. And she could stop trying to please her mother, to take her mother's place, to do for the boys what her mother wanted.

Her mother had made them into what they were, which was, she accepted with her new sense of clarity, monsters.

And she had no intention of having her life turned upside down any longer by them and their various appalling ways.

She had had enough.

# 34 ∫

'Bonjour, Mimi!'

Phoebe came out of the shower towelling her hair furiously as she greeted Mimi, who was waiting her turn in the passage.

'What an age you do take, Phoebe.' She felt out of sorts and tired after a bad night and an early wakening.

'I think in the shower,' said Phoebe grandly. 'Thinking can't be hurried. Oh, and Ranulf's gone,' she added casually.

'What? Oh, no, not that again. I'm not in the mood.'

Sylvester was much more interested when Phoebe told him the news at breakfast. 'When you say gone . . . ?'

'I mean he came into my room at about four o'clock this morning; it's funny, I don't remember him being so clanky, and he said goodbye. He was going back to England, mission accomplished. You could tell he was very pleased with himself. Smug, that's what he was.'

'A smug ghost?' said Mimi. 'Honestly, you must get top marks for English composition, your imagination is fantastic.'

Phoebe cast her a look of scorn. 'I'd never put anything like that in a story I wrote, for it would come straight back, and I'd have to do another one. Perhaps you did your homework twice over when you were at school, but once is quite enough for me, thanks all the same. Besides, composition is fiction, Ranulf isn't.'

Mimi made an irritated noise.

Sylvester was intrigued. 'Four o'clock, you say? I wonder. Have you seen Edmund recently, Mimi?'

'No, I have not, if you mean was he in our bedroom last night. He slept in his room downstairs, as he does every night now.'

'Nip along there, Phoebe, listen at the door, see if it sounds as though he's working.'

She was back in a flash to report silence.

'Did you try the door?'

'No,' said Phoebe. 'He's got very nasty-tempered while he's been working, I don't want to have my head snapped off.'

'Come on,' said Sylvester. He led the way to Edmund's door, followed by a curious Phoebe peering over his shoulder, and a rather annoyed Mimi.

Still silence. He grasped the handle in his large and muscular hand and, very softly, turned it.

The door wasn't locked. It opened, and Sylvester looked in.

The room was L-shaped, with a table where Edmund worked at one end. Glass sliding doors led on to a small private terrace at the side of the house, sheltered by trees. There were two chairs outside, facing each other as though their occupants had been engaged in conversation, but no one was there. The muslin which hung at the windows billowed gently in the breeze.

Round the corner, in the longer arm of the L, was the bed. Mimi looked and saw Edmund, fast asleep, stretched out on top of the bedclothes, unshaven and dressed in shirt and trousers. One arm had fallen down beside him so that his hand dangled on the floor. His eyes were shut.

'He's asleep,' whispered Phoebe. 'Funny, he's usually up and working by now.'

Mimi bent over him. 'Edmund,' she said softly. And then in a louder voice, 'Edmund! Wake up.'

Nothing. Not a flicker of an eye, not a twitch of a muscle.

She lifted his arm, which flopped down against him like a rag doll. 'He isn't asleep; he's in a coma. He's taken something. He's ill. Quick, oh, quick; call a doctor, an ambulance.'

Sylvester calmly rolled back one of Edmund's eyelids with a sure thumb. 'No, he isn't in a coma, nor has he expired. He's fast asleep, and by the look of him, he's going to sleep for hours and hours and hours.'

Mimi knew that Sylvester was right. He had wide experience of every kind of unconscious state, so he told her.

'You do, in my profession. Drink, drugs, overdoses, concussion – why, I remember the time one of the double bass players – but never mind that.' This was plain, ordinary old sleep. 'He's got a lot of catching up to do,' he pointed out reasonably.

'He shouldn't have got himself into such a state, it's very bad to get so exhausted. I knew he was pushing himself too hard.'

'Oh, pooh. If you ask me, the reason he's collapsed is that he's finished. That pile of typescript on the table looks very promising, I just had a quick look, and there are more than seven hundred pages of it.'

'He couldn't have written all that,' said Mimi, impressed despite herself.

'Why not? Never underestimate your husband. He's just the sort to spring a surprise on us all; you shouldn't have married a Mountjoy if you don't like surprises.'

Mimi resolutely refused to set foot outside the house all that day. She kept on going to Edmund's room to check that he was still breathing.

'I can't go out, he might wake up and need me.'

'What a bore you are,' said Sylvester amiably.

The afternoon came and went, and the brilliant turquoises and vibrant pinks of sunset gave way to the fragrant darkness of summer, and still he slept. A reluctant Mimi finally took herself to bed, convinced she wouldn't sleep for a single second. Naturally, once her head touched the pillow, she fell into a deep and dreamless sleep, not to wake up until . . .

. . . the sun was streaming through the windows and Edmund, freshly showered and shaven, was standing beside the bed with a cup of coffee for her.

'Edmund!'

She hurled herself out of bed, narrowly avoiding the contents of the coffee cup, and threw herself into his arms. 'Oh, Edmund.'

'Mmm,' he said appreciatively. 'Back in the land of the living, darling Mimi, and no prizes for guessing what we're about to do.'

# 35

'Edmund's finished his book, so I hear,' said Dr Daphne Whitgift, meeting her colleague in one of the university's many miles of undistinguished grey corridor. 'It's a big book; a very long one.'

'It's going to ruffle a few feathers.' Dr Cara Sicilienne smiled grimly at this pleasant thought.

'Because it's unorthodox?'

'No, because if it's any good, he'll make a great deal of money.'

Daphne, too, looked pleased, in an icy kind of way. 'Quite unforgivable, in our world.'

'They'll all be snuffling into their salary slips.'

They walked on, their heels, one pair flat and sensible, the other spiky and frivolous, clacking and slapping on the shiny vinyl flooring. 'He made a lot of money out of his first two books.'

'Yes, but everyone knew he'd tripped up on this one. Such satisfaction oozing through the department. Such protestations of sympathy, such gleeful rejoicing.'

Cara gave a joyful laugh which bounced off the walls and rang through the passageways, causing people within their cells on either side to stir and fidget, suddenly uncomfortable.

'They can all mumble about how he never really was a sound scholar.'

'Let them. Meagre people finding meagre pleasures. Fancy a drink?'

'Yes, I've got ten minutes before I address the second year on sexual symbolism in Fielding's novels.'

'Is there any?'

'No, but it'll draw the crowds, and who knows? If they think his books have anything to do with sex, one or two of them might even dip into *Tom Jones*.'

'Which is full of sex.'

'Full of bawdry, which is much more fun to read, but alarming and often distasteful to the modern mind.'

Mimi's mind was running on sex, or rather, she reproved herself, on love-making.

With Darius it would have been sex, with Edmund, it was something far different. She mused on several utterly rewarding sessions with him, which, together with his affectionate and revealing words reassured her as to the rival attractions of her and, for example, Inez.

She felt some guilt, not having mentioned Darius. It didn't seem the right time, and after all, she hadn't done anything.

No, you rat, said her conscience, but if Sylvester hadn't surged out of the cobbles, you would have, and then wouldn't you have been for it. Knowing what you now know about Darius and his little ways. Which, if you hadn't been so wrapped up in yourself, and so hurt by Edmund's exclusion of you so suddenly from his life, you would have spotted at once.

To be taken in, like some witless teenager.

So, there was guilt, but at present it merely added a lustre to her fervour, and so Edmund didn't notice, and merely thought that she was more lovely and interesting and desirable than ever. He even approved of her hair, a nice cut, he had said. That was in itself remarkable, for he never seemed to notice details of hair and grooming.

She reverted to her bright clothes.

'Do put away those dingy things,' he'd said. 'You really aren't a navy and brown person, it quite depresses me.'

He told her about his writing fit. 'It's like being another person,' he said. 'I was in a frenzy. I simply had to write it all down, and then another line and another. I quite see why some writers keep going on gin and Benzedrine like your mother.'

'My mother works hard at her books, but she's never been inspired like this. She'll be very envious.'

He pulled a face. 'The trouble is, I haven't read what I've written.'

'Not at all?'

'Not a word of it. I almost can't bear to, although I know I'll have to. It might all be the most appalling gibberish.'

'It'll need a lot more work, though, won't it? References and bibliography and all that kind of thing. And checking all the facts.'

'The facts all came from the horse's mouth,' he said. 'I wouldn't dream of tampering with the text. Of course you do realize that I've written a novel, not a scholarly work at all.'

This came as no real surprise to Mimi, it was so obvious now that he had told her. Scholars did not sit down for days on end and pour out the words like one possessed. Not that she'd ever heard of, anyhow.

'But if it's any good, how can I ever do it again?' Edmund sounded depressed. 'Now that the voice in my head has gone.'

'Ranulf, you mean.'

'You realized it was Ranulf?'

Mimi was silent.

Edmund wasn't surprised. There were those areas of life which could never be explained, only experienced and then immediately understood. Or, if not experienced, not even remotely grasped. Ranulf was one such, and she was a non-experiencer.

'Do you think you'll go off into fits like that again?'

'I don't know. I hope so. Will you mind, if I do?'

'Yes, but at least I'll know what you're up to. And I'll know it will come to an end. This time, I even imagined you might have to be carried off in a plain van. I could see myself ringing Dr Fuseli, pleading for a bed in his clinic.'

'I shall see old Fuseli when I'm next in London.'

'There isn't anything wrong with you, is there? That you haven't told me?' She was suddenly alarmed.

'No, of course not. I don't mean consult him, just see him to tell him what a fool he is.'

Their neighbour, Madame Lafargue, came to call. To say that Héloïse would be going back to school shortly, and that Phoebe very much wanted Héloïse to go and stay with her in Eyotshire, and Héloïse wanted her to come back to France, what did Mimi think?

Mimi could hear the note of doubt in her voice and she realized that Madame Lafargue wanted to know more about Phoebe's family. She reassured her about Quinta and Titus, wondering what on earth Phoebe had said to leave Madame so wary about her family life.

'She said some strange things, that her stepfather is always in chaos, is this possible?'

'No, no,' said Mimi, who couldn't help laughing. 'The chaos which she has mentioned is mathematical chaos. Her stepfather, Titus, is a distinguished mathematician, and that is his field.'

Relief spread over Madame's face. 'And her mother? She has been speaking of guts. Her mother uses guts for something, it sounds very brutal.'

Mimi couldn't help laughing. 'Phoebe's mother is a luthier.'

Understanding swept over the Frenchwoman's face. 'Oh, now I see,' she cried. 'She makes violins, musical instruments and uses gut strings. How very funny. Phoebe must have looked up the word in the dictionary.'

Edmund poured drinks and offered some wonderful olives and little crispy fishy things which Sylvester had found in the market. He and Sylvester gossiped amicably, Héloïse and Phoebe rolled on the lawn. It was all very peaceful.

'We shall be leaving quite soon,' said Mimi. 'Phoebe is much better, and she, too, needs to go back to school.'

'I heard that,' Phoebe called from the end of the garden. 'I hate school.'

'And your brothers?' enquired Madame Lafargue with a delicate lift of her eyebrows.

Mimi felt the familiar sinking in the pit of her stomach which attacked her every time she thought about her brothers.

'I expect, once we've gone, they will follow us back to England.'

'Pim likes very much to have them. She says Benedict is a good painter, and he is to do some designs for her pottery. She finds Ferdie's work very interesting, too.'

Mimi was surprised to hear that; most people recoiled at the sight of Ferdie's efforts, but maybe the French were made of sterner stuff.

'Of course, everyone in the village is very interested about their private lives, the sex.'

'What sex?'

'It is supposed that Pim and Marcel have been lovers. Some say they are brother and sister, and the idea of incest is very shocking and therefore very delightful for the neighbours. Now they have rearranged. Ferdie is homosexual, no?'

'Yes.'

'So, he sleeps with Marcel. And Benedict, what about him?'

'A bit of each, really,' said Mimi honestly.

'That explains it, for he sleeps with Pim but also, they say, with Marcel.'

'It all sounds rather complicated,' said Mimi desperately.

Sylvester came to her rescue. 'Ah, these artists,' he said genially. 'They have their own way of living. Tell me, Madame Lafargue, is the Château de Keroüalle typical of buildings of that period in this area?'

Clever Sylvester. Madame was more than happy to talk about architectural details of the distinctive local style, and the sexual combinations of Mimi's brothers were temporarily forgotten.

'You didn't tell me your brothers were here,' said Edmund, all his content and relaxedness gone.

'I didn't want to worry you. They came, wanting to move in, and I sent them away. I wouldn't have them bothering you while you were working.'

'Oh. But they haven't gone far?'

'No, unfortunately not.'

The subject lay like a shifting cloud between them. Intangible, but casting a shadow. At dinner, Edmund asked about Vincent.

There at least, Mimi was in the clear. 'He's left the house in Eyot, so Henrietta tells me. No one knows where he's gone.'

'Then we may expect him to turn up on the doorstep at any moment. You're going to have to do something about those brothers of yours, Mimi. This can't go on.'

'I know,' she said miserably, pushing at her food with an unenthusiastic fork.

'Don't worry about that,' said Sylvester, breaking the tension with a big and merry laugh. 'I've a score or two to pay off Vincent, and I think I can settle it all quite satisfactorily.'

'Are you up to some mischief? Plotting Vincent's downfall perhaps?' Mimi sounded hopeful.

'Not at all. Just arranging one or two things which will lead your brothers, and Vincent in particular, to sort themselves out. Now, don't fuss and fret, and stop being so pompous, Edmund. Have some delicious cognac and forget about the terrible trio. Enjoy the sun and the warmth and the countryside and the sea while you're here; you'll soon be back in the rain and wind and mists of northern England with brothers lurking in every shadow.'

Soon after that, Sylvester disappeared.

Phoebe clearly knew where he'd gone, but she wasn't saying. 'It'd be a date with Madame la Guillotine if I breathed a word,' she said, making dreadful throat-cutting gestures. 'You know how violent these big musicians can be if thwarted, so I shall ferme le bec and live to tell the tale.'

'Too bad,' said Edmund, packing Mimi and Phoebe and her friend into the car. 'He'll miss a day out at the boat museum, his loss.'

Mimi thought not. Sylvester adapted to all kinds of surprising and unexpected circumstances and places, but not this. Part of the museum was on water, with retired vessels moored alongside a quay. They went up and down and in and out of a trawler which had once sailed in tropical waters, bringing back sardines and tuna; through a lightship which had kept its lonely vigil in the Bristol Channel, sending out regular sweeps from the lamp tower to warn and guide other shipping; and peered into the deep hold of a wide-bottomed wherry which had carried loads of salt along coastal waters and up the great rivers of France.

Fascinating, but no one could claim that the steep and narrow companionways, tiny cabins and poky engine rooms had been fashioned for generously built cellists.

Mimi and Edmund followed Phoebe and Héloïse in a zigzag tour across the boats, and then headed for the indoor delights of the rest of the museum.

'They lived on the edge, the people who sailed in these boats,' said Edmund. 'How cosy our lives are in comparison. Of course, we're threatened by extinction from nameless weapons, and we're all terrified of germs and viruses and illness, but they're such intangible dangers, and we can't leap out and fight them with vigorous deeds and subtle plots and slashing swords.'

Just what had he been writing about?

'You see,' he continued, 'I just don't think most modern life forges your mind and heart and soul the way facing storms at sea in a fragile boat, or sailing beyond the limits of the known world once did. Look at the way my ancestors batted off to the Middle East and all across Europe. Terribly dangerous, and exciting and life-enhancing.'

'If you kept a life to enhance,' said Mimi.

Edmund's mind was back with Sir Hugo and his bastard half-brother and servant Ranulf as they set out on their travels and adventures and wars.

'Better to live every minute of forty years than merely to survive for ninety. That's the secret, not to lose one's spirit of adventure.'

'Do you miss your travels?'

He looked down at a coracle, wondering how you could ever control such a thing. 'No. Those kind of travels are for when you're young.'

'Challenges, then, are what you need.'

'Challenges,' he said, linking his arm with hers and strolling on. 'Like your fountains, when you think about it. Only a small business, but full of challenges, and risks, and always scope for new ideas and schemes, surely.'

She told him about what she'd seen and the contacts she'd made while he was slaving over a hot book, although she still kept quiet about her outings with Darius. Work was a safe enough subject. 'I shall ask Henrietta to stay on, to manage the day-to-day work. Then I can get out more into the market.'

'Did Henrietta say anything about the council fountain and all the fuss?'

'The fuss was a nine-day wonder, but since then it's been total silence from the council, so I don't hold out much hope.'

'Never mind. Gerry's boar is a very fine boar, and someone will want him.'

'Henrietta was right, the publicity did us nothing but good. I mustn't be away much longer, Henrietta is splendid, and Gerry is being a tower of strength, but it isn't fair to leave them too long.'

'Whenever you say the word, we can be off,' said Edmund. 'I don't propose to look at my book until I'm back in Eyot. I suppose we do have a house still standing?'

'I know exactly what you're getting at, and I'm not going to even think about them, it would spoil my day, and they've been quite destructive enough.'

'Did I dream it,' Edmund asked as they drove back from the museum, 'or did Inez come to the house while I was writing?'

Phoebe gave a vulgar wolf-whistle. 'Miss Well-Stacked of the Year? She certainly did. She was closeted with you for hours, and then when she came out, quiver, quiver, Mimi sent her away with a flea in her ear.'

'Mimi, that wasn't friendly.'

'I wasn't feeling friendly, to either of you.'

'You've got this strange animosity towards Inez, I can't think why.'

'Then you're very stupid,' she muttered to herself.

'Was she staying long in France?'

'I have no idea. She went off to stay with a cousin of hers in a village called Plotin.' Mimi sounded bad-tempered; she didn't care to think about Plotin or Inez or Darius.

'Perhaps I should look her up.'

'Perhaps you'll see her soon enough when we're back in England.'

# 36

On the other side of the Channel, in distant Eyotshire, plots were being hatched.

Councillor Henthorpe lived in Midwinter, Sylvester's village, and a phone call from Albert, the landlord, brought Lily tripping into the bar just when Henthorpe had downed his first pint and was beginning to feel better.

'Hello, Lily,' he said. 'Don't often get to see you in here. Sylvester away on his travels again? He fair gets about.'

'He's working abroad at the moment, yes,' said Lily.

Councillor Henthorpe, who was no fool, knew quite well Lily was there for a reason, and he moved away from the bar and chose a table with a settle along one side and two comfortable chairs opposite. 'Where we can't be overheard. What'll you have?'

'The usual, Harry.'

'Albert, half a pint of Irish stout for Lily here. And another pint for me.'

The drinks came, and Henthorpe waited while Lily took an appreciative draught from her glass. She came straight to the point. 'Are you still having trouble with Mrs Elgin over that fountain business?'

Henthorpe winced. 'Trouble? Aye, I am that, trouble with knobs on. What a pestiferous woman she is, and high on her moral crusade, letters to the papers, appearances on radio and TV, oh, she's a right menace that one. And we can't get nowt done about that bloody fountain, because every time we call the sub-committee she's off again, declaiming and denouncing like she was in chapel of a Sunday. Fair bore the pants off you, if you want it straight.'

'Doesn't she realize the newspapers got it wrong? That it was a deliberate piece of sabotage?'

'Aye, well, I think she does, but it doesn't matter. The firm that could even think of such a piece of work is immoral, and so anything they do for us is tainted. I'm that sorry about it, because we're going to end up with a heap of pebbles and a piddle of water, and it makes the council appear very backward-looking. A laughing-stock, that's what we'll be.'

'If it weren't for Mrs Elgin, do you think you'd get the boar design passed?'

'I do that. There's a lot of support for a boar, and I think that Gerry and Mimi have done a fine job, it'd be a fountain to be proud of. The boar's got a bit of a saucy look, I grant you, but why not? You don't get tusks and a hefty frame like that on you so as you can dance on your points. And if he's no beast to put up on Auntie Mabel's chimneypiece, so much the better. That's what we want. Good art, not afraid to tell the truth.'

'Well, Harry, it just so happens that I know a thing or two about Mrs Elgin's past, before she came to Eyot, when she lived – and worked – in London.'

Albert watched the two heads come closer together while he polished glasses. Two of a kind they were; he reckoned they'd have been at home back in Elizabethan days when there was a spy or a secret agent behind every curtain.

Henthorpe threw his head back and gave a great laugh. 'You're a treasure, Lily. Well, well, that's a turn-up for the books. Who would have thought it? Of course, I won't bring it out straight, no, no, I think a hint will suffice. And that way I've got a lever to use next time she gets uppity. I shall enjoy our next session; her and her moral crusade – bah.'

Mimi asked Edmund to drop her off in the village on their way back. 'You go on with the girls, Héloïse's mother will be wondering where she is.'

So he dropped her at the corner of the cobbled square with its rectangle of plane trees, and she walked across to the shops. She was just coming out of the boulangerie with two baguettes tucked under her arm when she was hailed by Sylvester.

'Hello,' she said. 'Where have you been?'

'Paris,' he said.

'Paris? Good heavens, all that way.'

'It isn't far. I went to see a bow I had heard about; very fine, I must say, but also very expensive, and I had a couple of other things I wanted to do. I took the train, you know, so quick and easy these days. Now, I'm glad to see you, I was just going to drop in on your graceless brothers. You can come with me, since you're here. It isn't far.'

'Oh, no, I don't want to see them. I rack my brains all the time, trying to think of a way to solve the sibling problem, and short of emigrating to the Antarctic, I can't see how it's to be done. And they'd probably follow me there. In anoraks.'

Sylvester took no notice, but pushed open the door of the pottery, making a chime of bells tinkle in the rear of the showroom. A thin, sardonic youth appeared, and in a swift interchange of rapid French, which filled Mimi with admiration, Sylvester learned that Ferdie and Benedict were both out at present, but due back soon. He gesticulated, and spoke a few more vigorous sentences, the thin youth smiled and nodded, and Sylvester joined Mimi by the pots.

'I like this centaur,' she said, holding up a prancing classical figure, with sharp little horns on his head, and a muscular chest adorned with curly hairs that ran into the back half of a stallion. 'Funny, the top part reminds me of Ferdie's work. You don't think . . . ?'

'Probably,' said Sylvester. 'A huge advance, I'd say, if the torsos are acquiring heads and limbs, even if of an equine kind.'

'Did I hear you asking Ferdie and Benedict to the house tonight?' Mimi asked as they left the pottery.

'I was, your French must be improving. They're coming up after dinner.'

'How could you do such a thing? Edmund will be furious, and the whole business will start up again.'

'Leave it to me. Now, I just need to drop into the hotel for a moment. Wait here.'

She ignored this command, and followed him into the tiny lobby. She listened, intrigued, as he booked a room 'avec un lit matrimonial'. 'Friends of mine coming to stay,' he explained airily to her. He booked the room in his own name, so she was none the wiser.

'Come along,' he said. 'My car is in the square.'

'I don't trust you in this bossy mood,' she said.

Edmund was yodelling in the shower when Mimi and Sylvester got back. Phoebe was lying in a post sun-and-sea haze on the sofa. Her beach haul of stones and a cuttlefish or two had been spread out by the sink in the kitchen area, and there were little heaps of sand on the tiled floor.

The glass doors which ran all along one side of the big sitting-room were open, birds were singing outside, it was all peaceful and normal.

'I shan't mention about the boys coming tonight,' Sylvester said to Mimi as he opened the fridge. 'And nor should you. Want a beer?'

'It's a bit sneaky,' she said, taking the beer. If Edmund knew they were coming, he would be in a temper all evening, but he might have got over the worst of it by the time they actually arrived. If it was sprung on him, he might be angry for much longer.

Oh, I'll leave it, she thought, feeling sleepy and relaxed, like Phoebe, after their day out. Coward, she told herself, taking another beer for Edmund and going upstairs to the shower.

'Beer outside the door,' she called. 'On the floor, so don't kick it over.'

'Excellent, and let's have an enormous dinner, I'm starving. We can sit outside under the stars, how I love France.'

Mimi didn't enjoy the meal which Edmund and Sylvester insisted on preparing as much as she should have done. She was too concerned about the confrontation which, she had a horrid suspicion, lay ahead of her.

After dinner, Phoebe went yawning off to bed, and while the other two cleared the table, Mimi wandered in and out of the room. She watched as the stars duly sprinkled the dark, warm skies, then came inside to the lights and lingering smells of their meal and the glasses of cognac which the kitchen staff were enjoying. She took a glass, but barely sipped it; she was full of tension, waiting for the sound of a car, a ring on the doorbell.

Sylvester had appointed himself washer-up while Edmund was stretched out on the terrace. He attacked the worst of the pans with clouds of soapy suds, hurled everything else with many clankings into the dishwasher. Then he put out glasses on a tray.

Rather too many, thought Mimi. Then her ear caught the sound of an engine. Phoebe, always wanting to know what was going on, flew downstairs in her pyjamas to see who it was. 'Someone's come to the wrong place,' she said, looking out of the window. 'It's a strange woman and a young man, nobody we know.'

Then came a loud ring on the bell, and a rattle of the letter box. She frowned, that particular sequence of sounds at the door was very familiar.

Then Sylvester was opening the door, standing with his arms outspread, greeting the arrivals with loud cries of welcome and enthusiasm.

Who was it?

# 37

Mimi stood stock-still and stared and stared.

'Darling Mimi, what a sweet place. Don't stand there looking like a fish with your mouth open, come and say hello.'

It was her mother, looking ridiculously young and trim and well in a pair of superbly cut trousers and silk T-shirt. What had happened to the baggy trousers and middle-aged skirts and tops from Jaeger and Dickins and Jones?

And the hair!

Her mother's formerly greying locks were now an expensive shade of pearly blonde; gone was the semi-fringe and bobbish shape, instead she had a perfect cut and exquisitely coiffed waves.

Mimi could hardly ever remember her mother wearing perfume, just a decorous dab of cologne on the inside of each wrist. And now she moved forward in a waft of delicious and expensive scent.

'I must say, you look quite wonderful,' said Sylvester appreciatively.

Edmund was staring quite as hard as Mimi. He had backed away behind the sofa, and he couldn't take his eyes off Finella and her companion.

The companion!

Who was this outrageously beautiful and exotic young man, with such glowing dark eyes, such a sheen of health on his silken olive skin, such a lithe body clad in such elegant clothes?

'Darling,' said Finella. 'This is Charles.' She pronounced it in the French way. 'Charles, my daughter Mimi. And the tall dark man over there is Edmund, my son-in-law, come and say hello, Edmund. And this is Sylvester Tate, the cellist.'

Charles took Mimi's hand and brushed it with his lips. Then he raised his hands in admiration towards Sylvester. 'Maestro,' he said in a slightly husky voice, as attractive as the rest of him, thought Mimi; what a delightful young man.

Edmund recovered his poise, greeted Finella with an affectionate kiss on the cheek, shook Charles heartily by the hand and retreated to the kitchen area, where Mimi joined him, leaving the other three to exchange extravagant compliments.

'Who is he?' he hissed at her, as he searched for glasses. 'And what *has* come over your mother?'

'Sylvester's already put the glasses out on a tray,' she said in a whisper. 'Doesn't she look wonderful? Charles must be her toy boy.'

He dropped the glass he was polishing, and it broke into smithereens on the tiled floor.

'Tiens,' said Charles, looking towards them with an entrancing look of amusement.

'Shit,' said Edmund, pushing the slivers to one side with his foot. 'Toy boy? At your mother's age? Why, he can't be more than about twenty-two.'

'That's how old toy boys are,' said Mimi. 'Otherwise, what's the point?'

'It's disgraceful.'

'No, it's not. If it was my father with a blonde bit on his arm, you wouldn't think anything of it at all.'

He seemed struck by this, although he knew, deep down, that the cases were not the same.

She began to laugh. 'How the boys are going to hate him.'

'Oh, good,' said Edmund, his face lightening at the thought. 'Pity they aren't here to see her.'

'Um,' said Mimi.

Edmund gave her a very severe look. 'Mimi, you haven't . . .'

'Only Ferdie and Benedict,' she said quickly. 'We've lost Vincent, remember.'

'You are a wretch, it's all extremely underhand. Did you know your mother was in France? Why didn't you tell me?'

'I knew she was in Paris, but not where. I didn't tell you

because I found out while you were beavering away, and then it slipped my mind. I swear I had no idea she was coming this evening. Sylvester's behind all this.'

'And isn't he in his element, like some wicked magician pulling off his tricks.'

There was another ring on the doorbell.

'More guests?' said Finella. 'A party, Sylvester, this is most unexpected.'

'I'll go,' said Edmund, frowning horribly and heading for the door. 'That's Benedict and Ferdie, I suppose.'

'Vincent,' cried Finella, coming into the hall as Edmund opened the door. 'How lovely.'

'Inez,' said Edmund, with a contrasting lack of enthusiasm. 'What are you doing here?'

'Goodness,' said Phoebe, who had retreated upstairs and was hanging over the railing.

Mimi came out of her room, where she had gone to tidy herself up a bit. She felt at a distinct disadvantage in her faded red shorts and plum coloured T-shirt, and had seen Charles's eyes running over her clothes with an amused look in them. So she had changed into a vivid green and very short skirt and a shocking pink shirt. At least they looked less creased, although she knew they were nowhere near her mother's league.

'It's that bosomy woman from the university,' said Phoebe, in tones of strong disapproval. 'Inez. I wonder where she picked up Vincent?'

Mimi pinned a smile on her face and ran down the stairs and into the sitting-room. Vincent gave her a smile with no warmth in it, and raised his eyebrows at her outfit before turning back to his mother. Inez had button-holed Edmund, who was looking alarmed. Charles came over to Mimi. 'Who is this woman?'

'She's a friend of my husband's. From England. She teaches at a university.'

Inez was looking even more voluptuous than usual, with her clinging top accentuating her splendid cleavage to a remarkable degree. Mimi glared at her.

'She is like a moo-cow,' pronounced Charles in her ear. 'Gross, she should have an operation, she is not chic at all.'

Mimi decided she liked Charles very much indeed.

Vincent, who could hardly take his eyes off Charles even while he was talking to his mother, didn't like him at all. Mimi wouldn't have been surprised if he'd bared his teeth at him and growled.

'What a happy gathering,' said Sylvester, who was looking immensely pleased with himself. 'Don't you like my surprise?'

'Where did you find Vincent? And why did he come with Inez?'

'You forget that Vincent is a friend of Darius's. I used my brain, and went over to Plotin to see if he was holed up there. And indeed he was. No sign of Darius and Giselle, who are away, but there were Vincent and Inez, who seems to have the knack of controlling him.'

'No!' said Mimi, looking at Inez with new respect.

Edmund had left the front door wedged open, and so Ferdie and Benedict were in their midst without any warning.

'Darlings,' cried Finella, hugging them hard, but carefully not disturbing her make-up or hair. 'Ferdie, pink shorts, and so very short. Benedict, you look quite human, what has happened to the holey jeans?'

Benedict, too, was wearing shorts, but smart navy French ones with a belt and a paler blue polo shirt tucked neatly into them. He looked quite civilized, for the first time in several years. He, like Vincent, couldn't take his eyes off Charles, but for quite different reasons.

Finella was giving an account of her travels. She brushed over the reasons for her sudden departure, Edmund noticed, not mentioning her secretly taken decision to sell her London flat and disappear into the blue.

On the banana boat, she had met Charles. At Tangier, they had both disembarked to visit Charles's family; he was the son of a Moroccan father and French mother. Then they had made their way back to Paris, where Finella was in the process of buying a flat, and where she planned to settle.

Vincent's eyes gleamed at the thought of Paris. 'Which arrondissement, Mama?'

'Seventeenth, darling, second floor, quite delightful. But, sadly, no room for you boys, where are you all living now? Are you quite settled?'

Vincent took little notice of there being no room; it hadn't deterred him before and wouldn't now. He would happily fold himself into a broom cupboard if he could live at someone else's expense in Paris.

'We went to stay with Mimi,' said Ferdie. 'Who has been quite beastly to us, you should know this.'

Benedict murmured his dissent in dreamy tones, uninterested in domestic details, he was still drinking in Charles's beauty.

'Ferdie's quite right,' said Vincent in his smooth way. 'Mimi has no family feeling, and she behaved in a most disgraceful and inhospitable way, quite deplorable. What harm was there in her own family coming to stay for a few days? She treated us as though we were Huns or a horde of Mongols.'

'No, parasites,' snapped Edmund. 'Few days indeed. Weeks and weeks. And before you think of it, you are not coming back. If you set foot in my house, I shall send for the police and have you thrown out.'

'Do calm down,' said Vincent. 'Nobody would choose to stay in your quite ghastly gothic house unless they had to, and as for Eyot!' He shuddered. Inez gave him a cool look, but said nothing.

'Dear Ma,' said Benedict, who had a lovely smile, although it rarely lit up his serious face. 'Can you manage without Ferdie and me? For if Edmund is going to be unkind, then we can't go back to Eyot, and so it will be best if we stay here, in the village with Pim and Marcel.'

'No,' said Mimi quickly. 'Not at my expense you don't. Three weeks, and that's your lot, I can't even afford that.'

'You make us sound like spongers,' complained Ferdie. 'As it happens, you won't need to pay, because we're going to live en famille with Pim and Marcel, and work for the pottery as well as doing our own stuff. Marcel is going to sit for me, I've never had a better model.'

'And we can easily go to Paris to see Mummy and Charles,' said Benedict in blissful tones.

'Hardly Charles,' said Vincent. 'He will have his own life in Paris.'

'No, darling,' said Finella. 'Charles will be sharing my flat.'

'I thought you said there was no room.'

'Room for Charles, but not for you.'

Vincent shrugged, furious, but controlling his temper. 'Very well, if you say so. It's nothing to me, I have other plans.'

'He means Elvira,' Mimi whispered to Edmund.

The phone rang, startling them and interrupting what might have developed into a promising family row; it was clear that Vincent was not going to let the matter of Charles pass on the nod.

He's afraid Charles will get his hand on Finella's loot, thought Edmund, with glee; it was a rare pleasure to see Vincent ill at ease.

'For you, Sylvester,' said Mimi. 'It's Lily.'

Sylvester disappeared with the phone into the hall, and all the others could hear was the intermittent rumbling of his voice. Then he came back into the room, rubbing his hands together. 'How lucky I put some champagne in to chill,' he said. 'Good news all round. First, Mimi, Henthorpe has whipped your boar fountain through the council sub-committee and the full council as well, bang-bang, just like that!'

'No! How? What about Mrs Elgin?'

'You have to thank Lily. She told Henthorpe that Mrs Elgin had, in earlier days, had a beat off Piccadilly.'

'How very surprising,' said Edmund. 'And how did Lily know that?'

'Best not to enquire,' said Sylvester. 'Confronted, in private, by Henthorpe with this interesting piece of information, Mrs Elgin crumpled and became putty in Henthorpe's hand, willing to back him to the hilt in return for his keeping quiet about her past.'

Mimi was delighted. Edmund slid an arm round her waist, and gave her a hug. 'I like that boar very much,' he said. 'Every time I go past it, I shall think of Valdemar.'

'And,' said Sylvester, 'more hot news. Gerry and Elvira got married today.'

Edmund was perplexed, what was it with these young men?

Mimi, after a moment's stunned reflection, decided it would be excellent for Gerry. And for Elvira, to whom he would, she was prepared to bet, prove a devoted husband.

Sylvester busied himself with corks. 'Look at Vincent's face,' he said to Edmund in passing. 'That's paid off a few old scores.'

'Hasn't it just?' said Edmund with huge satisfaction.

It was three o'clock in the morning before they all left. Sylvester was still full of beans, Mimi felt as though six steam-rollers had gone over her, and Edmund was sprawled on the sofa, humming to himself.

'That's all worked out better than I could have hoped,' said Sylvester.

'No need to be smug,' said Mimi. 'After all, you can't take the credit for my mother meeting up with Charles, isn't he a lamb?'

'No,' said Edmund. 'I'm not at all sure I approve of that, it's bound to end in tears.'

'Nonsense,' said Sylvester. 'Finella's quite able to look after herself, and what an improvement in her appearance. If she turns up at literary dos looking like that, it'll put thousands on her sales. Wait until Junius gets sight of her, he'll probably have a heart attack, you know how catty he always is about dowdy clients.'

'Nothing dowdy about her now,' said Mimi sleepily. 'Only Vincent to worry about. Iron bars at all the windows, and a man trap inside the doors, do you think, Edmund?'

'I wouldn't worry about Vincent,' said Sylvester. 'He's had a nasty shock, and Inez is at hand to pick up the pieces. She was telling him that she's recently inherited a house from an aged aunt which needs doing up and furnishing from top to bottom. And the aunt conveniently left her a lot of money as well; Vincent will be installed within the week, you mark my words. And she'll have married him within the year. Just as I foretold, Mimi, you have to agree that Inez is ideal for Vincent, since she has no sense of humour at all.'

Edmund was very struck by this. 'Do you know, Sylvester, you're quite right. Inez is the most boring woman I ever met.'

Mimi gave a great sigh of pleasure; the relief, the happiness! 'Oh, Edmund, no more fears of any of my brothers turning up on the doorstep, how truly wonderful.'

'Good thing you haven't got much family,' said Sylvester to Edmund. 'Can't see Lady Wray wanting to move in.'

Mimi went pale at the thought.

'We shall have the house all to ourselves again,' said Edmund. 'What a pleasing prospect. I shall miss Phoebe, but it's time she went home; Ranulf's gone, and best of all . . .'

'No brothers,' said Mimi.

# POSTSCRIPT ∫

Dr Cara Sicilienne and Dr Daphne Whitgift met in the foyer of the concert hall and climbed the stairs together to the entrance.

'*The Times* have sent me the proofs of Edmund's book. They want a big review from an eminent historian, they say. Flattery, so that they can try to get away with a low fee. I should have done it for nothing, but I shan't tell them that.'

'The *Guardian* have asked me to write about it. Outrageous coverage for an historical novel, but of course he's a Name, and a man; it puts it into quite a different category from all the other poor scribblers.'

'I shall slam it, of course, I'm planning a stinker.'

'Excellent. I shall praise it highly.'

'You could recommend it for a prize.'

'Good God, do you want it to die on the shelves? No, no, I shall pitch it exactly right, so that everybody from office girls to the literati will rush out and buy it.'

'It will do extremely well.'

'Bound to.'

Junius came downstairs to greet Edmund and Mimi, wreathed in smiles. 'Congratulations, Edmund, I really didn't think you had it in you.'

'Thank you, Junius, so kind always.'

'I've booked a table, and I'm longing for the latest news of your dear mother, Mimi. Is it true that she's moved into a Louis Quinze apartment with two aromatically oiled black men? I want to hear all about it.'